THE SAINT IN ACTION

FOREWORD BY
JONATHAN RIGBY

THE ADVENTURES OF THE SAINT

Enter the Saint (1930), *The Saint Closes the Case* (1930),
The Avenging Saint (1930), *Featuring the Saint* (1931),
Alias the Saint (1931), *The Saint Meets His Match* (1931),
The Saint Versus Scotland Yard (1932), *The Saint's Getaway* (1932),
The Saint and Mr Teal (1933), *The Brighter Buccaneer* (1933),
The Saint in London (1934), *The Saint Intervenes* (1934),
The Saint Goes On (1934), *The Saint in New York* (1935),
Saint Overboard (1936), *The Saint in Action* (1937),
The Saint Bids Diamonds (1937), *The Saint Plays with Fire* (1938),
Follow the Saint (1938), *The Happy Highwayman* (1939),
The Saint in Miami (1940), *The Saint Goes West* (1942),
The Saint Steps In (1943), *The Saint on Guard* (1944),
The Saint Sees It Through (1946), *Call for the Saint* (1948),
Saint Errant (1948), *The Saint in Europe* (1953),
The Saint on the Spanish Main (1955), *The Saint Around the World* (1956),
Thanks to the Saint (1957), *Señor Saint* (1958), *Saint to the Rescue* (1959),
Trust the Saint (1962), *The Saint in the Sun* (1963),
Vendetta for the Saint (1964), *The Saint on TV* (1968),
The Saint Returns (1968), *The Saint and the Fiction Makers* (1968),
The Saint Abroad (1969), *The Saint in Pursuit* (1970),
The Saint and the People Importers (1971), *Catch the Saint* (1975),
The Saint and the Hapsburg Necklace (1976), *Send for the Saint* (1977),
The Saint in Trouble (1978), *The Saint and the Templar Treasure* (1978),
Count On the Saint (1980), *Salvage for the Saint* (1983)

THE SAINT IN ACTION

LESLIE CHARTERIS

SERIES EDITOR: IAN DICKERSON

The characters and events portrayed in this book are fictitious. Any similarity to real persons, living or dead, is coincidental and not intended by the author.

Text copyright © 2014 Interfund (London) Ltd.
Foreword © 2014 Jonathan Rigby
Preface first published in the Hodder edition of *The Saint in Action*, 1962
Introduction to "The Unlicensed Victuallers" first published in *The First Saint Omnibus*, 1939
Publication History and Author Biography © 2014 Ian Dickerson
All rights reserved.

No part of this book may be reproduced, or stored in a retrieval system, or transmitted in any form or by any means, electronic, mechanical, photocopying, recording, or otherwise, without express written permission of the publisher.

Published by Thomas & Mercer, Seattle

www.apub.com

ISBN-13: 9781477842768
ISBN-10: 1477842764

Cover design by David Drummond, www.salamanderhill.com

Printed in the United States of America.

To Patricia Charteris
hoping she may meet a Saint someday

PUBLISHER'S NOTE

The text of this book has been preserved from the original edition and includes vocabulary, grammar, style, and punctuation that might differ from modern publishing practices. Every care has been taken to preserve the author's tone and meaning, allowing only minimal changes to punctuation and wording to ensure a fluent experience for modern readers.

FOREWORD TO THE NEW EDITION

Anyone taking even a cursory interest in the Leslie Charteris bibliography will quickly stumble upon numerous sources of confusion. Many of them arise from Charteris's unwillingness—or, more accurately, his publishers' unwillingness—to leave a title alone.

That magazine stories should undergo title changes when promoted to book form is perhaps unsurprising. But Charteris's book titles were fiddled with, too, particularly when it became clear that he may have stumbled in not applying the marketable "Saint" name to all the volumes featuring the character. As a result, plenty of Charteris's pre-war books were re-branded for post-war audiences. *The Last Hero*, for example, became *The Saint Closes the Case. She Was a Lady* (never a good title) became *The Saint Meets His Match. The Holy Terror* became *The Saint vs Scotland Yard* . . . and so it went on.

But, of Charteris's twenty-one pre-war Saint titles, three remained conspicuously unaltered. I like to think that Charteris made a point of not changing these ones because they so perfectly encapsulate the devil-may-care appeal of his chosen hero. Let's face it, *The Brighter Buccaneer*, *The Ace of Knaves*, and *The Happy Highwayman* are so good they really don't need the added assistance of the Saint name. Admittedly, *The Ace of Knaves* was known in some US editions as *The Saint in Action*, but this was one of the few Saint re-titlings that didn't stick. Indeed, this 2014 reissue marks the first time it has been used in the UK, twenty years after Charteris's death.

In essence, *The Brighter Buccaneer*, *The Ace of Knaves*, and *The Happy Highwayman* are all the same title, pinning down precisely the rollicking, and occasionally amoral, adventurer who blazes his way through the pages within. They also involve the kind of wordplay in which Charteris delighted. The first and last are simple alliterations, while *The Ace of Knaves* punningly combines a non-existent playing card with a Shakespearean synonym for "rogue." Indeed, the phrase was so memorable it was later appropriated as one of the Joker's aliases in the Batman comic books.

Punning and alliteration may not in themselves qualify as high style, but you don't have to look at Charteris's pre-war Saint books for very long before realising that here was a light fiction stylist of the highest order. The very earliest Saint stories may have betrayed a tendency towards rather clotted and overlong sentences, while the Saint himself had a distressing fondness for composing facetious poems and inflicting them on the reader at unnecessary length. But these were the fledgling gaucheries of a writer who, after all, was a mere twenty years of age when he invented Simon Templar.

Soon enough Charteris proved himself a master of three literary forms—the short story, the novella, and the full-length novel. For dazzling proof of this, try (just taking three titles at random) "The Green Goods Man" (1932), "The Elusive Ellshaw" (1934), and *The Saint Plays with Fire* (1938). (It will come as no surprise that these three were originally known as "The Very Green Goods Man," "The Race Train Crime," and *Prelude for War.*) With Simon Templar as his dashingly piratical mouthpiece, Charteris used these and other stories as a means of expressing his contempt for the flabby evasions and hidden corruption of contemporary life. In the process, the Saint earned the sobriquet "the Robin Hood of modern crime" while Charteris was hailed as the natural successor to Edgar Wallace.

To me, though, Charteris's real literary master was P. G. Wodehouse.

As a boy my bedside table was rarely without a Wodehouse, as often as not coupled with an Ian Fleming, both books being read in tandem. *Moonraker* might rub shoulders with *Joy in the Morning*, *Dr No* with *The Luck of the Bodkins*, and so on. Had I also been familiar with Charteris at that early age, I would have made a marvellous discovery—for here was a writer who combined the cruel action-thriller excitement of James Bond with Galahad Threepwood's highly developed sense of the absurd.

In *The Ace of Knaves*, for example, you'll encounter one of Charteris's most memorable creations, the Saint's hapless would-be nemesis, Claud Eustace Teal. "He bit on his chewing gum," writes Charteris, "with the ferocious energy of a hungry cannibal tasting a mouthful of tough missionary." Elsewhere, a beautiful film star looks at the Saint "with so much loathing and hatred and disgust that Simon knew just what it felt like to be one of those wriggly things with too many legs that make their abode under flat stones."

Pure Wodehouse.

The genius of Charteris, however, is that he subverts this breezy style with grisly underworld details and thus creates a style all his own. "In the course of a long and wide experience," pronounces the Saint with perfect sang-froid, "I've rarely seen a head bashed in with so much thoroughness. I shouldn't be surprised if they found his brains coming out through his eyes when they turned him over."

And Charteris tightens the screw yet further by having the Saint playfully characterise the monster responsible for this hideous head-bashing as, of all things, Pongo. What Wodehouse fan can fail to be reminded of that mild-mannered habitué of the Drones Club, Pongo Twistleton?

On top of this, Charteris's relish for language finds him tossing in ten-dollar words like pachydermatously, fuliginous, and epizootic (the last two on consecutive pages), describing the noise of a lorry's engine as "scrangling," calling a consignment of illegal liquor "contraband stagger soup," and having a minor hood mistake his f's for m's when using phrases like "none of your muckin' business." Lovely stuff.

The Ace of Knaves was first published in June 1937 and finds Charteris, and the Saint, at the height of his powers. Throughout all three of the novellas contained in it, Charteris's prose offers a sparkling combination of the lean and laconic with the florid and fruity.

"The Spanish War" originated as "Return of the Saint" in the 13 February 1937 issue of *The Thriller* and is, at bottom, a classic clash between Templar and Teal, with the Spanish Civil War as an unlikely catalyst. It also features a mild instance of the kind of racism that cropped up so frequently among Charteris's contemporaries. Himself an Anglo-Chinese, Charteris almost never succumbed to this kind of thing, though one could perhaps point to the torturer Ngano in "The Million Pound Day" (aka "Black Face") and the revoltingly lecherous Abdul Osman in "The Death Penalty." Here, however, there's a very peculiar reference to Luis Quintana's teeth as a "characteristic Spanish row of irregular fangs covered with greenish-yellow slime." Immediately after *The Ace of Knaves*, Charteris published the novel *Thieves' Picnic* (aka *The Saint Bids Diamonds*), which contains more slurs against the natives of Tenerife (where Charteris had recently taken a Christmas vacation) than one would have thought possible.

Unusually, "The Unlicensed Victuallers" had had no prior existence as a magazine story. This bracing night-time tale of liquor smuggling in 1930s Dorset is distinguished by three things. First, there's the intriguing figure of society girl-turned-smuggler Brenda Marlow, who seems like a trial run for the scintillating Lady Valerie Woodchester in Charteris's classic novel *The Saint Plays with Fire*. Second, the Saint falls, uncharacteristically, into a very transparent trap. Finally, the outrageously brutal ending can leave the unsuspecting reader slack-jawed with amazement even today. Here, the Saint's amoral code dispenses the roughest of rough justice, literally fighting fire with fire.

"The Beauty Specialist," which started life as "The Z-Man" in the 27 March 1937 edition of *The Thriller*, is a gruesome delight from start to finish, with a particularly odious and sadistic villain whom Simon compares to both Count Dracula and Boris Karloff. The milieu of the British film industry gives the story added flavour, with Beatrice Avery, Irene Cromwell, and Sheila Ireland roughly comparable to such real-life stars as, say, Jessie Matthews, Vivien Leigh, and Merle Oberon.

The film industry was no doubt much on Charteris's mind at the time, since film rights to the Saint had recently been snapped up by RKO. The first Saint film, *The Saint in New York*, was completed in March 1938 and starred Louis Hayward as the ideal cinematic Simon Templar. Twenty-odd years later, of course, another definitive Saint turned up on TV in the form of Roger Moore. And with him came—inevitably—yet another round of re-titlings.

"The Spanish War" became a 1963 episode called "The Work of Art," in which the

Spanish Civil War was supplanted by Algeria's more topical struggle for independence from France, with the black-browed Martin Benson ideally cast as Quintana. The same year, "The Beauty Specialist" became "Marcia." This one was named after the story's deceased film star (whom Charteris had called Mercia) and featured budding star Samantha Eggar as "Claire" Avery. It also offered a delightfully detailed insight into *The Saint*'s home studio, Elstree, as would other film industry episodes like "Starring the Saint" and "Simon and Delilah." Then in 1964 "The Unlicensed Victuallers" was radically adapted as

"The Hi-Jackers," which replaced Dorset with Munich's Oktoberfest and turned Brenda Marlow into Mathilde Baum. Why? To facilitate the casting of German beauty Ingrid Schoeller.

Consistently glossy and charming as *The Saint* series was (and remains), it suffered from the same in-built problem that afflicted the contemporaneous BBC series *The World of Wooster*. Roger Moore and Ivor Dean may have been ideal as Templar and Teal, just as Dennis Price and Ian Carmichael were perfectly suited to Jeeves and Wooster. But there was really no substitute for Charteris's—and Wodehouse's—prose.

For that, of course, you have to go back to the original books. And, in the annals of the Saint, *The Ace of Knaves* is one of the very best. In fact, its US first edition carried a two-word endorsement ("Simply corking!") from—guess who?

That's right. P. G. Wodehouse.

—Jonathan Rigby

THE SAINT IN ACTION

PREFACE

Although this is by no means one of the first Saint books—in fact, it stands seventeenth in the series—I still think it may be helpful to preface this umpteenth reprinting with a reminder that it was first published more than a quarter-century ago, and its adventures take place amid the current history of those times.

The Spanish War referred to in the first story is therefore the one which began in 1935. The truck driver's wages of ten pounds a week mentioned in the second story were not bad wages in those days. Nor would the £10,000 quoted in the last story have seemed quite as small a bite of a film star's fortune as it does today. The reader will come upon many other such symptoms of a certain antiquity.

I am leaving them unchanged, as I have decided to do in other reprints, because after all it's obvious that all the Saint's adventures could not have happened last week, and that is what life was like in those days.

—Leslie Charteris (1962)

THE SPANISH WAR

1

Simon Templar folded his newspaper with a sigh and laid it reverently to rest in the wastebasket.

"We live in a wonderful country," he observed. "Did you read how two policemen and one policewoman practically lived in a night-club in Brighton for about three weeks, drawing their wages from the ratepayers all the time and drinking gallons of champagne at the ratepayers' expense, until they finally managed to lure some poor fathead into the place and get him to buy them a drink after time? And that's what we pay taxes for. Our precious politicians can go to Geneva and swindle the Abyssinians with all the dignity of a gang of bucket-shop promoters, and slap the poor deluded Spaniard on the back and tell him he's just dreaming about Italians and Germans helping the rebels in his so-called civil war, but the honour of England has been vindicated. A bloke is fined fifty quid for selling a whisky and soda at half-past eleven and another bloke is fined a fiver for drinking it, two policemen and one policewoman have had a wonderful free jag and helped themselves towards promotion, and the world has been shown that England respects the Law. Rule, Britannia."

Patricia Holm smiled tolerantly.

"I love you when your gorge rises," she said, and the Saint chuckled.

"It's a beautiful gorge, darling," he answered. "And talking about the Law, it seems a long time since we saw anything of dear old Chief Inspector Teal."

"He doesn't go abroad very much," Patricia pointed out. "If you stayed at home for a bit I expect you'd see plenty of him."

Simon nodded.

"There's plenty of him to see," he agreed, "and I suppose we'll be seeing it. I can't go on being respectable indefinitely."

He got up from the breakfast table and stretched himself lazily by the open windows.

The spring sunshine lay in pools between the trees of the Park and twinkled on the delicate green of the young leaves that were still too freshly budded for the London air to have dulled their colour, and the same sunshine twinkled in the smile with which the Saint looked back at Patricia. It was a smile that made any disclaimer of respectability seem almost superfluous. Respectability was a disease that could never have attacked a man with a smile in which there was so much unconquerable devilment it couldn't have found a foothold anywhere in any one of the seventy-four inches of slimly muscular length that separated his crisp black hair from the soles of his polished shoes. And with that smile laughing its irresistible way into her eyes, Patricia felt again as fresh and ageless as if she were only meeting it then for the first time, the gay disreputable magic of that incomparable buccaneer whom the newspapers had christened the Robin Hood of modern crime, and whom the police and the underworld alike had called by many worse names.

"I suppose you can't," she said resignedly, and knew that she was stating one of the few immutable certainties of this unsettled world.

Simon lighted a cigarette with an impenitent grin, and turned to the door as Orace's walrus face poked itself into the room.

"Someone wantin' to see yer," said Orace, and the Saint raised his eyebrows. "Does he look like a detective?" he asked hopefully.

Orace shook his head.

"Nossir. 'E looks like a gennelman."

Simon went through into the living-room and found his visitor standing by the table flicking over the pages of the *New Yorker*. He dropped the magazine and turned quickly as the Saint came in. He was a youngish man with brown curly hair and a lantern jaw and rimless glasses. The Saint, whose life had depended more than once on his gift for measuring up strangers with a casual glance, guessed that Orace's diagnosis was probably correct, and also that his visitor was slightly agitated.

"Mr Templar? I've never had the pleasure of meeting you, but I've seen your picture and read about you in the papers. I've really got no business to come and take up your time, but—"

The Saint nodded. He was used to people who really had no business to come and take up his time—it was one of the penalties of fame, but it had often turned out to be a profitable penalty. He held out his cigarette-case.

"Sit down and let's hear what's on your mind," he said soothingly. "I've never met you either, so anyway we start square."

"My name's Graham—Geoffrey Graham." The young man took a cigarette and sat on the arm of a chair as if he expected to bounce off at any moment. "I don't know how much you want to know about me—I'm an articled pupil in an architect's office, and I live in Bloomsbury—my family live in Yorkshire and they aren't very well off—"

"Have you murdered somebody?" asked the Saint gravely.

"No. No, I haven't done that—"

"Or burgled a bank?"

"No, but—"

"It might have been quite exciting if you had," said the Saint calmly. "But as things are, suppose you tell me what the trouble is first, and then we'll decide how far back to go into the story of your life."

"Well—"

The expectation was justified. The young man did bounce off the chair. He pulled a bundle of large folded papers out of his pocket, disengaged one of them, and held it out.

"Well, look," he said. "What d'you think this is?"

Simon unfolded the document. It was printed on crisp heavy paper, and very beautifully engraved; it looked as if it might have been valuable, but most men would have studied it for some time before venturing to define it. Simon held it up to the light, rubbed it between his fingers, and flipped it back on to the table.

"It seems to be one of the new American Government short-term loan thousand-dollar bearer bonds," he said, in much the same way as he might have said, "It seems to be a bus ticket to Wimbledon," but his blue eyes had settled into a quiet and rather watchful interestedness.

Graham pulled out a handkerchief and wiped his forehead.

"My God," he said. He breathed heavily once or twice. "Well, that's what I'd come to the conclusion it was, only I couldn't believe it. I thought I'd better make sure. You know, I've read about those things in stories, like everybody else, but I'd never seen one before. My God!"

He blinked down at the handful of papers which he was still clutching, and threw them down on the table beside the specimen.

"Look," he said in an awe-stricken voice. "There's thirty-four more of 'em. That's thirty-five thousand dollars—seven thousand pounds—isn't it?"

Simon picked up the collection and glanced through them.

"It was when I was at school," he said. "Are you making a collection or something?"

"Well, not exactly. I got them out of a fellow's desk."

"There must be money in architecture," said the Saint encouragingly.

"No, it wasn't at the office. This was a fellow who lived in the same boarding-house with me when I was living in Bayswater. You see—"

The Saint studied him thoughtfully. His uninvited callers in the past had included more than one optimistic gentleman who had tried to sell him a machine for making diamonds or turning water into lubricating oil, and he was always glad to listen to a new story. But although the opening he had just listened to might well have served as a prelude to one of those flights of misdirected ingenuity which were the Saint's perennial joy and occasional source of income, there seemed to be something genuine about the young man in front of him which didn't quite fit in with the Saint's shrewdly discriminating suspicions.

"Why not start at the beginning and go on to the end?" he suggested.

"It's quite simple, really," explained Graham, as if he didn't find it simple at all. "You see, about six months ago I lent this fellow a tenner."

"What fellow?"

"His name's David Ingleston. I knew him quite slightly, the way you know people in a boarding-house, but he seemed all right, and he said he'd pay me back in a week. He hasn't paid me back yet. He kept promising to pay me back, but when the time came he'd always have some excuse or other. When I moved my digs to Bloomsbury it got worse—if I rang up or went to see him he'd be out, or he'd have been sent abroad by his firm, or something, and if I wrote to him he didn't answer, and so on. I'm not very well off, as I told you, and a tenner means quite a bit to me. I was getting pretty fed up with it." The young man stared resentfully at the sheaf of bonds on the table, as if they personified the iniquity of their owner.

"Well, the other day I found out that he was back in England and that he'd moved into a flat in Chelsea. That made it seem worse, because I thought if he could afford to move into a flat he could afford to pay me my ten quid. I rang him up and I happened to catch him at home for once, so I told him what I thought of him. He was very apologetic, and he asked me to go round and have a drink with him last night and he'd pay me the tenner then. I was there at half-past eight, and he was out, but the maid said I could wait. I kicked my heels for half an hour, and then I began to get angry. After I'd waited an hour I was thoroughly furious. I guessed that he'd forgotten the appointment, or he just wasn't going to keep it, and I could see I'd be waiting another ten years before I got my tenner back. The only thing I could think of was to take it out of him some other way. I couldn't see anything worth pinching that was small enough for me to sneak out under my coat, so I pulled open a drawer of the desk, and I saw those things."

"So you borrowed them for security."

"I didn't really stop to think about it. I didn't know what they were, but they looked as if they might be valuable, so I just shoved them into my pocket. Then the maid came in and said she was going home because she didn't sleep in the flat, and she didn't think she'd better leave me there alone. I was just boiling by that time, so I told her she could tell Ingleston I'd have something to say to him later, and marched off. When I got home and had another look at what I'd pinched I began to get the wind up. I couldn't very well take the things into a bank and ask about them, but I thought that you . . . Well, you know, you—"

"You don't have to feel embarrassed," murmured the Saint kindly. "I have heard people say that they thought my principles were fairly broad-minded. Still, I'm not thinking of sending for the police, although for an amateur burglar you do seem to have got off to a pretty good start."

The young man's lantern jaw became even longer and squarer.

"I don't want Ingleston's beastly bonds," he said, "but I do want my tenner."

"I know," said the Saint sympathetically. "But the Law doesn't allow you to pinch things from people just because they owe you money. It may be ridiculous, but there it is. Hasn't Ingleston rung you up or anything since you pushed off with his bonds?"

"No, but perhaps he hasn't missed them yet."

"If he had, you'd probably have heard from him—the maid would have told him you'd been waiting an hour for him last night. Let's hope he hasn't missed them, because if he felt nasty you might have had the police looking for you."

Graham looked slightly stunned.

"But I didn't mean to keep the things—"

"You pinched them," Simon pointed out. "And the police don't know anything about what people mean. Do you realise that you've committed larceny on a scale that'd make a lot of professionals jealous, and that you could be sent to prison for quite a long time?"

The other's mouth fell open.

"I hadn't thought of it like that," he said feebly. "It was all on the spur of the moment—I hadn't realised—My God, what am I going to do?"

"The best thing you can do, my lad," said the Saint sensibly, "is to put them back before there's any fuss."

"But—"

There was something so comical about the young man's blankly horrified paralysis that Simon couldn't help taking pity on him.

"Come on," he said. "He can't eat you, and the sooner he gets his bonds back the less likely he is to try. Look here—I'll drive over with you if you like and see that he behaves himself, and we'll take a tenner off him at the same time."

"It's awfully good of you," Graham began weakly, and the Saint grinned and stood up.

"We always try to oblige our customers," he said.

He picked up the bundle of bonds and stuffed them into his own pocket. On the way out he looked in at the dining-room to wrinkle his nose at Patricia.

"You'll have to button your own boots," he said. "I'm tottering out for an hour or so to do my Boy Scout act. Where's my bugle?"

He thought of it no more seriously than that, as a mildly amusing interlude to pass the morning between a late breakfast and a cocktail before lunch. The last idea in his head was that he might be setting out on an adventure whose brief intensity would rank with the wildest of his many immortal escapades, and perhaps if it had not been for all those other adventures he might have missed this one altogether. But the heritage of those other adventures was an instinct, the habit of a lifetime, a sixth sense too subtle to define, that fell imperceptibly and unconsciously into tune with the swift smoky rhythm of danger, and that queer intuition caught him like an electric current as the long shining Hirondel purred close to the address that Graham had given him. It caught him quicker than his mind could work—so quickly that before he could analyse his thoughts he had smacked the gear lever down into second, whipped the car behind the cover of a crawling taxi, and whirled out of sight of the building around the next corner.

2

"That was the house," Graham protested. "You just passed it."

"I know," said the Saint.

He locked the handbrake as the car pulled in to the kerb, and turned to look back at the corner they had just taken. The movement was automatic, although he knew that he couldn't see the entrance of the house from where they had stopped, but in his memory he could see it as clearly as if the angle of the building which hid it from his eyes had been made of glass—the whole little tableau that had blazed those high-voltage danger signals into his brain.

Not that there had been anything sensational about it, anything that would have had that instantaneous and dynamic effect on the average man's reactions. Just seven or eight assorted citizens of various but quite ordinary and unexciting shapes and sizes, loafing and gaping inanely about the pavement, with the door of the house which Simon had been making for as a kind of vague focus linking them roughly together. A constable in uniform standing beside the door, and a rotund pink-faced man in a bowler hat who had emerged from the hall to speak to him at the very moment when the Saint's eye was grasping the general outlines of the scene. Nothing startling or prodigious, but it was enough to keep the Saint sitting there with his eyes keen and intent while he went over the details in his mind. Perhaps it was the memory of that round man with a face like a slightly apoplectic cherub, who had come out to speak to the policeman . . .

Graham was staring at him perplexedly. "What's the matter?" he asked.

The Saint looked at him, almost without seeing him, and a faint aimless smile touched his lips.

"Nothing," he said. "Can you drive a car?"

"Fairly well."

"Drive this one. She's a bit of a handful, so you'd better take it easy. Don't put your foot down too quickly, or you'll find yourself a mile or two ahead of yourself."

"But—"

"Go back to my place. You'll find a girl there—name of Patricia Holm. I'll phone her and tell her you're on your way. She'll give you a drink and prattle to you till I get back. I'd like to pay this call alone."

"But—"

Simon swung his legs over the side and pushed himself off on to the pavement.

"That seems to be quite a favourite word of yours," he remarked. "On your way, brother. You can tell me all about it presently."

He stood and watched the Hirondel take a leap forward like a loosed antelope and then crawl on up the road with a very mystified young man clinging grimly to the steering-wheel, and then he turned into a convenient tobacconist's and put a call through to Patricia.

"I'm sending my Boy Scout material back for you to look after," he said. "Feed him some ginger ale and keep him happy till I get back. I wouldn't flirt with him too much, because I think he's a rather earnest soul. And if there should be any inquiries, tell Orace to hide him in the oven and don't let anybody know we've got him."

"Does this mean you're getting into trouble again?" she demanded ominously. "Because if you are—"

"Darling, I am about to have a conference with the vicar about the patterns for the next sewing bee," said the Saint, and hung up the receiver.

He lighted a cigarette as he sauntered down to the corner and across the street towards the house which he had been meaning to visit. The scene was still more or less the same, one or two new idle citizens having joined the small accumulation of inquisitive loafers, and one or two of the old congregation having grown tired of gaping at nothing and moved off. The policeman still stood majestically by the door, although the man in the bowler hat no longer obstructed the opening. The policeman moved a little to do some obstructing of his own as the Saint ambled up the steps.

"Do you live here, sir?"

"No," said the Saint amiably. "Do you?" The constable gazed at him woodenly.

"Who do you want to see?"

"I should like to see Chief Inspector Teal," Simon told him impressively. "He's expecting me."

The policeman studied him suspiciously for a moment, but the Saint was very impressive. He looked like a man whom a Chief Inspector might have been expecting. He might equally well have been expected by a Prime Minister, a film actress, or a man who trained budgerigars to play the trombone, but the constable was not a sufficiently profound thinker to take this universal view. He turned and led the way into the house, and Simon followed him. They went through the hall, which had the empty and sanitary and fresh-painted air common to all houses which have been recently converted into flats, and through the half-open door of a ground-floor flat a strip of curl-papered female goggled at them morbidly as they went by. At the top of the empty and sanitary and freshly painted stairs the door of another flat was ajar, with another policeman standing beside it.

"Someone to see the Inspector," said the first policeman, and, having discharged his duty, went downstairs again to resume his vigil.

The second policeman opened the door, and they went into the hall of the flat. Almost opposite the entrance was the open door of the living-room, and as the Saint reached it he saw four men moving about. There was a man fiddling with a camera on a tripod near the door, and across the room another man was poring over the furniture with a bottle of grey powder and a camel-hair brush and magnifying glass. A tall, thin, melancholy looking man with a large notebook stood a little way apart, sucking the end of a pencil, and the man with the bowler hat and the figure like an inverted egg whom Simon had seen from his car was peering over his shoulder at what had been written down.

It was on the last of these men that the Saint's eyes rested as he entered the room. He remained indifferent to the other stares that swivelled round to greet him with bovine curiosity, waiting until the bowler hat tilted towards him. And as it did so, a warm and friendly smile established itself on the Saint's face.

"What ho, Claud Eustace," he said affably.

The china-blue eyes under the brim of the bowler hat grew larger and rounder as they assimilated the shock of identification. In them, even a man with the firmest intentions of believing nothing but good of his fellow men would have found it hard to discern any of that spontaneous cordiality and cheer with which a well-mannered wanderer in the great wilderness of life should have returned the greeting of a brother voyager. To be precise, they looked as if their owner had just discovered that he was in the act of absent-mindedly swallowing a live toad.

A rich tint of sun-kissed plum mantled the face below the eyes, and the man seemed to quiver a little, like a volcano seeking for some means of self-expression. After one or two awful seconds he found it.

"What the hell are you doing here?" blared Chief Inspector Claud Eustace Teal.

3

It must be admitted in Mr Teal's defence that he was not normally a man who blared, or whose eyes tended to perform strange antics. Left to himself, he would have been a placid and even-tempered soul, with all the sluggish equanimity appropriate to his girth, and as a matter of fact he had during his earlier years with the Criminal Investigation Department developed a pose of exaggerated sleepiness and perpetual boredom of which he was extremely proud. It was the advent of the Saint on Mr Teal's halcyon horizon which had changed all that, and made the detective an embittered and an apoplectic man.

Not that there was one single crime on the record, one microscopic molecule of a misdemeanour, for which Chief Inspector Teal could have taken official action against the Saint. That was a great deal of the trouble, and the realisation of it did nothing to brighten the skies above the detective's well-worn and carefully laundered bowler. But it sometimes seemed to Mr Teal that all the griefs and misfortunes that had afflicted him in recent years could be directly traced to the exploits of that incredible outlaw who had danced so long and so derisively just beyond Mr Teal's legal reach—who had mocked him, baffled him, cheated him, eluded him, brought down upon him the not entirely justified censure of his superiors, and set him more insoluble problems than any other man alive. Perhaps it was some of these acid memories that welled up into the detective's weary brain and stimulated that spontaneous outburst of feeling. For wherever the Saint went there was trouble, and trouble of a kind with which Mr Teal had grown miserably familiar.

"Claud!" said the Saint reprovingly. "Is that nice? Is it kind? Is that the way your dear old mother would like to hear you speak?"

"Never mind my mother—"

"How could I, Claud? I never met her. How's she getting on?"

Mr Teal swallowed, and turned towards the policeman who had brought Simon in. "What did you let him in for?" he demanded, in a voice of fearful menace.

The policeman swayed slightly before the blast.

"Richards brought him up, sir. I understood you were expecting him—"

"And so you are, Claud," said the Saint. "Why be so bashful about it?" Teal stared at him malevolently.

"Why should I be expecting you?"

"Because you always are. It's a habit. Whenever anybody does anything, you come and unbosom yourself to me. Whenever any crime's been committed, I did it. So just for once I thought I'd come and see you and save you the trouble of coming to see me. Pretty decent of me, I call it."

"How did you know a crime had been committed?"

"It was Deduction," said the Saint. "You see, I happened to be ambling along by here when I saw a policeman at the door and a small crowd outside, and your intellectual features leering out of the door to say something to the said cop, so I went into a tea-shop and had a small cup of cocoa while I thought it over. I admit that the first idea that crossed my mind was that you'd been thrown out—I mean that you'd retired from the Force and gone in for Art, and that you were holding an exhibition of your works, and that the crowd outside was waiting for the doors to open, and that you were telling the cop to keep them in order for a bit because you couldn't find your false beard. It was only after some remarkable brain work that I avoided falling into this error. Gradually the real solution dawned on me—"

"Now you mention it," Teal said ominously, "why did you happen to be ambling along here?"

"Why shouldn't I, Claud? I have to amble somewhere, and they say this is a free country. There are several thousands of other people ambling around Chelsea, but do you rush out into the streets and grab them and ask them why?"

Mr Teal's pudgy fists clenched inside his pockets. It was happening again—the same as it always had. He set out to be a detective, and some evil spirit turned him into a clown. It wasn't his fault. It was the fault of that debonair, mocking, lazily smiling Mephistopheles who was misnamed the Saint, who seemed to have been born with the uncanny gift of paralysing the detective's trained and native caution and luring him into howling gaucheries that made Mr Teal go hot and cold when he thought about them. And the more often it happened, the more easily it happened next time. There was an awful fatefulness about it that made Mr Teal want to burst into tears.

He took hold of himself doggedly, glowering up at the Saint with a concentrated uncharitableness that would have made a lion think twice before biting him.

"Well," he said, with a restraint that made the veins stand out on his forehead, "what do you want here?"

"I just thought I'd drop in and see how you were getting on with your detecting. Quite a jolly little murder it looks, too, if I may say so."

For the first time since the casual glance he had taken round the room when he came in, his cool gaze went back to the crumpled shape on the floor.

It lay on the floor, close to the fireplace and a side table on which stood a bottle of whisky and a siphon—the body of what seemed to have been a man of medium size and build, wearing an ordinary dark suit. His hair looked as if it might have been a pale gingery colour, but it was difficult to be sure about that, because there was not much of it that was not clotted with the blood that had flowed from his smashed skull and spread in a pool over the carpet. There was not much of the back of his head left at all, as a matter of fact, for the smashing had been carried out very methodically and with the obvious intention of making sure that there would never be any need to repeat the dose. A little distance away lay the instrument with which the smashing had been done: it looked like an ordinary cheap hammer, and the wooden handle was so clean that it might well have been bought new for the purpose.

The rest of the room was in disorder. Books had been pulled out of their shelves, the carpet was wrinkled as if it had been pulled up to examine the floor underneath, cushions had been taken out of the chairs, and there were gashes in the upholstery. All the drawers of the desk were open—one of them had been pulled right out and left on the floor, and another was upturned on the table. A mass of papers was scattered around like a stage snowfall. A yard from the dead man's right hand, a tumbler lay on its side at the edge of a pool of moisture where its contents had soaked into the carpet.

"Quite a jolly little murder," Simon repeated. Teal went on watching him suspiciously.

"Do you know anything about it?"

"Not a thing," said the Saint honestly. "Do you?"

Chief Inspector Teal dug into his waistcoat pocket and extracted from it a small pink rectangular packet. From this he drew a small pink envelope, unwrapped it, and fed the contents into his mouth. There was a short interval of silence, while his salivary glands responded exquisitely to the stimulus and his teeth mashed the strip of gum into a conveniently malleable wedge.

The delay, coupled with the previous pause while the Saint had been studying the scenery, gave him a chance to complete the recovery of his self-possession, and Mr Teal had been making the most of his respite. Some of the rich purple had faded out of his face, and his eyelids had started to droop. His brain was reviving from its first shock and beginning to function again.

"It looks like an ordinary murder and robbery to me," he answered, with a gruff straightforwardness which he hoped was convincing. "Hardly in your line, I should say."

"Anything is in my line if it helps you," said the Saint generously. "Mmm . . . robbery. The place does look as if it had been taken apart, doesn't it?" He drifted about the room, taking in details. "Couple of nice silver cups on the mantelpiece. Gold cigarette-case. Burglars certainly are getting choosey these days, aren't they, Claud? Why, I can remember a time when none of 'em would have turned up their noses at a few odds and ends like that."

"They may have been looking for something more valuable," Teal said temptingly.

The Saint nodded.

"Yes, that's possible—you must have been reading a book or something."

"Have you any idea what that could have been?"

Simon thought for a moment.

"I know," he said suddenly. "It was the plans for the new death ray which the master spy with the hare-lip stole from the War Office in Chapter Three."

Mr Teal felt the arteries in his neck throbbing, but with a superhuman effort he clung to his precariously rescued sang-froid, chewing fiercely on his blob of spearmint.

"Oh yes," he said, with desperate moderation. "But we don't really believe in things like that. They must have thought he had something here that they could get money for—" "They?" said the Saint, as if the point had just occurred to him. "I see—you've already found that there were several blokes involved in it."

"I was saying that to be on the safe side. Of course, we haven't found any evidence yet—"

"Nobody would expect you to," Simon encouraged him liberally. "After all, you're only detectives, and that isn't your job. If this had been a night-club where the deceased was serving drinks after hours, it would have been quite a different matter. But making allowances for that—"

"What would you see?"

Simon pointed.

"There's whisky and a siphon on that small table. And one glass with what looks like whisky in it. Just one. On the floor there's another glass, surrounded by a certain amount of dampness. What happens when a bloke's dishing up a round of drinks? Normally, he pours out the whisky into however many glasses he's using. Then he squirts the soda into the glass of the first victim, tells him to say when, hands him his dose of medicine, and goes on to the next. And so on."

"So you think there was only one other man here, and the murderer hit him while he was filling the first glass?"

"I didn't say so," responded the Saint airily. "I didn't say 'man' in the first place. It might have been some of these hairy Olympic female champions—some of 'em sling a pretty hefty hammer, I believe. And all the rest of them may have been teetotallers, so they wouldn't be getting a drink."

Teal edged his gum into a hollow tooth and held it there heroically.

"All the same," he persisted, "you do think it looks as if he, or she, or they, were on fairly friendly terms with . . ."

He hesitated.

"With Comrade Ingleston?" Simon prompted him kindly. "How did you know that?"

The brassy note was creeping back into Teal's voice, and he tried to strangle the symptom with a gulp that almost ruptured his larynx. The ensuing silence made him feel as self-conscious as if he had blared out like a bugle, but the Saint was only smiling with unaltered affability.

"How did I know they were friendly? Well, after all, when you start pouring out drinks—"

"How did you know his name was Ingleston?"

"I was just guessing," said the Saint apologetically. "I took it that the motive was robbery, going on what you said. Therefore the robberee was the murderee, so to speak. Therefore the corpse was the owner of this flat and all that therein is. Therefore he was the owner of that photo."

The detective blinked at him distrustfully for a second or two, and then went back to the mantelpiece and peered at the picture he had indicated. It was a framed photograph of a plump swarthy man in horn-rimmed spectacles, and across the lower part of it was scrawled:

A mi buen amigo
D. David Ingleston,
con mucho afecto de
LUIS QUINTANA

Mr Teal was no linguist, but he scarcely needed to be.

"Just another spot of this deduction business," Simon explained modestly. "Of course, these tricks must seem frightfully easy to you professionals, but to an amateur like myself—"

"1 was only wondering how you knew," Teal said shortly.

The brassy note was still jangling in his vocal chords, but the texture of it was different. He seemed disappointed. He was disappointed. He hit on his chewing-gum with the ferocious energy of a hungry cannibal tasting a mouthful of tough missionary.

"It does look as if the murderer or murderers were on friendly terms with Ingleston," he said presently. "Apart from the glasses, none of the windows seems to have been tampered with, and the front door hasn't been touched."

"How was the murder discovered?"

"When the maid came in this morning. She has her own key."

"You've checked up on Ingleston's friends?"

"We haven't had time to do much in that line yet. But the maid says that a friend of his waited over an hour for him here last night, until she sent him away because she wanted to go home. She says that this fellow seemed to be in a rage about something, and when he went off he said he'd have something to say to Ingleston later, so he may have waited in the street until Ingleston came home and followed him upstairs."

The Saint nodded interestedly. "Did she know who he was?"

"Oh yes, we know who he was," said Mr Teal confidently. "It won't take long to find him."

His drowsy eyes were fastened unwinkingly on the Saint's face, watching for the slightest betrayal of emotion, but Simon only nodded again with benevolent approval.

"Then there really doesn't seem to be anything for me to do," he drawled. "With that Sherlock Holmes brain of yours and the great organisation behind you, I shall expect to read about the arrest in tomorrow morning's papers. And a good job too. These ruffians must be taught that crime will not be allowed to go unpunished so long as there is one honest bowler hat in Scotland Yard. Farewell, old faithful."

He buttoned his coat and held out his hand.

"Is that all you've got to say?" barked the detective, and Simon raised his eyebrows.

"What more can I add? You've got a gorgeous collection of clues, and I know you'll make the most of them. What poor words of mine could compete with the peals of praise that will echo down the corridors from the Chief Commissioner's office—"

"All right," said Teal blackly. "I'll know where to find you if I want you."

He stood and watched the Saint's broad, elegantly tailored back pass out through the door with a feeling as if he had recently been embalmed in glue. It was not the first time that Mr Teal had had that sensation after an interview with the Saint, but many repetitions had never inured him to it. All the peace and comfort had been taken out of his day. He had set out to attend to a nice, ordinary, straightforward, routine murder, and now he had to resign himself to the expectation that nothing about it would turn out to be nice or ordinary or straightforward or routine. Nothing that brought him in contact with the Saint ever did.

He turned wearily round, as if a great load had been placed on his shoulders, to find his subordinates watching him with a kind of smirking perplexity. Mr Teal's eyes glittered balefully.

"Get on with your work!" he snarled. "What d'you think this is—an old maids' home?"

He strode across to the telephone, and switched his incandescent glare on to the fingerprint expert. "Have you finished with this?"

"Y-yes, sir," stammered the man hastily. "There's nothing on it except the deceased's own prints—"

Mr Teal was not interested in that. He grabbed off the microphone and dialled Scotland Yard.

"I want somebody to tail Simon Templar, of Cornwall House, Piccadilly," he snapped, when he was through to his department. "Put a couple of good men on the job, and tell 'em to keep their eyes open. He's a slippery customer, and he'll lose them if they give him the chance. I want to know everything he does for twenty-four hours a day until further notice . . . Yes, I do mean the Saint—and if he gives them the slip they'll need some saints to pray for them!"

At that moment Simon Templar was not thinking about the possible consequences of being followed night and day by the heavy-footed minions of the C.I.D. His mind was entirely occupied with other consequences which struck him as being far less commonplace.

He had hailed a taxi outside the house, and as he was climbing in he heard a curious sharp crack of sound in front of him. He felt a quick stinging pain like the jab of a needle in his chin, and something like an angry wasp zoomed past his ear. As his head jerked up he saw a new spidery pattern of cracks in the window a couple of feet from his eyes—an irregular star-shaped spangle of lines radiating from a neat hole perforated in the glass, about the size of a .38-calibre bullet.

4

A split second later, the Saint's glinting gaze was raking the street and surrounding pavements instinctively, before he realised a moment afterwards that the shot could only have come from another car, which had crept up alongside the taxi so that some philanthropist could fire at him through the offside window as he boarded the cab from the pavement. As he started to search the scenery for the offending vehicle, a bus crashed past, shutting off his field of vision like a moving curtain, and as it went on its bulk effectively obliterated any glimpse he might have had of a car making off in the same direction.

Fortunately the gun must have been silenced, and the taxi driver must have taken the accompanying sound effects for a combination of the cough of a passing exhaust and the clumsiness of his passenger, for he had not even looked round. As the Saint settled on to the seat and closed the door through which he had entered, he grated the gears together and chugged away without any apparent awareness of the sensational episode that had taken place a few inches behind his unromantic back.

Simon took out a handkerchief and dabbed his chin where it had been nicked by a flying splinter of glass. Then he reached forward, unlatched the damaged door, and slammed it again with all his strength. The glass with the bullet-hole in it shattered with the impact and tinkled down into the road.

This time the driver did look round, jamming on his brakes at the same time. "'Ere," he protested plaintively, "wot's all this?"

"I'm sorry," said the Saint in distress. "The door wasn't fastened properly, and I must have banged it a bit too hard. I'll have to pay you for it."

"That you will," said the driver. "Free pahnds each, them winders cost."

"Okay," said the Saint. "You'll get your three pounds."

"Ar," said the driver.

He ground the gears again and sent the cab spluttering on, slightly mollified by the prospect of collecting double the cost of the repair, and the Saint sat back and took out a cigarette.

As far as he was concerned, it was worth the bonus to dispose of a witness who might have inconvenient recollections of a fare who allowed himself to be shot at "fru winders," but there were other points less easy to dispose of, and he was still considering them when he opened the door of his flat in Cornwall House.

He found Patricia with her feet up on the settee, smoking a cigarette, while Geoffrey Graham, balanced on springs on the edge of a chair as usual, appeared to be expounding the principles of architecture.

". . . You see, it isn't only functional, but the rhythmic balance of mass has to have a definite harmonic correlation—"

"Yippee," said the Saint gravely. "But what about the uncoordinated finials?"

The young man jumped up, turned pink, and spilt some beer from the tankard he was clutching. Patricia looked up with a rather wan smile.

"You haven't been very long," she said. "Mr Graham and I were only just getting to know each other."

"I should have said you were getting pretty intimate, myself," murmured the Saint.

"When you decide that it isn't only functional, and start to get a spot of harmonic correlation into your rhythmic masses—"

"That's enough," said Patricia.

"That's what I thought," said the Saint. "However . . ."

He grinned, and sat down beside her. Even under the mask of irrepressible flippancy which rarely left him, she could feel the keyed alertness vibrating within him like a charge of electricity.

"What's been happening?" she asked. "I've been on a party."

Graham's eyes beamed behind his glasses.

"Did you see Ingleston?"

"Oh yes. And very handsome he looked. You did a lovely job on the back of his head."

"I did a—"

"No, I don't really believe that. But I just wanted to see how you'd take it, to make sure." Simon reached for the cigarette-box. "Somebody else did, though. In the course of a long and wide experience, I've rarely seen a head bashed in with so much thoroughness. I shouldn't be surprised if they found his brains coming out through his eyes when they turned him over."

The young man's mouth fell slowly open, as if his chin was being lowered like a drawbridge.

"You don't say he's—dead?"

"If you're sensitive about it, we'll say he has awoken to life immortal. But the one certain thing is that he'll never pay you your tenner now, unless he's left it to you in his will. I had an idea something had gone screwy—that's why I sent you back here. It was sheer luck that I happened to see Chief Inspector Teal's tummy bulging out of the front door as we were driving up, otherwise the party might have been even breezier than it was."

Graham seemed to wobble a little as the full meaning of the Saint's words worked into his brain. His face went paler, and he steadied himself against the back of a chair. "Do you mean he was murdered?"

"That was the idea I was trying to put over," Simon admitted. "Directly I saw Claud Eustace floating around I knew something had blown up—he doesn't go chasing out with his magnifying glass and pedigree bloodhounds because somebody's lost a collar-stud. And there he was, with his photographers and fingerprinters and the body in the library, just like the best detective stories. So we had a cheery little chat."

"I think I need a drink," said Patricia faintly.

She got up and fetched a bottle of sherry and some glasses, and the Saint blew a smoke-ring and spoilt it with a chuckle.

"Are you out on bail, or did you just run away?" she inquired. "I mean, I don't want to interfere with you, but it'd be sort of helpful to know."

"Not a bit of it, darling. It wasn't that sort of chat. He puffed and trumpeted to some extent at the start, but that was only natural. I soothed him with my well-known charm, and then he got awfully cunning. If you've ever seen Claud Eustace being cunning, you won't want to go to the circus any more. He opened his heart to me and talked about the case and asked me all kinds of innocent questions, and he was working so hard at being affable that the perspiration was fairly streaming down his face; every time I gave him an innocent answer his eyes got smaller and brighter and I thought he was going to burst a blood-vessel. Of course, in order to keep the conversation going and bait his traps for me he had to give me a certain amount of information, and I was supposed to drop a few bricks in reply, but it didn't exactly work out that way, and eventually I thought I'd better push off before he had a seizure." The Saint's eyes danced behind the veils of smoke drifting across his face. "However, I didn't do too badly out of the exchange myself, and one of the useful bits of gossip I picked up was the name of the chief current suspect."

"Who's that?" asked Graham feverishly.

"You!"

The word hit Graham in the midriff and almost doubled him up. He gaped at the Saint with his Adam's apple jigging up and down like a yo-yo for some seconds before his voice came back.

"Me?" he croaked.

"Who else? You were the last person in the flat. You were very steamed up about seeing Ingleston. You were fuming when the maid slung you out. The last thing you told her was that you'd have something to say to Ingleston later. It's the sort of clue that even a policeman couldn't miss. They're looking for you now . . . Which reminds me."

He reached out for the telephone and called the porter's desk downstairs.

"That you, Sam? . . . Simon Templar speaking. You know that bloke who came to see me earlier this morning, who went out with me? . . . No, you're wrong. He didn't come back. In fact, he never came here at all. You never saw him in your life. Nobody's been to see me today. Have you got that? . . . Good man."

Graham was still breathing heavily. "But . . . but . . ."

"I know," said the Saint patiently. "But let's take things one at a time. Teal's sure to make inquiries here—in fact, I wouldn't mind betting that he's already got a team of flatfeet galumphing along here to pick up my trail. So long as they can't definitely hook you up with me, it'll be something in your favour, my reputation being what it is. They'll draw your digs and your office of course, but that doesn't matter. It's a good job you didn't leave those bonds at home, though, or they'd have had a warrant out for you by this time."

"Wouldn't it be better for him to get back as quickly as possible?" suggested Patricia. "If they think he's trying to dodge them it'll only make it look worse."

"The trouble is, there may be people looking for him who'd be a tot more dangerous than poor old Teal," said the Saint.

He spoke quite casually, but there was a shade of meaning in his voice that cut a tiny crease between Patricia's eyebrows and made Graham stiffen up.

Simon opened out his blood-spotted handkerchief, and touched the cut on his chin.

"Hadn't any of you noticed the damage to my beauty?" he inquired. "Or did you think I'd been having a shave while I was out?"

They looked at him in perplexity merging into a groping fragment of comprehension.

And the Saint smiled.

"I collected that on my way home—just after I left Ingleston's, to be accurate. I was getting into a taxi when some sportsman came by and turned on the tap. All I got hit by was a bit of broken glass, but that wasn't his fault. If he'd been a better shot it would have been the last time I made the headlines."

Complete understanding left them still silent, absorbing the implications according to their different temperaments and backgrounds. The frown smoothed out of Patricia's forehead, to be replaced by an expression of martyred resignation. Graham put down his tankard and mopped his brow with an unsteady hand.

"But who—"

"It's pretty obvious, I think," said the Saint. "Somebody knocked Ingleston off—we know that. For the sake of simplicity, let us call him

Pongo. Pongo was hanging around last night, waiting for Ingleston to come home, and he saw you come out. He'd have been watching the place pretty closely, so he wouldn't have forgotten your face, even if it didn't mean much to him at the time. Later on Ingleston arrives, Pongo accosts him and goes in with him—the evidence shows that he was somebody Ingleston knew—and while Ingleston is pouring out some drinks, Pongo gets to work on him with a hammer he's brought along for the purpose. Then after Ingleston has been removed, Pongo gets on with the real business of the evening and starts looking for whatever he came to find. He tears the whole place apart—it looked as if a tribe of monkeys had been through it—but my guess is that he doesn't find what he's looking for, because it's already gone."

"You mean those bonds I took?"

"Exactly. So after a while Pongo gives it up and amscrays, muttering curses in his beard. But he isn't ready to quit altogether, so this morning he's back on watch, waiting to see if he can get a line on the lost boodle. And what does he see but a car containing yourself, the bloke who came out of the place last night, and me. We look as if we were going to pull up at the door, and then we suddenly whizz on and stop around the next corner. All very suspicious. Pongo curls his moustachios and lurks like anything. I hop out of the car, and you go on with it. Pongo has one awful moment while he wonders which way he ought to go and whether he can split himself in half, and then he decides to stick to me—(a) because I'm a new factor that might be worth investigating, (b) because I'm obviously going back to the scene of the crime and you aren't, and possibly (c) because he knows who you are and knows he can pick you up again if he wants to. Pongo sees me speak to the cop at the door and go in; presently I come out again, so he takes his chance and lets fly."

"But why?"

The Saint shrugged.

"Maybe he didn't like my face. Maybe he knew who I was and was scared things might get too hot if I was butting in. Maybe he'd already trailed you here and he'd only just made up his mind what to do about both of us, which would mean you're next on his list. Maybe a lot of things. That's one of the questions we've got to find the answer to."

"But what's it all about?"

"It appears to be about seven thousand quids' worth of bearer bonds, which is enough reason for a good many things to happen. What I'd like to know is how a man who couldn't pay you a tenner collected all that mazuma. What sort of a job was he in?"

"He was with a firm of sherry importers in the City."

"Sherry!"

The Saint was motionless for a moment, and then he took another cigarette. He couldn't have explained himself what it was that had struck that sudden new crispness into his nerves—it was as if he was trying to make his conscious mind catch up with a spurt of intuition that had outdistanced it.

"You told me that Ingleston had been abroad recently," he said. "Would he have been likely to go to Spain?"

"I expect so. He'd been sent there several times before. He spoke Spanish very well, you see—"

"Did he have a lot of Spanish friends?"

"I don't know."

"He had one, anyway—there was a signed photograph inscribed in Spanish on his mantelpiece. Did you ever hear of Luis Quintana?"

"No."

"He's a representative that the Spanish rebels sent over a few weeks ago . . ."

Simon jumped up and moved restlessly across the room.

There was a fierce drive of energy in the restrained movements of his limbs that had to reach some hidden objective quickly or burn itself to exhaustion.

"Sherry," he said. "Spain. Spanish rebels. American bearer bonds. And mysterious Pongos cutting loose with hammers and pop-guns. There must be something to mix them together and make soup."

He took the bundle of bonds out of his pocket and studied one of them again more closely. And then he was wrapped in stillness for so long that the others felt as if they were gripped in the same trance, without knowing why.

At last he spoke.

"They look genuine," he said softly. "Engraving, ink, paper, everything. They look all right. You couldn't say they were fakes without some special tests. And yet they might be . . . But there's only been one man in our time who could do a forgery like this—if it is a forgery."

"Who was that?" said Patricia.

The Saint met her gaze with blue eyes glinting with lights that held the essence of the mystery which he himself had just been trying to fathom.

"He was a Pole called Ladek Urivetzky—and I read in the paper that he was executed by a firing-squad in Oviedo about a month ago."

5

And an elegant bowl of soup it made when you got it all stirred up, Simon reflected that evening, as he was being trundled down the dim baronial corridors of Cornwall House. But of all the extraneous characters who had been spilled by some coincidence or other into the pot, he was the only one who could make that reflection with the same ecstatic confidence.

"It doesn't seem to make sense," Patricia had said helplessly, when he contributed the last item of certain knowledge that he had.

"It sings songs to me," said the Saint.

But he had gone into no more details, for the Saint had a weakness for his mysteries. They had only been able to make desperate guesses at what was in his mind, knowing that there must be something seething there from the mocking amusement in his eyes and the unholy Saintliness of his smile. It was as if a rocket had exploded inside him, flooding all the dark places in his mind with light when he had caught up in that dynamic moment with the lead his instinct for adventure had given him.

At this particular time, however, neither his eyes nor his smile could have given any information to anyone who might have been watching him, for they were completely hidden by the white beard and moustache and dark glasses which left very little of his face uncovered. He had put on those useful pieces of scenery with some care before he let himself through a panel in the back of a built-in wardrobe in his bedroom which brought him into a similar built-in wardrobe in the bedroom of the adjoining flat, which was occupied by an incurable invalid of great age who rejoiced in the name of Joshua Pond, as any inquisitive person might have discovered from the head porter, Sam Outrell, or the register of tenants. What it would not have been so easy for the inquisitive person to discover was that Mr Pond's existence was entirely imaginary, and took concrete form only when it suited the Saint's purposes. Mr Pond rarely went out at all, a fact that was easily explained by his antiquity and failing health.

Securely screened behind his smoked glasses and masses of snowy facial shrubbery, with a white muffler wound round his neck and a black homburg planted squarely on his head, Mr Pond sat in his wheeled chair and was tenderly propelled down the passage by Sam Outrell and a smart young chauffeur in livery. Two men in overalls working on some telephone wiring with a mass of tools spread round them looked up as the door of the flat opened, and ignored him as he went by. The chair was pushed into the lift, and passed out of their ken. In the lobby downstairs, a man reading a newspaper looked up as the lift doors opened, and returned automatically to his reading. The chair passed him, and was wheeled out into the street, where a sedate black limousine stood waiting. Sam Outrell and the chauffeur each took one of the invalid's elbows and helped him to totter through the door of the car. The chauffeur wrapped a rug around his knees, Sam Outrell closed the door and saluted, the chauffeur took the wheel, and the car whisked away into the night, followed by the disinterested eyes of another large man who stood making a half-hearted attempt to sell newspapers on the opposite side of the street.

"And what exactly," asked the chauffeur, as the car streaked westwards along Piccadilly, "are we out for tonight?"

The Saint laughed.

"I'm sorry I had to drag you away from that cocktail-party, Peter, old lad, but Claud Eustace is having one of his spasms. Did you see 'em all? Four of 'em—about three square yards of feet all told. That is, if there weren't any more."

He was looking back through the rear window, deciding whether they were being followed. Presently he was satisfied, and turned round again.

"Take a cruise through the Park, Peter, while I peel off my whiskers."

He stowed the outfit carefully away in a concealed locker in front of him, ready to be put on again when it was required. The venerable black homburg joined it, along with the grey suede gloves, and he took off the lightweight black overcoat and laid it folded on the seat beside him. In a few minutes he was smoothing down his own dark hair and lighting a cigarette.

"What's Teal having a spasm about this time?" demanded Peter Quentin. "And why didn't you let me in on it before?"

"It's only just begun," said the Saint.

He told the story from the beginning, in a synoptic, rapid-fire outline which omitted no important details, except the connecting links which his own imagination was still working on.

"Sherry, Spain, Spanish rebels, American bearer bonds, mysterious Pongos with hammers and artillery, and a Polish forger who was stood up against a wall in Oviedo," he repeated at the end of it. "And a Spanish civil war still going on and getting bloodier and messier every day, in case you've forgotten it. I've seen a lot of odd things mixed up together in my time, but I think this is in the running for a prize."

"But who's doing what?" said Peter.

"That's what I'm still trying to get straight," said the Saint frankly. "Oviedo's changed hands about half a dozen times, and I don't remember who was holding it when Urivetzky was wiped out. I don't know which side Urivetzky was on, or why he should have been mixed up in it at all—except that there seem to be amateurs from half the countries in Europe taking sides in the picnic anyway. But I have got an idea what's in the wind, and I'm going to know some more before I go to bed."

The car slowed up, and Peter said, "Shall I go round again while you're thinking?"

Simon flicked the stub of his cigarette through the window.

"I did all my thinking before I sent for you," he said. "You can cut out here—we're going to Cambridge Square."

"I have heard of it," said Peter with heavy irony. "But not from you. What's it got to do with this party? I thought you said Graham's digs were in Bloomsbury."

"So they are," said the Saint equably. "And Quintana's digs are in Cambridge Square."

There was a certain pregnant interval of silence while Peter brought the car out of the Park and squeezed it through the tide of traffic swirling around Hyde Park Corner.

"I always thought you were daft," he said, as they floated out of the maelstrom into the calmer waters of Grosvenor Place. "And now I know it."

"But why?" asked the Saint reasonably. "Comrade Quintana seems to have been quite a pal of Ingleston's, so he ought to be interested in the news about his boy friend. Or if he's already heard it, he'll want someone to condole with him in his bereavement. But if he has heard it, I should be interested to know how—I sent for all the evening papers, and there wasn't a line about the murder in any of them."

"Why shouldn't he have heard about it from the police?"

"He might have. And yet somehow I don't think so. I stuck that photograph right under Teal's bloodhound nose, and he was too busy boiling with thwarted rage because I'd accounted for knowing the name of the corpse to be able to smell a clue when he'd got one. Of course, he may have done some more sniffing since then, but even then it may take him some time to realise who Luis Quintana is. And anyway we've got to chance it, because Quintana's our own best clue . . . You can stop the car here, Peter—I won't drive up to the door."

"What's making you so modest all of a sudden?" Peter inquired innocently as he applied the brakes.

The Saint smiled, and stepped out on to the pavement.

"It comes naturally to me," he said. "And this isn't going to be an official visit."

"I'll bet you don't even know what sort of a visit it is going to be," said Peter accusingly, and Simon grinned at him without shame.

"I don't—which only makes it more interesting. Wait for me here, old lad, and I'll tell you all about it later."

He was only confessing the simple truth, but in the way he looked at it there was nothing about it to depress the spirits. The Saint had always been like that—daft, as Peter had called him, but daft with a magnificent insolence of daftness that had driven more than one of his adversaries to desperation as they essayed the hopeless task of predicting his unpredictable impulses. Having nothing to make plans for, the Saint had seen no reason to expend his energy on making them, particularly when so much of it would have been spent on meeting hypothetical difficulties while the real ones were probably never thought of. He had obtained Quintana's address from a friend on a newspaper, and all he knew about it was that it was number 319 in the square. He had no idea what type of house it was, and on that depended the development of his campaign. On that, and on whatever other schemes crossed his mind on the way.

He sauntered along the south side of the square, assimilating numbers and opening his mind impartially to the free influx of inspiration. Number 319, he discovered, stood in the very southeast corner of the square, at the right-angle junction of the two streets that entered the square at that point. It was a broad two-storied house of vaguely Georgian architecture, flanked by the wings of wall common to that type of façade which apparently screened a small surrounding garden. Across the front, an entrance driveway ran in past the front door under a pillared portico. And as the Saint stood on the corner, lighting a cigarette and taking in every detail of the building with the trained eye of a veteran, a taxi turned into the drive and coughed itself to a standstill under the porch. Simon moved a little so that he could see between the pillars, and for one moment only he saw the passenger who got out of the cab, as he paid off the driver before he turned and went up the steps through the front door, which had been opened for him as soon as the taxi pulled up.

For one moment only—but that was enough to make the Saint catch his breath so quickly that the lighter in his hand went out. For the man who had gone in, the man whose face he had seen for that paralysing instant, was Ladek Urivetzky, the supreme forger of the twentieth century, the man who was reported to have been eliminated by a firing-squad in Oviedo four weeks ago.

6

Simon had no doubt of it. He had never met Urivetzky in person, but his memory for faces was as accurate as a card index, and his private collection of photographs and descriptions of outstanding members of the international underworld contained items that would have been envied by more than one official bureau of records. And that sallow, thick-lipped, skull-like face with the curved scar under the left eye was as unmistakable as any face could be without previous first-hand examination.

For some seconds the Saint stood motionless, while the door closed and the empty taxi rattled on out of the driveway and departed into the night. Then he moved on, with a tremor of exquisite excitement tugging at his nerves.

He made a complete circuit of the block in which the house stood. It was quite a small block, and the rest of the buildings in it consisted of the ordinary, monotonously identical, tall, narrow houses common to that part of London. Built in an unbroken row one against the other, they formed a solid three-sided wall with no openings other than a couple of narrow alleys in one side which led into little courtyards of mews garages buried in the heart of the block. Nowhere did the place seem less effectively protected than it did at the front.

Standing once more on the corner from which he had started off, the Saint drew his cigarette to brightness and studied the façade again with that tingle of reckless ecstasy working its way deep into the profoundest recesses of his being.

Somehow or other he had to get into Quintana's house, and if the only way to get in was at the front, then he would get in at the front. Not that the front door entered into his plans—

Any vague idea he might have set out with of brazenly bluffing his way into the owner's presence had been annihilated beyond resurrection by that one breath-stopping glimpse of Urivetzky's arrival. The brazenness and the bluff might come later, and probably would, but before that the Saint wanted to know what a man who was supposed to be dead was doing at the house of a man whose friend really was dead, and why a man who was admitted to have been the greatest forger of his time was visiting the friend of a man who had had an unaccountable collection of bonds which might have been forged, and why one thread in the lives of all these strangely assorted people linked them together, when that thread had its roots in a country where death had lately become a commonplace—and the Saint wanted to know all these things without announcing his intrusion. Wherefore he stood and dissected the possibilities with that stir of lawless delight roaming through his insides. On each side of the house, the ground floor was wider than the upper part of the buildings, so that its flat roof formed a kind of terrace on to which upstairs windows opened. And beyond the garden wall there were two tall trees, growing so close to the side of the house that it looked as if one could step off one of their branches on to the terrace as easily as stepping across a garden path. . .

The Saint crossed the road.

He had no qualms about the enormity of what he proposed to do. What occupied his mind much more were the chances of being allowed to commit his crime. There seemed to be an entirely unnecessary number of street lamps clustered around that corner, and while they could never have competed with the noonday sun, they were bright enough to illumine the scene for the eyes of any passer-by, who might tend to regard the sight of a man climbing over a wall as a spectacle to which the attention of the neighbourhood might justifiably be directed. But Cambridge Square is a quiet place, and at that hour it was sunk in its regular post-prandial coma. The Saint slowed his steps to allow a lone prowling taxi to drag itself past him, and at the same time he measured the wall with his eye. It was not more than seven feet high, and the top was protected with curved iron spikes set in the brickwork—but they were spikes of an old-fashioned pattern which had been clearly designed for a day when burglarious agility was still an undeveloped art. To a wall-climber of the Saint's experience, they were not much more of an obstacle than a row of feathers . . .

The prowling taxi had hauled itself wearily on, and the nearest other car was the limousine in which Peter Quentin was waiting. For the moment, there was no other human being nearer than that. Simon Templar's glance swept once over the panorama, and he knew that it was no use waiting for a better opportunity. The rest was on the lap of the gods.

He made a leap for the top of the wall, caught the base of one spike with his right hand and the curve of another with his left, and was over like a flash of dark lightning. A roving cat could hardly have cleared the obstacle with more silent speed.

His feet padded down with the same catlike softness on the paved path on the other side, and for a second he crouched there without movement, exactly as he had landed, listening for any trace of a disturbing sound in the world outside. But his straining ears caught nothing that stood out from the vague normal background of London noise, and in another moment he was darting across an open patch of grass like a fleeting shadow to the foot of one of the trees he had marked down in his survey.

Its branches grew so low down that his hands could reach the lowest of them with the help of an easy jump, and with only a moment's pause he was working himself up into the short young foliage with the swift suppleness of a trained gymnast. In less than a minute from the time when he had surmounted the wall, he was poising himself for the short leap on to the terrace that was his first objective.

Until then, he had been screened by the wall and the new leaves that partly clothed the tree, but now he was in the open again, plainly visible to anyone who looked up or looked out, even when he had crossed the terrace to the partial shelter of one of the dark window-doorways that opened on to it. He tried the handle cautiously, but it was fastened on the inside. For some time, which was probably a minute or two, but which seemed like a week, he had to work on it with a slender tool which he took from his pocket, before the window opened and let him into the dark room beyond.

He closed the window after him and stood looking out through it, scanning the square below. Beside the limousine near the corner he saw a dark shape pacing to and fro, and saw also the erratically fluctuating pin-point of a lighted cigarette-end, and the sketch of a smile touched his lips. Peter was doubtless collecting enough material to give a heart specialist a year's course of study, but there was the consoling thought that a few more repetitions of the same stimulus would probably give him a lifelong immunity of incalculable value . . . Otherwise, there were no visible signs of commotion. If any stray wanderers in the vicinity had witnessed any excerpts from the recent unrolling of events, they had apparently decided that such affairs were none of their dull and respectable business, and had proceeded untroubled on their prosaic ways.

The Saint turned away from the window and unclipped the pencil flashlight from his breast pocket. Its dim, subdued gleam swivelled once round the room—and snapped out again suddenly.

He was in some kind of formal reception-room, a gaunt, bare chamber with gilt-edged mirrors and velvet drapes and stuffy uninviting chairs ranged around the walls to leave most of the floor clear. There was nothing remarkable about it except its monumental ugliness, which would have impressed the spiritual descendants of Queen Victoria as being delightfully respectable and dignified. Facing the Saint, as he stood by the window, was a door which presumably led out to a landing or corridor, and on his right was another door communicating with an adjoining room. It was through this communicating door that he had heard the sound of voices which had made him extinguish his torch with involuntary abruptness.

He had heard the answer to a muffled question quite distinctly, spoken in good English but with a strong foreign accent:

"I met him in Sevilla when he was visiting Jerez for his company."

A slow smile of deep contentment touched the Saint's lips, and he put his torch away with an inaudible sigh. If he had known all the inside geography of the house and had moreover been gifted with second sight, he couldn't have organised his entrance more accurately and appropriately. It was one of those moments when his guardian angel seemed to have hooked him bodily on to the assembly line of adventure and launched him on to an unerringly triumphant sequence of developments like the routine of some supernal mass-production factory.

In a few swift, noiseless steps he was at the door, with his ear close to the panels, in time to hear the first thin grumbling voice say, "In a case like this, you should have more sense. You say you work for what you think is good for your country, but you are as stupid as a little child. I am only working for money for myself, but even I am more careful. Or is that the reason why I cannot afford to be stupid?"

"My dear Urivetzky!" The second voice was conciliatory. "It was not so easy as you think. We had to find agents quickly, and at a time when we could take no risks, when everything had to be done in secret, when, if we made a mistake, we could have been imprisoned or even executed. Ingleston had many friends in Sevilla, expropriated aristocrats, and they assured me that he was in sympathy with our cause. I heard the highest recommendations of him before I spoke to him, and we wished to use foreigners whenever possible because they would arouse no suspicion. But every man can be tempted—"

"It is the business of a leader to choose men who are difficult to tempt," Urivetzky retorted sourly. "Anyone who was not stupid would know that when you entrust a man with bearer bonds which are not traceable, which can be used for any purpose by the man who possesses them, that you must take care how you choose him."

"I am not so experienced in these matters as yourself." The other's voice had an edge to it. "Unfortunately all the gold of Spain is held by the Banco de España, in Madrid, which is held by the Reds, and we shall never know what they have done with it. I regret the necessity for these tricks, but we have no choice."

"Pah! You have choice enough. How many thousand Germans and Italians are fighting on your side?"

"They are in sympathy with us, but even they would not help us for nothing." Urivetzky grunted.

"I also regret your necessities, if they are necessities," he said. "And I shall regret them more if your other agents have been as badly chosen."

"They have not been badly chosen. At this moment I have nearly forty thousand pounds in American and English money in my safe, all of it paid over to me by our other agents. Ingleston was the only mistake we have made."

"And he won't trouble us anymore," said a third voice, speaking for the first time.

It was a moment after the Saint had decided that it was time for him to locate the keyhole and add another dimension to the drama which was being unfolded for his benefit. He found the hole just as the third voice reached his ears, and scanned the scene through it with some interest.

The room beyond was smaller than the one which he was in, and from the more habitable furnishings and the lines of bookshelves along the walls it appeared to be a small private study.

Urivetzky sat in an arm-chair with his back to the keyhole—the hairless cranium which showed over the back of the chair could only have belonged to him. In a swivel chair behind the desk sat another man whom the Saint recognised at once from the photograph he had seen as Luis Quintana himself: he was smiling at the time, exposing the characteristic Spanish row of irregular fangs covered with greenish-yellow slime, like rocks left naked at low tide, which ought to be exhibited in museums for the education of Anglo-Saxon maidens who have been misled by ceaseless propaganda into believing in the dentifricial glamour of the Latin grin.

Simon observed those details with his first perfunctory glance. From a curiosity point of view, he was more immediately interested in the third member of the party, who sat puffing a cigar in the chair directly facing him. He was a man with a square-looking body and a close-cropped square-looking grey head; the expression of his mouth was hidden by a thick straggling moustache, but his black eyes were flat and vicious. And the Saint knew intuitively that he must be the unidentified assassin whom for the purposes of convenient reference he had christened Pongo.

"The other bonds have not yet been found," Urivetzky said acidly.

"They will be found," Quintana reassured him.

"They had better be found. Otherwise this will be the finish. I am not interested in your country, but I am interested in my living."

The Rebels' Representative raised his eyebrows.

"Perhaps you exaggerate. If these forgeries are so perfect—"

"Of course they are perfect. No man in the world could have done better. But they are forgeries. Why are you so stupid? A bond is a work of art. To those who have eyes, it has the signature of the creator in every line. So is a forgery a work of art. Look at a connoisseur in an art gallery. Without any catalogue, he will study the pictures and he will say, 'That is a Velasquez, that is a Rembrandt, that is an El Greco.' So there are men in the world who will look at forgeries of bonds, and say, 'That is a So-and-so, that is a Somebody, that is a Urivetzky.' It makes no difference if the Urivetzky is most like the original. There are still men who will recognise it."

"It is hardly likely to fall into their hands. And it was to disarm their suspicion that we had the story sent out that you had been killed."

"And so perhaps you make more suspicion. This man Templar is not a fool—I have heard too much of him."

"He will be taken care of also," said the man known as Pongo. "I have been working all day—"

He was interrupted by a knock on the door. A servant came in as Quintana answered, and turned towards the eliminator of problems.

"There is someone to speak to you on the telephone, Señor," he said. The square man gestured smugly at Urivetzky.

"You see?" he said. "Perhaps this is the report I've been waiting for."

He got up and went out, and the Saint straightened the kinks out of his neck and spine. He had done as good a job of eavesdropping as he could have hoped to do, and he had no complaints. Nearly all the questions in his mind had been answered.

But on Quintana's own statement, there were nearly forty thousand pounds in ready cash in the safe, and they were forty thousand reasons for some deep and sober cogitation before he retired from the scene into which he had so seasonably introduced himself. After all, there was still the outstanding matter of a tenner which the late Mr Ingleston had owed, and in the light of what Simon had learned he could see even less reason than before why it should not be repaid with interest . . . And there was also the telephone conversation to which Señor Pongo had hastened away, which might be worth listening to.

The voices went on coming through the door while he stood for a while undecided. "Even you take risks," Quintana was saying. "If I had known that you would drive here—"

"That was no risk. There are no policemen looking for me, and taxi drivers are not detectives."

This might be the best chance he would have to do something about the safe, while the odds in the study were reduced from three to two. But Pongo might return at any moment— and by the same token, his telephone conversation wouldn't last for ever. Whereas the safe and its contents would probably manage to keep a jump ahead of disintegration for a few minutes more.

Simon made his choice with a shrug. He tiptoed back across the room, towards the door that opened on to the landing. He had no idea what was on the other side of it, but that was only an incidental gamble among many others.

Even so, he was still destined to be surprised.

The carpet outside must have been very thick, or the door very solid, for he heard nothing until he was a couple of yards from it. And then the door was flung open and Pongo rushed in.

The light from the landing caught the Saint squarely and centrally as it streamed in, but Pongo was entering so hastily that he was well inside the room before he could check himself.

Simon leapt at him. His left hand caught the man by the lapels of his coat, and at the same time he side-stepped towards the door, pushing it shut with his own shoulder and turning the key with his right hand. But the shock had slowed up his reaction by a fatal fraction, and the other recovered himself enough to let out a sharp choking yelp before the Saint shifted his grip to his throat.

The Saint smiled at him benevolently and reached for his gun. But his fingers had only just touched his pocket when light flooded the room from another direction, and a voice spoke behind him.

"Keep still," rasped Luis Quintana.

7

The Saint let his hand drop slowly, and turned round. Quintana and Urivetzky stood in the communicating doorway, and Quintana held a gun.

"Good evening, girls," said the Saint winsomely. Urivetzky let out an exclamation as he saw his face. "The Saint!"

"In person," Simon admitted pleasantly. "But you don't have to stand on ceremony. Just treat me like an old friend of the family."

Released from the numbing grip on his windpipe, the square man retreated to a safe distance, massaging his throat tenderly.

"I mistook the door," he exploded hoarsely. "I opened this one—and he was inside. He must have been listening. How much he has heard—"

"Yes," said Quintana, with slow significance.

The Saint continued to stand still while Pongo stepped up to him again and took away his gun. The man's exploring hands also found the cigarette-case in his breast pocket and took it out, and Simon took it gently back from him and helped himself to a cigarette before returning it with a deprecating bow.

He felt for his lighter, in a bland and genial silence which invited the others to make themselves at home while they selected the next way of breaking it, and his self-possession was so unshaken that it looked as if his stillness was dictated less by the steady aim of Quintana's gun than by a wholly urbane and altruistic desire to avoid embarrassing the company by seeming to rush them into a decision. What was going on in his own mind was his own secret, and he kept it decorously to himself.

But it seemed as if he had been somewhat rash in crediting his guardian angel with the organising ability of Henry Ford.

Certainly a good deal of the system was there, but somewhere along the moving belt something seemed to have gone haywire. Simon experienced some of the emotions that a Ford executive would have experienced if, watching a chassis travelling down the assembly line, at the point where it should have had its tail-light screwed on, he had seen it being rapidly outfitted with a thatched roof and stained-glass windows. Perhaps it was really an improvement, but its advantages were not immediately apparent. Perhaps the fact that Pongo should have chosen to charge through the wrong door in his excitement was really a blessing in disguise, but to the Saint it seemed to have created a situation from which a tactful and prudent man would extract himself with all possible speed. The only question it left was exactly how the withdrawal should be organised.

It was the square man who first reasserted himself.

"How long has he been here?" he demanded grimly. The Saint smiled at him.

"My dear Señor Pongo—"

The square man drew himself up.

"My name is not Pongo," he said with dignity. "I am Major Vicente Guillermo Gabriel Pérez, of the Third Division of the army of the Spanish Patriots."

"Arriba España," murmured the Saint solemnly. "But you won't mind if I call you Pongo, will you? I can't remember all your other names at once. And the point, my dear Señor Pongo, is not exactly how long I've been here but how long you've been here."

There was a moment's startled silence, and then Quintana said coldly: "Will you be good enough to explain?"

Simon gestured slightly with his cigarette.

"You see," he said, "unless you have a very good alibi, Pongo, I shall naturally have to include you with the rest of the menagerie. And that will cost you money."

Major Vicente Guillermo Gabriel Pérez's flat vicious eyes stared at him with a rather stupid blankness. The other two men seemed to have been similarly afflicted with a temporary paralysis of incomprehension. But the Saint's paternal geniality held them all together with the unobtrusive dominance of a perfect host. With the same natural charm, he tried to relieve them of some of their perplexity.

"We have here," he explained, "Comrade Ladek Urivetzky, once of Warsaw and subsequently of various other places. A bloke with quite a reputation in certain circles, if I remember rightly. I think the last time I heard of him was in connection with the celebrated City and Continental Bank case, when he got away with about fifty thousand quid after depositing a bundle of Danish Premium Bonds for security. All the boys at Scotland Yard were looking for him all over the place, and I expect they were still looking for him until they heard that he'd been mopped up in Oviedo. Now it seems that he isn't dead at all. He's right here in London, playing happy families with the Representative of the Spanish rebels and," Simon bowed faintly in the direction of the square man, "Major Vicente Guillermo Gabriel Pongo, of the Third Division of the army of the Spanish Whatnots. So I have a feeling that Chief Inspector Teal would be interested to know why two such illustrious gentlemen are entertaining a notorious criminal."

There was another short strained stillness, before Quintana broke it with a brittle laugh.

"If you think that we are here to be bluffed by a common burglar—"

"Not common," Simon protested mildly. "Whatever else I may be, I've never been called that. Ask Comrade Urivetzky. But in any case, there are worse crimes in this country than burglary."

"What do you mean?"

"I mean—murder."

Major Pérez kept still, watching him with evil intentness.

"What murder?"

"Pongo," said the Saint kindly, "I may have a face like an innocent little child, which is more than you have, but appearances are deceptive. I was not born yesterday. I've been listening in this room for some time, and I'd done a good deal of thinking before that, and I think I know nearly as much about this racket of yours as is worth knowing."

"What racket?" The Saint sighed.

"All right," he said. "Let's have it in words of one syllable. A good many things have been done in Spain to get funds for your precious revolution, and since nearly all the official Spanish dough is in Madrid a good many of your tricks have had to sail pretty close to the wind. Well, your contribution was to think up this idea of pledging forged bonds around the place, to get money to pay the Germans and Italians for their guns and aero-planes and tanks and bombs and poison gas and other contributions to the cause of civilisation. Somebody thought of hiring Comrade Urivetzky to do the forging, and you were all set."

He leaned back against the mantelpiece and blew a smoke-ring at a particularly hideous ormolu clock.

"The next thing was to get stooges to pledge the bonds, because if any of them were spotted you didn't want all your credit to be shot to hell at once. Among others, you collected Comrade Ingleston. You met him on one of his trips to Spain— he spoke Spanish very well, and he had plenty of friends among your crowd, Sevilla being a red-hot monarchist and fascist stronghold, unless it's changed since I was last there. You made him a proposition, and he took it on. Unfortunately he wasn't such an idealist as you may have thought, and when he began to find himself with pocketfuls of bearer bonds he heard the call of easy money. He started to go short on his returns. You got suspicious and started to keep tabs on him, and before long there wasn't much doubt left about it. Ingleston was playing you for suckers, and something had to be done about it. Pongo did it."

There was no doubt now that he was holding his audience. They were drinking up every word with a thirsty concentration that would have made some men hesitate to go on, but the Saint knew what he was doing.

"Last night," he proceeded with easy confidence, "Pongo was waiting for Ingleston in the street when he came home. He hailed him like a brother, and was invited upstairs. While Ingleston was pouring out a drink, Pongo jumped on him from behind with a hammer. Then after Ingleston was dead he had a look round for the last consignment of forged bonds. He was unlucky there, of course, because I'd already got them."

"That is very interesting," Quintana said deliberately.

"You've no idea how interesting it is," answered the Saint earnestly. "Suppose you just look at it all at once. Here's Ladek Urivetzky, a well-known forger and a wanted man, taking shelter here and being like a brother with the pair of you. Here's Ingleston murdered by a Major of the Third Division of the army of the Spanish Patriots, also among those present. Well, boys, I'm well known to be a broad-minded bloke, and I can't say that any of it worries me much. Forgers and fascists are more or less in the same class to me, and Ingleston seems to have been the kind of guy that anyone might bump off in an absent-minded moment. I don't feel a bit virtuous about either side, so I haven't got any sermons for you. But what I don't like is you boys thinking you can make yourselves at home and raise hell in this town without my permission. London is the greatest city in the world, and our policemen are wonderful, so I'm told," said the Saint proudly, "and I don't like to have them bothered. So if you want to have your fun I'm afraid you've got to pay for it."

"Pay for it?" repeated Major Pérez, as if the phrase was strange to him. The Saint nodded.

"If you want to go on amusing yourselves, you have to pay your entertainment tax," he said. "That's what I meant when we started talking. If you're well in this with the others, you'll have to be assessed along with them."

They went on watching him with their mouths partly open and their eyes dark with pitiless malignance, but the Saint's trick of carrying the battle right back into the enemy's camp held them frozen into inactivity by its sheer unblushing impudence.

"And how much," asked Quintana, with an effort of irony that somehow lacked the clear ring of unshaken self-assurance, "would this assessment be?"

"It would be about forty thousand pounds," said the Saint calmly. "That will be a donation of twenty thousand pounds for the International Red Cross, which seems a very suitable cause for you to contribute to, and twenty thousand pounds for me for collecting it. If I heard you correctly, you've got that much cash in your safe, so you wouldn't even have the bother of writing a cheque. It makes everything so beautifully simple."

Quintana's ironic smile tightened.

"I think it would be simpler to hand you over to the police," he said.

"Imbecile!" Urivetzky spoke, breaking his own long silence. "What could you tell the police—"

"Exactly," agreed the Saint. "And what could I tell them? No, boys, it won't do. That's what I was trying to show you. I suppose they couldn't hurt you much, on account of your position and what not, but they could make it pretty difficult for you. And there certainly wouldn't be anything left of your beautiful finance scheme. And then I don't suppose you'd be so popular with the Spanish Patriots when you went home. Probably you'd find yourselves leaning against a wall, watching the firing squad line up." The Saint shook his head. "No—I think forty thousand quid is a bargain price for the good turn I'd be doing you."

Major Pérez grinned at him like an ape.

"And suppose you didn't have a chance to use your information?" he said. The Saint smiled with unruffled tranquillity.

"My dear Pongo—do you really think I'd have come here without thinking of that? Of course you can use your artillery any time you want to, and at this range, with a bit of luck, you might even hit me. But it wouldn't do you any good. I told some friends of mine that I'd be back with them in ten minutes from now, and if I don't arrive punctually they'll phone Scotland Yard and tell Chief Inspector Teal exactly where I went and why. You can think it over till your brains boil, children, but your only way out will still cost you forty thousand quid."

8

The silence that followed lasted longer than any of its predecessors. It was made up of enough diverse ingredients to fill a psychological catalogue, and their conflicting effects combined to produce a state of explosive inertia in which the dropping of a pin would have sounded like a steel girder decanting itself into a stack of cymbals.

The Saint's cigarette expired, and he pressed it quietly out on the mantelpiece. For a few moments at least, he was the only man in the room who was immune to the atmosphere of the petrified earthquake which had invaded it, and he was clinging to his immunity as if it was the most precious possession he had—which in fact it was. Whether the hoary old bluff which he had built up with such unblinking effrontery could be carried through to a flawless conclusion was another question, but he had done his best for it, and no man could have done more. And if he had achieved nothing else, he had at least made the opposition stop and think. If he had left them to their immediate and natural impulses from the time when they found him there, he would probably have been nothing but a name in history by this time; they might still plan to let him end the adventure in the same way, but now they would proceed with considerable caution. And the Saint knew that when the ungodly began to proceed with caution, instead of simply leaning on the trigger and asking questions afterwards as common sense would dictate, was when an honest roan might begin to look for loopholes. If there was anything that Simon Templar needed then, it was loopholes, and he was watching for them with a languid and untroubled smile on his lips and his muscles poised and tingling like a sprinter at the start of a race.

Pérez spoke again, after that momentous silence, in a babble of rapid-fire Spanish. "He means his friends at his apartment."

"How many of them are there?" asked Quintana, in the same language.

"There is a girl and a manservant. Those are the only ones who live there—I made inquiries. No one else has been there today except Graham."

Quintana glanced at the Saint again, but the Saint, who understood every word as easily as if it had been spoken in English, frowned back at him with the worried expression of a man who is trying hard to understand and failing in the attempt.

"You are sure there is no mistake?" Quintana insisted.

"That would be impossible. I heard about Graham from Ingleston, and he is not the type of man who would be an associate of the Saint. I followed him to the Saint's apartment this morning, and Fernández followed him back there when the Saint went in to Ingleston's. Fernández and Nayder have been watching there ever since, pretending to repair telephone wires."

"But your telephone call—"

"That was Fernández, to know how much longer he should stay there. Also he was suspicious because an old man muffled up so that he could not be recognised had been brought out of the next apartment, and Fernández had been thinking about it and wondering if it was one of the Saint's gang. Now we know that it must have been the Saint himself."

"No one else has gone out the same way?"

"No."

Quintana gazed at the Saint thoughtfully, stroking the barrel of his automatic with his left hand.

"You will excuse us not speaking English, Mr Templar," he said at length. "Naturally it is easier for us to speak our own language. But I was just trying to find out how good your case was. Major Pérez assures me that we are more or less in your hands."

The Saint, who knew that Major Pérez had done no such thing, returned his gaze with a bland and gullible smile. "That was what I was trying to make you see, dear old bird," he said, but his pulses were beating a little faster.

"If you will come into the next room," said Quintana, "we had better see if we can settle this matter like gentlemen."

Urivetzky's brow blackened incredulously, and he made an abrupt movement.

"Fools!" he snarled. "Would you let this man—"

"Please," said Quintana, turning towards him. "Would you allow me to handle this affair in my own way? We are not criminals—we are supposed to be diplomats."

As he had turned, the Saint could only see him in profile, but Simon knew, as certainly as if he could have seen it, that the side of his face which only Urivetzky could see moved in a significant wink. He knew it, if from nothing else, from the way Urivetzky's scowl slowly smoothed out into inscrutability.

"Perhaps you are right," Urivetzky said presently, with a shrug. "But these ways are not my ways."

"Sometimes they are necessary," said Quintana, and turned to Pérez. "You agree, Major?"

The Spanish Patriot, with his eyes still fixed on the Saint, brought his features into perfunctory and calculating repose. "Of course."

Quintana bowed.

"Will you come this way, Mr Templar?"

Simon hitched himself off the mantelpiece and strolled across to the communicating door. Quintana moved aside to let him pass, and immediately fell in behind him and followed him in to the study. Urivetzky came after him, and Pérez completed the procession and closed the door. It was rather like a special committee going into conference, or an ark taking in its crew.

No one who watched the Saint dissolve into the most comfortable armchair would have imagined that there was a single shadow of anxiety in his mind. But behind that one and only shield which he had, he was wondering with a cold prickle in his nerves where the next shot was coming from.

He knew that there was something coming. He had put over his own bluff, but even he couldn't convince himself that it had gone over quite so triumphantly. Except in story-books, things simply didn't happen that way. Men like Quintana and Urivetzky and Pérez didn't crumple up and stop fighting directly they met an obstacle. And in the very way they had so suddenly seemed to crumple up, there was enough to tell him that he would need every mental and physical gift that he had to keep ahead of them through the next couple of moves.

With nothing but an air of lazy good humour, he stretched out his hand towards Pérez.

"Could I have my cigarette-case back now?" he drawled. "Or were you thinking of giving it to somebody for a birthday present?"

"By all means," said Quintana. "Give it back to him, Pérez."

Simon took back the case and opened it with a certain feeling of relief which he kept strictly to himself. At least, with that in his hands, he had something on his side, little as it was.

"And now," he said, through a veil of smoke, "what about this forty thousand quid?"

"That can be arranged fairly quickly."

Quintana had sat down in the swivel chair behind the desk. He leaned back in it, turning his gun between his hands as if he had ceased to regard it as a useful weapon, but Simon knew that he could bring it back to usefulness quicker than the distance between them could be covered.

"Mr Templar, you are a bold man. Let me point out that you are now inside the residence of the Representative of the Spanish Nationalist Party. If I shot you now, and the fact was ever discovered, I doubt whether anything very serious could ever happen to me."

"Except some of the things I was telling you about," murmured the Saint. The other nodded.

"Yes, it would be very inconvenient. But it would not be fatal; I am only mentioning that to show my appreciation of your—nerve. And for some other reasons. Now, the alternative to killing you is to pay you your price of forty thousand pounds. But we could not do that without satisfactory guarantees that your own side of the bargain would be kept."

"And what would they be?"

"Very simple. We have all heard of your reputation, and in your own way you are said to be a man of honour. I expect your associates are of the same type. Well, in diplomatic circles, when such situations arise, as they sometimes do, it is customary to bind the agreement with a solemn written undertaking that it will be kept. I shall therefore have to require that undertaking not only from yourself but also from these other persons who you say are in your confidence. They will come here personally and sign it in my presence."

The Saint moved very little. "When?"

"I should prefer it to be done tonight."

"And the money?"

"That will be yours as soon as the undertaking is signed." Quintana stopped playing with his gun, at a moment which left its muzzle conveniently but inconspicuously turned in the Saint's direction. "I suggest that you should telephone them at once, since the time limit you left them was so short. You will say nothing to them except that you require them to come here at once. Provided that there are no—accidents, the whole thing can be settled within half an hour."

The Saint's deep breath took in a long drift of smoke. So that was the move. It was something to know, even if the knowledge made nothing any easier.

He said, without a trace of perturbation: "How do I know that you've really got the cash to do your share?"

Quintana looked at him with the raised eyebrows of faintly contemptuous reproach, and then he got up from the desk and went to the safe and unlocked it. He came back with a heavy sheaf of banknotes bound together with an elastic band and threw it down on the blotter in front of him as he sat down again.

"There is the money. You can take it away with you as soon as the formalities are complete. And for your own sake it would be better to complete them quickly. That is a condition I cannot argue about. Either you will accept your price on my terms, or you will be shot before your friends communicate with Scotland Yard. In that case, the trouble we shall be caused will be of no benefit to you. Choose for yourself."

He spread out his arms in a suave diplomatist's bow, gargled his tonsils, and spat gracefully at the porcelain cuspidor beside the desk.

The Saint trimmed his cigarette-end in an ash-tray.

An immense calm had suddenly come over him, in strange contrast to the tension he had been under before. Now that his questions had been answered, everything had been smoothed out into a simplicity in which tension had no place. His bluff had gone over—up to a point. But Quintana's answer was complete and unarguable. Simon knew that it was a lie, that Quintana had no intention of keeping his side of the bargain, that he never meant to hand over the money in front of him, that to telephone the others to come over and sign fabulous undertakings would only be leading them into the same trap that he himself was in. But he also knew, equally well, that if he rejected the condition he would be shot without mercy—and that Quintana might get away with it. It was a trap that he was expected to walk into like the greenest of greenhorns, and yet to stand back and announce that he had heard better fairy-tales at his nurse's knee would merely be making the preliminary arrangements for his own funeral service.

"You are lucky to get your price so easily," whined Urivetzky. "The conditions are only reasonable," said Pérez.

Simon looked from one to the other. They had grasped the trend of Quintana's strategy as quickly as he had himself, and they were hunched forward, taut with eagerness, to see how he would respond. And the Saint knew that this was one occasion when his fluent tongue would take him no further—when the only response that would save his life would be the response they wanted. How long even that would save his life for was another matter, but the alternatives were instant and inexorable. They could be read like a book in the hollow-eyed intentness of Urivetzky's skull-like face and the savage vindictiveness of Pérez's stare.

The Saint smiled.

"Why, yes," he agreed sappily. "That seems fair enough."

It was as if an actual physical pressure had been released from the room. The others drew back imperceptibly, and the air seemed to lighten, although, the claws were still there.

Quintana opened a drawer of the desk and took out a telephone.

"This is a private line which cannot be traced," he said. "I am telling you that in case you should have any idea of going back on your bargain."

"Why should I?" Simon inquired guilelessly. "I want that money too much."

"I am only warning you. If in the course of this conversation you should say anything which might make us suspect that you were trying to evade our agreement, you will be killed at once. If you have no intention of double-crossing us the warning can do you no harm."

He pushed the telephone across the desk, and Simon picked up the receiver.

Without a shadow of hesitation he dialled the private number of Chief Inspector Claud Eustace Teal.

9

The only thing left was to pray that Teal would be there. Simon glanced at his watch while he waited for the connection. Mr Teal was not a man who had many diversions outside his job, and at that hour he should have been peacefully installed beside his hearth, chewing spearmint and doing whatever homely things Chief Inspectors did when they were off duty. And while the Saint was holding his breath, the answer in a familiar sleepy voice came on the line.

"Hullo."

"Hullo," said Simon. "This is the Saint." There was a moment's pause.

"Well, what do you want?" Teal asked nastily.

"I'm okay," said the Saint. "Can I speak to Patricia?"

"She's not here."

Simon took a pull at his cigarette.

"Oh, hullo, Pat," he said. "How are you?"

"I tell you, she isn't here," yowled the detective. "Why should she be? I've got enough to do—"

"I'm fine, darling," said the Saint. "I'm with Quintana now."

"Who?"

"Luis Quintana . . . at 319 Cambridge Square."

"Look here," Teal said cholerically, "if this is another of your ideas of a joke—"

"I've talked things over with him," said the Saint, "and he's ready to do business. I've told him that we'll keep everything quiet—about Urivetzky being alive, and about those forged American short-term loan bearer bonds, and about Pérez murdering Ingleston—all for forty thousand pounds cash. It seems fair enough to me, if it's all right with the rest of you."

There was another silence for a second or two, and then Teal said, in a different voice, "Are you talking to me?"

"Yes, darling," said the Saint. "I'm in his study now, and he's ready to hand over the money at once. There's only one condition. He knows that you know all about these things, and he wants you all to come over and sign an undertaking to keep your mouths shut as well as mine. I guess we'll have to agree to that."

"You want me to come over to 319 Cambridge Square?" said Teal slowly. "Yes, Pat. At once. Quintana insists on it, and I can't argue with him."

"Shall I bring some help?"

"Yes, bring the others. He wants you all to sign. You needn't send your names in— they'll be expecting you. Will you come on over?"

"They've got a gun on you, I suppose," Teal said intelligently. "That's the idea," said the Saint. "As quick as you can, darling. 'Bye."

He dropped the microphone back and pushed the telephone away with a smile of satisfaction.

"They'll be here in a few minutes," he announced.

Urivetzky unlocked his fingers and leaned back, and Pérez, who had sat down on the arm of the same chair, crossed his legs and took out a cigarette. Quintana nodded, and put his gun down on the desk where it was still within easy reach. Every one of the individual reactions held an unspoken triumph that would have shrieked aloud its confirmation of the Saint's deductions—if he had wanted any confirmation. They were like three spiders waiting for the entrance of the flies.

None of them spoke. An atmosphere of guarded relaxation settled upon the scene, in which they waited, in savoury anticipation, for the logical outcome of their own ingenuity.

The Saint himself was not reluctant to be spared the trouble of making conversation. At ease in his chair, with an outward confidence and equanimity that was even more convincing than theirs, with his head thrown back so that he could build intermittent smoke-ring patterns towards the ceiling, he watched in his imagination the machinery that his telephone call had set in motion.

Now Teal was hanging up the receiver after another telephone call. Now he would be kicking off his carpet slippers and going quietly frantic over the obstinacy of his boot-laces. And over in the gloomy, soot-grimed building on the Embankment that was called Scotland Yard, there would be a suppressed crescendo of traffic in certain bare, echoing corridors, and big, heavy-footed men would be buttoning their prosaic and respectable coats and reaching down for their prosaic and respectable hats; and a car or two would start up and swing round in the courtyard and stand there unexcitedly ticking over; and a man would hurriedly finish his beer in the canteen and stump up the stairs. Perhaps in his study in Hampstead an Assistant Commissioner would be frowning over the telephone and fiddling with his moustache and giving counsel in a worried Oxonian bleat. "Well, I don't know . . . Yes, but . . . ticklish business, you know . . . international complications . . . Home Secretary . . . Foreign Office . . . Yes, I know, got to do something, but . . . Bonds? Forgery? Murder? . . . I don't know . . . discretion . . . unofficial . . . tact . . . Well, for God's sake be careful . . ." And Teal would be waiting, fidgeting on his doorstep, till the cars drove up and he stepped in with a curt, businesslike greeting, and they went on, threading rapidly through the traffic, filled with stolid, unromantic, uncommunicative men. "Your policemen are wonderful." Now they would be well on their way—it wouldn't take them long to get to Cambridge Square, via the modest lodgings in Victoria where Teal had his home. All these things happening in London, between the drab narrow streets, under the pulse of the city, while seekers after excitement crowded into movie theatres and sleek men and shrill women danced on overcrowded floors and smug or frustrated nonentities paced under the bright lights or hurried through quiet squares. All this happening under the deep, monotonous murmur of London, which penetrated even through closed windows and solid walls a continuous thrum of life of which one would be unaware unless it stopped, out of which an isolated squeal of brakes or the toot of a passing horn close by came sometimes like an abrupt reminder of its far-spread reality . . .

The time passed so quickly, Simon thought, and stole another glance at his watch. At any moment now they would be here. And then there would be trouble for himself, whoever else was in it. He had still been guilty of burglary, and there were several items of information which he had condoned or concealed. And on the desk in front of him there were still forty thousand pounds in ready cash, which any efficiently organised buccaneering concern could have used.

He had done the only thing he could have done, in the circumstances. And Chief Inspector Teal, not being completely solid ivory above the bowler hat-brim, had grasped enough of the idea to save the situation, as the Saint had known he would. But it didn't end there.

Even at that moment, probably, Teal was gloating over the fact that for the first time in his life the Saint had had to appeal to him and the majesty of the Law for help, and he was doubtless elaborating in his mind the various sarcastic comments with which he would rub home the unpleasantness that could be visited on the Saint impartially with any other malefactors who might be collected at the same time. On that visitation at least the Assistant Commissioner must have been insistent—if Mr Teal needed any encouragement.

But the Saint had done what Quintana wanted. And after he had done it, the certainty of success had had its own demoralising effect on the opposition. The sharp edge of vigilance on which Simon had felt his life balancing had been dulled—little enough, he knew, but with a subtle definiteness.

Quintana was rocking his swivel chair backwards and forwards, his hands supporting him on the edge of the desk. Urivetzky was lounging back as the Saint was, his hands folded and his deep-set eyes lost in thought. Pérez was sprawling, his cigarette drooping limply from the corner of his mouth, his hands in his pockets. But in one of those same pockets, Simon knew, was a loaded automatic.

And at that moment, in a complete silence, the Saint heard the soft pad of footsteps outside that suddenly broke into the sharp rap of knuckles on the door.

It was one of the servants who looked in in answer to Quintana's summons.

"There are some people downstairs," he said in Spanish. "They will give no names, but they say you are expecting them."

"How many?" asked Quintana, without ceasing his measured rocking in his chair.

"Four."

"Let them come up."

The tension was back in the room, under the surface, evident in the slight motions which Urivetzky and Pérez made. Only the Saint did not stir from his reclining position, but his left hand, on the arm of the chair, imperceptibly tested the effort that would be necessary to raise him quickly out of it.

There was only one light in the room, he noted—a single bulb hung from the ceiling under a painted parchment shade.

As he was lying back, he could see under the shade, straight to the bulb underneath.

Quintana turned to Pérez.

"Search them before they come in," he said.

Pérez's flat eyes hid a gleam of approval. He got up and slouched through the door as other footsteps approached along the passage.

Quintana looked at the Saint.

"A formality," he said, "but we must be careful. There are only three of us."

There were only two of them now, to be exact, and Quintana was still balanced with his fingers against the edge of the desk, in a position where it would take him a fraction of a second longer to recover himself than if he had been sitting up. The last vital difference in the odds had been adjusted when Pérez left the room . . .

The Saint seemed to lounge even more lazily, while his left hand took a firmer grip of the arm of his chair. He waved his cigarette-case back aimlessly, so that it was near his ear.

"Of course," he said, very clearly, "I'm not worried about that. The only thing I'm bothered about is this bloke Graham. You know, the police might think he murdered Ingleston. We know that Pérez did it—"

"I should hardly call it murder," answered Quintana, and although he was taking no pains to clarify his voice it must have been lucidly audible through the open door. "Ingleston was a traitor, and traitors are executed. Pérez was simply carrying out the sentence of the Fascist government as I interpreted it."

"That's all I wanted to know," said the Saint, and with a crisp jerk of his wrist he sent his cigarette-case spinning diagonally upwards like a whirling shaft of silver, straight at the single light over the desk.

The plop of the exploding bulb thudded like a gunshot into the silence, and after it there was a flash of darkness, complete and blinding, before the dim quantity of light filtering through from the corridor outside could take effect on unadjusted eyes. And in that interval of darkness the Saint hurled himself out of his chair like a living thunderbolt.

He reached the bundle of banknotes on the desk as his cigarette-case went on to crash against the far wall, and they were in his pocket before it clattered to the floor. Quintana went first for his gun, but he was off balance; he had to take weight off his hands before they could grab, and that lost him a fraction of a second in which everything was lost. As Quintana raised the automatic, Simon went on with the same continuous hurtling movement that had swept the sheaf of money into his pocket, but at this stage all the power and impetus of the movement was gathered to a focal point in his left fist. The fist took Quintana squarely and centrally on the end of his nose, with every ounce of the Saint's flying bone and muscle behind it; something seemed to crumple like an eggshell, and Simon felt his knuckles sog into warm, sticky pulp.

Quintana went over backwards, smashingly, his legs flying in the air, taking the whole chair with him. The Saint's own momentum carried him halfway across the desk; he wriggled over, pushed his feet off on to the ground, and dived for the communicating door.

Urivetzky clawed at him as he went by, and Simon whipped round, sent him reeling with a right to the jaw, and was on his way with hardly a pause. An instant later, with the door slammed again behind him, he was scooting across the reception-room to let himself out through the tall windows on to the terrace. A faint muffled shout, scarcely audible in the deep interior of the house, was the only sound that followed him.

Outside, the sombre peace of Cambridge Square was as untroubled as it had always been, but Simon knew that it would not remain untroubled for long. He ignored the tree by which he had climbed up, placed one hand on the balustrade, and vaulted out into space. He dropped twenty feet, landed with feet braced and knees bent to absorb the shock, straightened lithely up, and dashed for the wall. Again he went over it with the swift sureness of a cat, and by the good grace of Providence the street on the other side was deserted. Simon turned to the left, instead of to the right where Peter Quentin was waiting farther off with the car, in order to avoid passing the front of the house, and before the first sounds of the hue and cry arose behind him he was strolling sedately round the next corner like any righteous citizen on his way home.

He walked around two blocks so as to approach the car from behind, and as he re-entered Cambridge Square he kept the car between him and the front of the house until the last moment when he stepped round it to open the door and get in.

"I was just getting ready to go home," Peter said, as he steered the limousine out from the kerb. "A couple of cars drove up a few minutes ago with what looked like policemen in them, so I thought they'd look after you."

"Maybe they were looking for a burglar," said the Saint, and passed his bundle of currency over Peter's shoulder. "Take care of this for me, will you? There's forty thousand quid there, so don't lose it. You'd better park it somewhere as soon as you can—I'd better not keep it myself tonight, because Claud Eustace will probably be looking for it."

The limousine swerved in a slightly hysterical arc as Peter felt the bundle and stuffed it into his pocket.

"Did they give you this to get rid of you?" he asked feebly.

"More or less." The Saint was slipping into his sober black overcoat and taking his patriarchal white whiskers out of the locker. "Now step on the gas and let's get home. And before you even start ladling me out of here, tell Sam Outrell to phone his father and rush him over to Cornwall House by the service entrance while Orace and I get rid of those phoney phone repairers—because I have a hunch there's going to be some argument about Joshua Pond!"

10

Chief Inspector Claud Eustace Teal fastened his chewing-gum well back in his mouth and prayed that his collar would stand the strain of the swelling which he could feel creeping up his neck.

"Are you trying to tell me that I'm raving mad?" he squawked.

He had not meant to squawk. But those same infuriating convulsions with which he was only too bitterly familiar were taking hold of his vocal chords again, robbing his voice of the rich, commanding resonance which for some reason he could never achieve when he faced that lazy derisive buccaneer who had long ago taken all the joy out of his life. And the sound of his own squawking filled him with such flabbergasted fury that it only increased his internal feeling of inflation till his collar creaked perilously on its studs.

"What—me?" protested the Saint, in shocked accents. "Claud, have I ever been rude to you? Have I ever hurt your feelings? I may think things, but I keep them to myself—"

"Listen." The detective took hold of himself with both pudgy hands. "I've spent two hours at Quintana's house—"

"Didn't you have fun?"

"I've spent most of that time talking to Quintana. I took Urivetzky away with me—he's in a cell at Cannon Row now—"

"You took who?"

"Urivetzky."

"What are Urivetzky?" asked the Saint. "They sound like a remedy for rheumatism. Have you been having some more trouble with that gouty toe of yours?"

"You know damn well who I mean!"

Simon scratched his head.

"Now I think of it, the name does sort of sound familiar," he admitted. "Was he the guy who pulled off that big forgery some time ago?"

"You know that as well as I do," Teal said grimly, "and you know we were looking for him until we heard he'd been shot in Spain. Well, it's all very well for you to hand him over—"

"Me?" repeated the Saint. "I never touched him."

"He had a cracked jaw when I picked him up. And where did you skin your knuckles?"

"Trying to do a bit of amateur repair work on the car. I don't know if you've ever noticed what a lot of nobbly bits there are in these new-fangled engines."

"You ——."

"I'm not, Claud, really I'm not. And you mustn't say things like that. They're slanderous." The Saint took out a cigarette. "You know, the trouble with you is that you're too modest. After you've done a brilliant piece of detective work running down this crook that everybody's been looking for for years, you come over all coy and try to pass the credit on to someone else. It won't do, Claud. Modesty is all very well, but in these days you have to advertise even if it hurts."

"Besides that," Teal proceeded, "I took a man called Pérez, and he's charged with murdering Ingleston last night."

The Saint frowned slightly.

"Ingleston?" he repeated. "I've heard of him, too . . . Oh yes—he was the bloke with the bent skull that we were looking at this morning. And you've got his murderer, too?" The Saint's smile acquired a spontaneous warmth that would have thawed anyone less obstinately prejudiced. "Claud, this has been a great day for you! And you came straight over to tell me before you told anyone else. Well, I think we ought to have a drink on it."

"Quintana told the whole story," Teal ploughed on doggedly. "There wasn't much else he could do, unless he'd tried to stand on 'diplomatic rights,' and he was too shaken by what you'd done to his nose to think about that. He was howling for a doctor and cursing his friends in Spanish and answering most of my questions at the same time. I may get into trouble later for taking advantage of him, but I've got his signed statement and I've got Pérez. I don't know how much Quintana's immunity is good for, since he's the representative of the rebel government, but we'll see about that. I heard what he said to you just before you smashed the light, and so did three other officers. And his statement brings you in on three other charges of burglary, demanding money with menaces—"

"There's only one thing about this story that worries me, as I told you before," said the Saint mildly, "and that is why I keep coming into it."

Mr Teal moved his gum over to the other side of his jaw, and his round, cherubic, pink face became pinker and more desperately cherubic.

"You know why you come into it," he said. "You were prowling around at Ingleston's this morning, trying to get in my way. You knew that we were looking for Graham, and didn't say anything about him."

"You didn't ask me, Claud. You know how sensitive you are about outsiders trying to show you how to do your job, so it wasn't my business to butt into your case without any invitation."

"You've been hiding him here all day—"

"I certainly haven't. Just because you didn't find him doesn't mean that I was hiding him. It was all perfectly open. You only had to come to the door and say, 'Knock, knock, is Graham there?' and we'd have said, 'Graham who?' and you'd have said, 'Graham the dawn,' and we'd have said 'Peep-bo, here he is,' and everything would have been all right."

"We made inquiries here, and the porter said no one had been to see you."

"He must have been mistaken. To err is human—"

Teal moved his gum again and almost swallowed it. "You've been harbouring a suspected person—"

"But what on earth," asked the Saint puzzledly, "is the poor boy suspected of? Buying a sweepstake ticket or something dreadful like that? I thought you'd got a bloke called Pérez who was supposed to have murdered Ingleston."

"Graham was suspected at the time, and you'd no business to be harbouring him. And now he's still believed to be in possession of seven thousand pounds' worth of American bearer bonds—"

"Bonds?"

"Yes, bonds. Forged bonds. And there's also forty thousand pounds in cash that you stole from Quintana's house tonight!"

"My dear Claud!" The Saint was earnestly sympathetic. "If you've been thinking things like that, I don't wonder that you're upset. Seven thousand pounds' worth of forged bonds and forty thousand quid in cash—*that* would be something to make a song about. But you're all wrong this time. We haven't got any bonds, and we haven't got anything like forty thousand pounds."

"No?" Teal's voice was savage. "Well—"

"Of course you can," said the Saint clairvoyantly. "Go ahead and search us. Search the place. I won't even ask you to show a warrant. If it'll set your mind at rest . . ."

Teal glared around the room as if he was ready to start in and tear it apart without further parley, but even in his glare there was the beginning of a kind of hopeless doubt. The very way that the Saint had so readily told him to go ahead was almost a guarantee that there would be nothing to find, that he would only be laying himself open to more derision from that maddeningly bantering tongue. He had to brace himself to keep plunging on before he thought too much about it and lost steerage way.

"We'll search the room all right while you're in the next cell to Urivetzky," he retorted venomously.

"And what's going to put me there?"

"I am! I know what you were doing at that house tonight—"

"How could I have been doing anything," Simon protested, "when I wasn't there?"

"I know you were there all right—"

Simon shook his head.

"Somebody must have been playing tricks on you. We've all been sitting quietly here, telling stories and talking about architecture."

Teal swallowed, choked, and got his voice back.

"Are you trying to tell me that I'm raving mad?" he bugled again. "After I spoke to you myself on the telephone?"

"Telephones are deceptive things," said the Saint sadly. "If someone was pretending to be me, naturally they'd imitate my voice—"

"I've got more than that. I've got statements from Quintana and Urivetzky and Pérez that you were there all the time."

Simon shrugged deprecatingly.

"After all," he said, "their reputations don't seem to be too good, and I suppose people like that will say anything if they think it'll take trouble away from themselves."

"Would they telephone me and ask me to come over and arrest them?" hooted Teal.

"I don't say they did, although people do lots of queer things. But somebody did it. Why, I don't know. But that's not my job. I'm not a detective, and this isn't my case. It'll be quite a little problem for you, Claud, and I'll be glad to let you know if I think of any theories. But did you see me there?"

"I heard your voice inside the room, and so did three other officers—"

"But that must have been my impersonator, Claud—the bloke who did all the tough stuff, cracking jaws and bopping people on the nose and so forth. I'm sure your officers think they were right, the same as you do—but what about your other officers?"

"What other officers?"

"I mean," said the Saint deliberately, "all those great flat-footed morons who've been plastering the scenery around this building ever since I saw you this morning. You've had them watching me like a flea under a microscope, and I suppose they're as sane as anyone else at Scotland Yard. And unless every one of them is a perjurer, I'll bet you can't bring on one of them who won't swear that I haven't put my nose outside all evening. Now suppose you laugh that off!"

His voice crisped to a subtle sting on the last words, but it was nothing to the tightening that crawled over Chief Inspector Teal. It was as if the detective suddenly soared out of all his gnawing hesitations on a great expansion of sublime triumph. He seemed to grow bigger as his chest swelled, and his round face was red with ecstasy.

"Now I'll tell you why I'm laughing!" he blazed back. "I know how you got out of here without my men seeing you!" That was something else I got from Quintana, because his men were watching this flat, too. I know how you were wheeled out in a false beard before these things happened, and how you were wheeled back just a little while ago! I know all about this precious Mr Joshua Pond, who's supposed to live in the flat next door. And I know that he doesn't exist! I know that the only Joshua Pond in this building is you! And that's what's going to put you where you belong!"

The detective's crescendo of exclamation marks ended in a falsetto squeak like a stabbed canary, but Teal was past caring. The exultation of conquest was singing in his head like strong drink. For once, at last, he had in his hands the final proof that would wreck the Saint's last fatal alibi. And Teal was glad of it. It was the moment for which he had lived more years than he wanted to remember, but it would atone for all of them.

"How's that going to do anything to me?" Simon asked abruptly.

"Because this Joshua Pond hasn't been out again since my men saw him come in. And I'm going right next door to ring his bell and see if he's there. And if he isn't there, I'll have all the evidence I want!"

"But suppose he is?" said the Saint anxiously. "I don't know anything about him, but he might object to being disturbed—"

"If he's there," Teal answered recklessly, "I'll admit that I'm raving mad. I'll admit that I've been dreaming all night. But I shan't have to!"

"Give Joshua my love," said the Saint softly. "Show him your tummy—he might like it." He picked up another cigarette and glanced around at Patricia Holm and Geoffrey Graham as Teal flung himself out of the room. And his smile had the superb inimitable madness on which all his life was based.

Teal was already thumbing the bell of the next apartment. And the door opened.

A very old man, in his shirt and trousers, with a voluminous growth of white whisker almost covering his face, looked out at him.

Something insane and unprecedented took possession of Mr Teal—something which, if he had stopped to think about it, had already seized him on two previous similar occasions during his long feud with the Saint. But Mr Teal was not stopping to think. He was not really responsible for his actions. He was no longer the cold, remorseless Nemesis that he liked to picture himself as he lurched forward with one wild movement, grasped a section of the old man's beard with one hand, and pulled to tear it off.

The only trouble was that the beard did not come off, and the next thing that Mr Teal was aware of was that his face was stinging from a powerful smack.

"Well, dang me!" squalled the ancient. "I never did heeear of such a thing in all my liiife. Haven't you got nothing better to do, young man, than come around pulling respectable folks' beeeards? You wait till I fetch a policeman to ye. I'll see that you learn some manners, danged if I doan't!"

Mr Teal stood there, hardly conscious of his tingling cheek, hardly hearing the old man on the telephone inside the apartment as he upbraided the porter for letting in "danged young fules to come and pull my beeeard." The exultant delirium of a few seconds ago seemed to have curdled to a leaden mass in his stomach. He knew, without stirring another muscle, that the supreme moment he had dreamed of had not yet come. He knew that he was doomed to leave the Saint free once again to organise more tragedies for him. He didn't know how this one had been organised, but he knew that it had been done, and he knew that his very watchdogs were the best evidence against him. And Mr, Teal knew, with the utter deadness of despair, that it had always been fated to be the same.

THE UNLICENSED VICTUALLERS

INTRODUCTION

When I was a boy (only a few hundred years ago) it was practically one of the immutable laws of life that every right-minded boy was a readymade customer for a story about Smugglers. So this is a story about Smugglers, and I have included it in this compendium on the assumption that none of us has grown very much older, and in the hope that our minds are not much worse than they used to be, if as bad. The Smugglers, of course, are a trifle streamlined and efficient, and they do not have wooden legs or black patches over one eye, but I trust that in all other respects their villainy will be found to be as satisfactory as that of the older models.

Aside from that, this story doesn't really seem to need any special introduction.

I notice, however, that it does contain one curious interlude which may provoke some comment.

The remarkable ability of Mr Hoppy Uniatz to consume alcohol, without visible discomfort, in quantities which would keep any six ordinary citizens in a state of permanent paralysis, has long been a source of amazement not only to the Saint himself but also to several habitual readers of these chronicles. Indeed, certain sceptical persons, who seem to doubt the historical solemnity of these records, have claimed that it is impossible for any human being to assimilate so much embalming fluid without becoming completely mummified—a somewhat ridiculous contention to us, of course, who have been eyewitnesses on so many occasions when Mr Uniatz has demonstrated that it can be done by doing it.

Simon Templar, for his part, has seemed to lean towards the theory that with Mr Uniatz's brain in its normally petrified condition, any further ossification would scarcely be perceptible. But this theory hardly seems tenable when one stops to consider that there are several nervous reflexes, perhaps unconnected with conscious cerebration, such as lifting a bottle to the mouth or bopping a guy on the coconut, which are normally suspended during complete alcoholic paralysis, but which in the case of Mr Uniatz appear to be immune to interference.

Personally, I do not feel qualified to venture an opinion on such a profound physiological puzzle. But by way of additional data for more learned scientists, and also to partly correct those critics who believe that Mr Uniatz has never shown any reaction to his intake of alcohol, I feel bound to draw attention to the curious interlude which I was referring to.

There is one point in this story at which, after a longish session with a cargo of contraband tiger's milk, Mr Uniatz, to my mind, indicates that his apparent immunity may be merely a matter of degree. I don't say that he shows signs of getting tight. But there is a slight exuberance, a faint exhilaration, a gentle glow, which might tempt one towards the daring hypothesis that his absorption of alcohol does not affect him simply because he does not drink enough. I don't really know, but there it is.

—Leslie Charteris (1939)

1

Somewhere among the black hills to the south-west dawned a faint patch of light. It moved and grew, pulsing and brightening, like a palely luminous cloud drifting down from the horizon, and Simon Templar, with his eyes fixed on it, slid his cigarette-case gently out of his pocket.

"Here it comes, Hoppy," he remarked.

Beside him, Hoppy Uniatz followed his gaze and inhaled deeply from his cigar, illuminating a set of features which would probably have caused any imaginative passer-by, seeing them spring suddenly out of the darkness, to mistake them for the dial of a particularly malevolent banshee.

"Maybe dey got some liquor on board dis time, boss," he said hopefully. "I could just do wit' a drink now."

Simon frowned at him in the gloom.

"You've got a drink," he said severely. "What happened to that bottle I gave you when we came out?"

Mr Uniatz wriggled uneasily in his seat.

"I dunno, boss. I just tried it, an' it was empty. It's de queerest t'ing . . ." An idea struck him. "Could it of been leakin' woujja t'ink, boss?"

"Either it was, or you will be," said the Saint resignedly.

His eyes were still fixed on the distance, where the nimbus of light was growing still brighter. By this time his expectant ears could hear the noise that came with it, a faraway rattle and rumble that was at first hardly more than a vibration in the air, growing steadily louder in the silence of the night.

He felt for a button on the dashboard, and the momentary whirr of the starter died into the smooth sibilant whisper of a perfectly tuned engine as the great car came to life. They were parked on the heath, just off the edge of the road, in the shadow of a clump of bushes, facing the ghostly aurora that was approaching them from where the hills rose towards the sea. Simon trod on the clutch and pushed the gear lever into first, and heard a subdued click beside him as Mr Uniatz released the safety catch of his automatic.

"Howja know dis is it?" Mr Uniatz said hoarsely, the point having just occurred to him.

"They're just on time." Simon was looking down at the phosphorescent hands of his wrist-watch. "Pargo said they'd be leaving at two o'clock. Anyway, we'll be sure of it when Peter gives us the flash."

"Is dat why you send him down de road?"

"Yes, Hoppy. That was the idea."

"To see de truck when it passes him?"

"Exactly."

Mr Uniatz scratched his head, making a noise like wood being sandpapered. "How does he know it's de right truck?" he asked anxiously.

"By the number-plate," Simon explained. "You know—that bit of tin with figures on it." Mr Uniatz digested this thought for a moment, and relaxed audibly.

"Chees, boss," he said admiringly. "De way you t'ink of everyt'ing!"

A warm glow of relief emanated from him, an almost tangible radiation of good cheer and fortified faith, rather like the fervour which must exude from a true follower of the Prophet when he arrives in Paradise and finds that Allah has indeed placed a number of supremely voluptuous houris at his disposal, exactly as promised in the *Qur'an*. It was a feeling which had become perennially new to Mr Uniatz, ever since the day when he had first discovered the sublime infallibility of the Saint and clutched at it like a straw in the turbulent oceans of Thought in which he had been floundering painfully all his life. That Simon Templar, on one of those odd quixotic impulses which were an essential part of his character, should have encouraged the attachment, was a miracle that Mr Uniatz had never stopped to contemplate; he asked nothing more than to be allowed to stay on as an unquestioning Sancho Panza to this dazzling demigod who could Think of Things with such supernatural ease.

"Dis is like de good old days," Hoppy said contentedly, and the Saint smiled in sympathy.

"It is, isn't it? But I never thought I'd be doing it in England."

Suddenly the haze of light down the road flared up, blazed into blinding clarity as the headlights of the lorry swung round a bend like searchlights. It was still some distance away, but the road ran practically straight for a mile in either direction, and they were parked in the lee of almost the only scrap of cover on the open moor.

Simon held up one hand to shield his eyes against the direct glare. He was not looking at the headlights themselves, but at a point in the darkness a little to the right of them, waiting for the signal that would identify the lorry beyond any doubt. And while he watched the signal came—four long equal flashes from a powerful electric torch, strong enough for him to see the twinkle of them even with the lorry's headlights shining towards him.

The Saint drew a deep breath.

"Okay," he said. "You know your stuff, Hoppy. And don't use that Betsy of yours unless you have to."

He flicked his lighter and touched it to the end of the cigarette clipped between his lips. The light thrown upwards by his cupped hands brought out his face for an instant in vivid sculpture—the crisp sweep of black hair, the rake-hell lines of cheekbone and jaw, the glimmer of scapegrace humour in the clear and mocking blue eyes. It was a face that fitted with an almost startling perfection, as faces so seldom do, not only into the mission that had brought him there that night, but also into all the legends about him. It was a face that made it seem easy to understand why he should be called the Saint, and why some people should think of him almost literally like that, while others called him by the same name and thought of him as a devil incarnate. It might have been the face of a highwayman in another age, waiting by the roadside on his black horse for some unsuspecting traveller—only that the power of a hundred horses purred under the bonnet waiting for the touch of his foot, and the travellers he was waiting for were not innocent even if they were unsuspecting.

The flame went out, dropping his face back into the darkness, and as he slipped the lighter back into his pocket he sent the car whirling forward in a short rush, spinning the wheel to swing it at right angles across the road, and stopped it there, with the front wheels a foot from the grass verge on the other side.

"Let's go," said the Saint.

Hoppy Uniatz was already half-way out of the door on his side. This at least was something he understood. To him, the higher flights of philosophy and intellectual attainment might be for ever barred, but in the field of pure action, once the objects of it had been clearly and carefully explained to him in short sentences employing only the four or five hundred words which made up his vocabulary, he had few equals. And the Saint grinned as he disembarked on to the macadam and melted soundlessly into the night on the opposite side of the road from the one Mr Uniatz had taken.

The driver of the lorry knew nothing of these preparations until his headlights flooded the Saint's car strongly enough to make it plain that the roadway was completely blocked. Instinctively he muttered a curse and trod and hauled on the brakes, and the lorry had groaned to a standstill only a yard from the obstacle before he realised that he might have been unwise.

Even so, there was nothing much else that he could have done, unless he had driven blindly on off the road on to the open heath, with the chance of landing himself in a ditch. Belatedly, it dawned on him that even that risk might have been preferable to the risk of stopping behind such a suspicious-looking barricade, and he groped quickly for a pocket in his overalls. But before he could get his gun out the door beside him was open, and another gun levelled at his middle was dimly visible in the reflected light of the headlamps.

"Would you mind stepping outside?" said a pleasant voice, and the driver set his teeth.

"Not on your mucking life—"

He had got that far when a hand grasped him by the front of his clothing. What followed was something that puzzled him intermittently for the rest of his life, and he would brood over it in his leisure hours, trying to reconcile his own personal impressions with the logical possibilities of the world as he had previously known it. But if it had not been so manifestly impossible, he would have said that he seemed to be lifted bodily out of his seat and drawn through the door with such force that he sailed through the air almost to the edge of the road in a graceful parabola comparable to the flight of the cruising flamingo, before a large portion of the county of Dorset rose up and hit him very hard in several places at once.

As he crawled painfully up on to his hands and knees, he saw the performer of this miracle standing over him.

"'Ere," he protested dazedly, "wot's the idear?"

"The idea is that you ought to be a good boy and do what you're told."

The voice was still cool and genial, but there was an undertone of silky earnestness in it which the driver had overlooked before. Staring up in an effort to make out the details of the face from which it came, the driver realised that the reason why it seemed so curiously featureless was that a dark cloth mask covered it from brow to chin, and something inside his chest seemed to turn cold.

Simon took hold of him again and lifted him to his feet, and as he did so a shrill yelp and a thud came from the other side of the lorry. . .

"That will be your mate going to sleep," said the Saint cheerfully. "Will you have one of our special bedtime stories, or will you just take things quietly?"

His left hand had been sliding imperceptibly over the man's clothing while he spoke, and before the driver knew what was happening the automatic which he carried in his overalls had been whisked away from him. All he saw of it was the glint of metal as it vanished into one of the Saint's pockets, but he clutched at the place where it had been and found nothing there. The Saint's soft laugh purled on his eardrums.

"Come along, sonny boy—let's see what you've got in that beautiful covered wagon."

With that stifling lump of ice swelling under his ribs, the driver felt himself being propelled firmly towards the rear of the van. Simon slipped a tiny flashlight out of his pocket as they went, and as they reached the back of the lorry the masked face of Mr Uniatz swam round from the other side into the bright beam.

"I heard music," said the Saint. Hoppy nodded.

"Dat was de udder guy. He tries to make a grab at my mask, so I bop him on de spire wit' my Betsy an' he dives."

"That's what I love about you," murmured Simon. "You're so thoughtful. Suppose he'd got your mask off, he might have died of heart failure, and that would have been bloody awkward. You ought to keep that face-curtain on all the time—it suits you."

He gave the driver a last gentle push that almost impaled him on the muzzle of Mr Uniatz's ever-ready Betsy, and turned his attention to the rear doors of the van. While he was fumbling with them, footsteps sounded on the road behind him and another flashlight split the darkness and focused on the lock from over his shoulder.

"What ho," said Peter Quentin.

"Ho kay," said the Saint. "The operation went off without a hitch, and one of the patients has a bent spire. Keep that light steady a minute, will you?"

Actually it was not a minute, but only a few seconds, before the lock surrendered its share of the unequal contest with a set of deft fingers that could have disposed of the latest type of burglar-proof safe in rather less time than an amateur would have taken to empty a can of asparagus with a patent tin-opener. Simon pocketed the instrument he had been using, swung the doors wide, and hauled himself nimbly up into the interior of the van.

"What have we won this time?" Peter asked interestedly.

The Saint's torch was sweeping over the rows of cases stacked up inside.

"Looks like a good night's work, soaks," he answered. "There's quite a load of Bisquit Dubouché, and a spot of Otard . . . a whole raft of Veuve Clicquot . . . Romanée-Conti . . . Chambertin . . . Here's a case of Château d'Yquem—"

"Is dey any Scotch?" inquired Mr Uniatz practically.

"No, I don't think so . . . Oh yes, there are a few cases in the corner. We don't seem to have done too badly."

He switched off his flashlight and returned to spring lightly down to the road and shut the doors again. For a moment he stood gleefully rubbing his hands.

"Bisquit Dubouché," he said. "Veuve Clicquot, Chambertin. Romanée-Conti. Château d'Yquem. Even Hoppy's Scotch. Think of it, my perishing pirates. Cases and cases of 'em. Hundreds of quids' worth of bee-yutiful drinks. And not one blinkin' bottle of it has paid a penny of duty. Smuggled in under the noses of the blear-eyed coastguards and pot-bellied excise men. Yoicks! And all for our benefit. Do we smuggle? Do we defraud the Revenue? No, no—a thousand times no. We just step in and grab the loot. Have a drink with me, you thugs."

"That's all very well," Peter Quentin objected seriously. "But we went into this hijacking game to try and find out who was the big bug who was running it—"

"And so we shall, Peter. So we shall. And we'll have a drink with him. And a cigar and a set of silk underwear, like we got last time. How are those lace panties wearing, Hoppy?"

Mr Uniatz made a plaintive noise in his throat, and the Saint pulled himself together.

"All right," he said, "Let's be on our way. Peter, you can carry on with the lorry. Park it in the usual place, and we'll be over in the morning and help you unload. Hoppy and I will take this team along and see if we can find out anything from them."

He turned away and led off along the roadside to move his car out of the way. In the blackness beside the truck he almost stumbled over something lying on the ground, and recalled Hoppy's account of his interview with the driver's mate. As he recovered his balance, he switched his torch on again and turned it downwards.

The sprawled figure in grimy overalls lay with its face turned upwards, quite motionless, the mouth slightly open. The upper part of the face was hard to distinguish under the brim of a tweed cap pulled well down over the eyes, but the chin was smooth and white. He could only have been a youngster, Simon realised, and felt a fleeting twinge of pity. He bent down and shook the lad's shoulder.

"How hard did you bop him, Hoppy?" he said thoughtfully.

"I just give him a little pat on de bean, boss—"

"The trouble is, everybody hasn't got a skull like yours," said the Saint.

He dropped on one knee and pulled down the zipper from the neck of the overalls, feeling inside the youngster's shirt for the reassurance of a heartbeat. And the others heard him let out a soft exclamation.

"What's the matter?" Peter Quentin demanded sharply.

"Well, we certainly won something," said the Saint. "Look."

He took hold of the shabby tweed cap and jerked it off, and the ray of the torch in Peter's hand jumped wildly as a flood of golden hair broke loose to curl around the face of a girl whose sheer loveliness took his breath away.

2

Mr Uniatz sucked in his breath with a sound like an expiring soda siphon, and Peter Quentin sighed.

"Nunc dimittis," he said weakly. "I can't stand any more. The rest of my life would be an anti-climax. I always knew you were the luckiest man on earth, but there are limits. I believe if you trod on a toad it'd turn out to be a fairy princess."

"You ought to see what happens when I tread on a fairy," said the Saint.

Actually his thoughts were chasing far ahead of his words. The miracle had happened—if it was a miracle—and the story went on from there. He was too hardened a traveller in the strange country of adventure to be dumbfounded by any of the unpredictable twists in its trails. But he was wondering, with a tingle of inward exhilaration, where this particular twist was destined to lead.

He turned up the edge of his mask to light another cigarette, and his mind went back over the events that had brought him out that night, not for the first time, to make the raid that had culminated in this surprise. The laden trucks thundering northwards from the coast, filled to capacity with those easily marketable goods on which the English duties were highest— wines and spirits, cigars and cigarettes, silks and embroideries and Paris models . . . The rumours in the Press, that leaked out in spite of the efforts of the police, of a super-smuggler whose cunning and audacity and efficient organisation were cheating the Revenue of thousands of pounds a week and driving baffled detectives to the verge of nervous breakdowns . . . The gossip in pubs along the coast, and the whispers in certain exclusive circles to which no law-abiding citizen had access . . . The first realisation that he had enough threads in his hands to be irrevocably committed to the adventure—that the grand old days of his outlawry had come back, as they must always go on coming back so long as he lived, when his name could be a holy terror to the police and the ungodly alike, and golden galleons of boodle waited for his joyous buccaneering forays . . .

And now he was wondering whether he dared to hope that the due he had been seeking for many weeks had fallen into his hands at last, in the shape of that slim golden beauty in the oil-stained overalls who lay unconscious under his hands.

He went on thinking without interrupting his examination. She was alive, anyway— her pulse was quick but regular, and she was breathing evenly. There was no blood on her head, and her skull seemed to be intact.

"That cap probably helped," he said. "But it only shows you how careful you have to be when you're patting people on the bean, Hoppy."

Mr Uniatz swallowed. "Chees, boss—"

"It's all right," Peter consoled him. "You wouldn't have missed anything if you had brained her. If there's going to be any more fun, he'll have it."

The Saint straightened up and turned to the driver of the lorry, who was standing woodenly behind him with his ribs aching from the steady pressure of a Betsy which in spite of Mr Uniatz's chivalrous distress had never shifted its position.

"Who is she?" Simon asked.

The driver glowered at him sullenly. "I don't know."

"What happened—did you find her growing on a tree?"

"I was just givin' 'er a lift."

"Where to?"

"That's none o' your mucking business."

"Oh no?" The Saint's voice was amiable and unruffled. "Pretty lucky she was all dressed up ready to go riding in a lorry, wasn't it?"

The man tightened his jaw and stood silent, scowling at the Saint with grim intensity.

He was, as a matter of fact, just starting to experience that incredulity of his own recollections of his recent flight through the air which had been referred to before: he was a big man, and he was thinking that he would like to see an attempt to repeat the performance.

The jar of Hoppy's gun grinding roughly into his side made him half turn with a darkening glare.

"Dijja hear de boss ask you a question?" inquired Mr Uniatz, with all the dulcet persuasiveness of a foghorn.

"You ruddy bastard—"

"That'll do," Simon intervened crisply. "And I wouldn't take any chances with my health if I were you, brother. That Betsy of Hoppy's would just about blow you in half, and he's rather sensitive about his family. We'll go on talking to you presently."

He turned to the others.

"I don't know how it strikes any of you bat-eyed brigands," he said, "but I've got a feeling that this is the best break we've had yet. After all, a lot of weird things happen in this world of sin, but you don't usually find girls in overalls riding on smugglers' trucks with a cargo of contraband stagger soup."

"You do when you hold 'em up," said Peter stoically.

"She didn't know I was going to hold it up, you fathead. So she's here for some other reason. Well, she might be just a girl friend of the Menace here, but I don't think it's likely. Take a look at her, and then look at him. Of course, if she turned out to be blind and deaf and half-witted—"

The driver growled viciously, and received another painful prod from Hoppy Uniatz's gun for his trouble.

"Well, if she isn't?" said Peter.

"Then she's something a hell of a lot more important. She's one of the nobs—or she knows 'em pretty well. It'd fit in, wouldn't it? Remember that last consignment we hijacked? All silk dresses and lace and crêpe de Chine underwhatsits. I always thought there might be a woman in it, and if this is her—"

"She," said Peter, helpfully.

The Saint laughed.

"The hell with your grammar," he said. "Let's get going— it'd spoil everything if somebody else came scooting over this blasted heath just now."

He turned away and picked the girl up in his arms like a baby —her body was still limp and lifeless, and it would save a certain amount of trouble if she remained in that state for a little while. So long as Hoppy hadn't struck hard enough for her to be unconscious too long . . .

He put her down in the car, in the seat beside his own, and closed the door. He had left the engine running in case of the need for a quick getaway, and he knew that in waiting so long he had already tempted the Providence that had sent him such a windfall. He straightened up briskly, and strolled to meet the others who were following him.

"This means that we change our plans a bit," he said. "I like my beauty sleep as much as any of you, even if I don't need it so much, but I've got to know where this is getting us before we go to bed. You can follow along with the lorry to the Old Barn, Peter, and Hoppy can take it up to town from there while we see if the fairy princess knows any new fairy tales."

Mr Uniatz cleared his throat. It sounded like the waste-pipe of a bath regurgitating, but it was meant to be a discreet and tactful noise. Almost the whole of the intervening conversation had been as obscure to him as a recitation from Euripides in the original Greek, but one minor omission stood out in front of him with pellucid clarity. Mr Uniatz was no genius, but he had an unswerving capacity for detail which many more brightly coruscating brains might have envied.

"Boss," he said, compressing philosophical volumes into their one irreducible nutshell. "Dis mug."

"I know," said the Saint hurriedly. "I was exaggerating a bit, I'm afraid. It isn't as bad as all that, really. I don't believe anyone would actually die of heart failure if they saw it. I've looked at it myself several times—"

"I mean," said Mr Uniatz shyly, emphasising his objective with another rib-splitting thrust of his Betsy, "dis mug here."

"Oh, him. Well—"

"Do I give him de woiks?" asked Mr Uniatz, condensing into six crystalline monosyllables the problem which dictators of every age and clime have taken thousands of words to propound.

Simon shrugged tolerantly.

"If he gets obstreperous, I should say yes," he murmured. "But if he behaves himself you can put it off for a while. We will have words with him first. If he can put us wise about whether the sleeping beauty is one of the first strings in this racket—"

"Or even the first string," said Peter Quentin thoughtfully.

The Saint put his cigarette to his mouth and drew it to a bright spark of light. For a few moments he was silent. It was a thought that had already occurred to him, long before, but he had been content to let the answer produce itself in its own good time. Even stranger things than that had happened, in the cockeyed world of which Simon Templar had made himself the uncrowned king, and when they did occur they were usually the forerunners of even more trouble than he had set out to ask for, which was plenty. But complications like that had to take care of themselves.

"Who knows?" said the Saint vaguely. "It might just as well have been the secretary of the Women's Temperance League, who isn't nearly so good-looking. On your way, Peter—"

"Hey!" bawled Mr Uniatz.

His voice, which could never at any time have rivalled the musical accents of a radio announcer, blared into the middle of the Saint's words with a blood-curdling intensity of feeling that made even Simon Templar's iron nerves wince. For a moment the Saint was paralysed, while he searched for some sign of the stimulus that was capable of drawing such a response from Mr Uniatz's phlegmatic throat.

And then he became aware that Hoppy was staring straight ahead with a frozen rigidity that was not even conscious of the sensation it had caused. A little to the Saint's left, the driver of the lorry was looking in the same direction with a glitter of evil satisfaction in his small eyes.

Simon swung round the other way, and saw that Peter Quentin also was gazing past him with the same petrified immobility. And as the Saint turned round further, he had a feeling of dizzy unreality that made his scalp creep.

As he remembered it, he had only taken a couple of steps away from his car when Peter Quentin and Hoppy Uniatz and the driver of the lorry had met him. But as he turned, he couldn't see the car at all where it should have been. The road all around him looked empty in the dull gleam of their torches, apart from the black bulk of the van which overshadowed them. It was another second before he saw where his car was. It had swung off on to the heath in a wide arc in order to straighten up, and while he watched, it bumped back on to the macadam and went skimming away up the road to the north-east, with no more than a soft flutter of gas from the exhaust to announce its departure.

3

"One of the things I envy about you," said Peter Quentin, with a certain relish, "is that magnetic power which makes you irresistible to women. Even if they've just been knocked unconscious, the moment they open their eyes and see what's found them—"

"It's a handicap, really," said the Saint good-humouredly. "Their instinct tells them that if they saw much of me they'd do something their mothers wouldn't like, so as often as not they tear themselves reluctantly away."

"I noticed she looked reluctant," said Peter. "She took your car, too—that must have been a wrench."

The Saint grinned philosophically, and tapped a cigarette on his thumbnail. His spirits were too elastic to know the meaning of depression, and the setback had intriguing angles to it which he was broad-minded enough to appreciate as an artist.

The lorry, with Peter at the wheel, churned on through West Holme on to the Wareham road, and Simon Templar lounged back on the hard seat beside him, with his feet propped up where the dashboard would have been if the lorry had boasted any such refinements, and considered the situation without malice. In the interior of the van, behind him, Hoppy Uniatz was keeping the original driver under control, and Simon hoped that he wouldn't do too much damage to the cargo. But even allowing for Mr Uniatz's phenomenal capacity, there was enough bottled kale there to save the night's work from being a total loss.

They were clattering through the sleeping streets of Ringwood before Peter Quentin said, "What are you going to do about the car?"

"Report it stolen some time tomorrow. She'll have ditched it by then—it's too hot to hold on to."

"And suppose she reports the lorry first?" Simon shook his head.

"She won't do that. It'd be too embarrassing if the police happened to catch us. We came out best on the deal, Peter. And on top of that, we've had a good look at her and we'd know her again."

"It ought to be easy," said Peter cheerlessly. "After all, there are only about ten million girls in England, and if we divide the country up between us—"

"We shan't have to go that far. Look at it on the balance of probabilities. If she stays in this game, and we stay in it, it's ten to one that our trails'll cross again."

Peter thought for a moment.

"Now you come to mention it," he said, "the odds are bigger than that. If she's got any sense, she'll find out who you are from the insurance certificate in the car. And then she'll be calling on you with a team of gunmen to ask for her lorry back."

"I had thought of that," said the Saint soberly. "And maybe that's the biggest advantage of all."

"It would save us the trouble of having to find someone to give it to," Peter agreed sympathetically.

But the Saint blew a cloud of smoke at the low roof of the tiny compartment, and said dreamily: "Just look at it strategically, old lad.

All the time we've known that there was some big nob, or bunch of nobs, organising this racket—some guy or guys who keep themselves so exclusive that not even their own mob knows who's at the top. They're the boys we're after, for the simple reason that because they've got the brains to run the show in a way that the saps who do the dirty work, like our pal in the back here, haven't got the intelligence to run it, they've also got the brains to see that they get the fattest dividend.

We've been messing about for some time, annoying them in small ways like this and trying to get a lead, and all the time we've been trying to keep ourselves under cover. Now I'm just beginning to wonder if that was the smartest game we could have played. In any case, the game's been changed now, whether we like it or not, and I don't know that I'm broken-hearted. Now we're on the range to be shot at, and while that's going on we may get a look at the shooters."

"Who'll still be just the saps who do the dirty work."

"I'm not so sure."

For once, Peter restrained the flippant retort which came automatically to his mind. He knew as well as any man that the Saint had been proved big enough game to bring the shyest and most cautious hunters out of hiding. There was something about the almost fabulous stories which had been built up around the character of the Saint that tended to make otherwise careful leaders feel that he was a problem of which the solution could not be safely deputed to less talented underlings.

"All the same," he said, "we were getting along pretty well with Pargo."

"He was still only one of the rank and file—or maybe you might call him a sergeant. It was a bit of luck that we found him driving the first lorry we hijacked with what I knew about his earlier career of crime, and he had sense enough to see that it was safer for him to take his chance with us than have himself parked in a sack outside

Scotland Yard, but I don't know that he could ever have got a line on the nobs . . . I made a date to meet him later tonight, by the way—when he rang me up about this lorry-load he said he'd be driving down from town in the small hours and might have some more tips, so I thought we'd better get together."

"Tell him to give us a ring when we're going to be bumped off," said Peter. "I'd like to know about it, so I can pay my insurance premium." The Saint looked at his watch.

"We've got an hour and a half to go before that," he said. "And we may get a squeal out of Hoppy's protégé before then."

His earlier relaxation, in which he had been not so much recovering from a blow as waiting for the inspiration for a fresh attack, had vanished altogether. Peter Quentin could feel the atmosphere about him, more than through anything he said in the gay surge of vitality that seemed to gather around him like an invisible aura, binding everyone within range in a spell of absurd magic which was beyond reason and was yet humanly impossible to resist, and once again Peter found himself surrendering blindly to that scapegrace wizardry.

"All right," he said ridiculously. "Let's squeeze the juice out of him and see what we get."

Near Stoney Cross they had swung off the main road into a narrow track that seemed to plunge into the cloistered depth of the New Forest, as if it would drift away into the heart of an ancient and forgotten England where huntsmen in green jerkins might still leap up to draw their bows at a stag springing from covert; actually it was a meandering and unkempt road that wandered eventually into the busy highways that converged on Lyndhurst. Somewhere along this road Peter Quentin hauled the wheel round and sent them jolting along an even narrower and deeper-rutted track that looked like nothing but an enlarged footpath. They lurched round a couple of sharp turns, groaned up a forbidding incline, and jarred to a sudden stop.

Peter switched out the lights, and the Saint put his feet down and stretched his cramped limbs.

"We all know about housemaid's knee," he remarked, "but did you ever hear about truck-driver's pelvis? That's what I've got. If I were a union man I should go on strike."

He opened the door and lowered himself tenderly to the ground, massaging the kinks out of his bones.

In front of him, a broad squat mass loomed blackly against the starlight—the Old Barn, which really had been a derelict thatched Tudor barn before Peter Quentin found it and transformed its interior into a cosy rural retreat with enough modern conveniences to compete with any West End apartment. It had the advantage of being far from any listening and peeping neighbours, and the Saint had found those assets adequate reason for borrowing it before. In that secluded bivouac, things could be done and noises could be made which would set a whole suburb chattering if they happened in it . . .

There was an inexorable assurance of those facts implicit in the resilience of the Saint's stride as he rambled towards the rear of the van. And as he approached it, in the silence which had followed the shutting off of the scrangling engine, he heard a hoarse voice raised in wailing melody.

"If I had de wings of a nangel,
From dese prison walls I would fly,
I would fly to de arms of my darling,
An dere I'd be willing to die . . ."

Simon unfastened the doors, while the discordant dirge continued to reverberate from the interior.

"I wish I had someone to lurve me,

Somebody to call me her own,
I wish—"

The Saint's torch splashed its beam into the van, framing the tableau in its circle of brilliance.

Mr Uniatz sat on a pile of cases, leaning back with his legs dangling and looking rather like a great ape on a jungle bough. In his left hand he held his Betsy, and the flashlight gripped between his knees was focused steadily on the lorry driver, who stood scowling on the opposite side of the van. One of the cases was open, and a couple of bottles rolled hollowly on the floor.

A third bottle was clutched firmly in Mr Uniatz's hand, and he appeared to have been using it to beat time.

His face expanded in a smile as he screwed up his eyes against the light. "Hi, boss," he said winningly.

"Come on out," said the Saint. "Both of you."

The lorry driver shuffled out first, and as he descended Simon caught him deftly by the wrist, twisted his arm up behind his back, and waited a moment for Peter to take over the hold.

He turned round as Hoppy Uniatz lowered himself clumsily to the ground.

"How much have you soaked up?" he inquired patiently.

"I just had two-t'ree sips, boss. I t'ought I'd make sure de booze was jake. Say, dijja know I could yodel? I just loin de trick comin' along here—"

The Saint turned to Peter with a shrug.

"I'm sorry, old son," he said. "It looks as if you'll have to take the truck on, after all. I've never seen Hoppy break down yet, but all the same it might be awkward if he met a policeman."

"Couldn't that wait till tomorrow?"

"I'd rather not risk it. The sooner the truck's cleared and out of the way the better."

"Okay, chief."

"Hoppy," said the Saint restrainedly, "stop that god-awful noise and take your boy friend inside."

Peter handed over the prisoner, and they walked back towards the front of the van. A last plaintive layee-o, like the sob of a lovesick cat, squealed through the stilly night before Peter climbed back into the driving seat and restarted the engine. Simon helped him to turn the truck round, and then Peter leaned out of the window.

"What happens next?"

"I'll call you in the morning when I know something," Simon answered. "Happy landings!"

He watched the lorry start on its clattering descent of the hill, and then he turned and went towards the house. In the bright spacious living-room the lorry-driver was lolling in a chair under Hoppy's watchful eye. Simon went straight up to him.

"Get up," he said. "I haven't told you to make yourself at home yet. You're here to answer some questions."

4

The man looked up from under his heavy brows, without moving. His mouth was clinched up so that his under-lip was the only one visible, and his big frame looked lumpy, as if all the muscles in it were knotted. He went on sitting there stolidly and didn't answer.

"Get up," said the Saint quietly.

The man crossed his legs and turned away to gaze into a far corner of the room.

Simon's hand moved quicker than a striking snake. It took hold of the driver and yanked him up on to his feet as if the chair had exploded under him. The man must have been expecting something to happen, but the response he had produced was so swift and unanswerable that for a moment his eyes were blank with stupefaction. Then he drew back his fist.

The Saint didn't stir or flinch. He didn't even seem to take any steps to meet that crudely telegraphed blow. From the slight tilt of his head and the infinitesimal lift of one eyebrow, he might almost have been vaguely amused. But his eyes held mockery rather than amusement—a curious cold glitter of devilish derision that had a bite like steel sword-points. There was something about it that matched the easy and untroubled and yet perfectly balanced way he was standing, something that seemed an essential offshoot of the supple width of his shoulders and the sardonic curve of his lips and the driver's disturbing memory of an apparently incredible incident only a short time before; something that belonged unarguably to the whiplash quality that had crackled under the quietness of his voice when he spoke . . . And somehow, for no other reasons, the blow didn't materialise. The driver's fist sank stiffly down to his side.

"Have a cigarette," the Saint said genially.

The driver stared at the packet suspiciously.

"Wot's all this abaht?" he demanded.

"Nothing, Algernon. Nothing at all. Hoppy and I are just a couple of humble philosophers looking for pearls of knowledge. By the way, is your name Algernon?"

"Wot's my name got to do with you?"

"It would help us to talk about you, Algernon. We can't just point at you all the time—it looks so rude. And then there's the blonde you didn't introduce us to. We want to know who she was, so we can give the vicar her phone number. What's her name?"

"Wouldn't you like to know?" snarled the driver belligerently.

Simon nodded with unaltered cordiality.

"You're asking as many questions as I am, Algernon," he remarked. "Which isn't what I brought you here for. But I don't mind letting you into the secret. I would like to know all these things. Go on—have a cigarette."

As the man's mouth opened for another retort the Saint flipped a cigarette neatly into it. The driver choked and snatched it out furiously. The Saint kindled his lighter. He held it out, and his cool blue eyes met the driver's reddening gaze over the flame. There was no hint of a threat in them, no offer of a challenge, nothing but the same lazy glimmer of half-humorous expectancy as they had held before, and yet once again they baffled the driver's wrath with a nonchalance that his brain was not capable of understanding. He put the cigarette back in his mouth and bent his head sulkily to accept the light.

Mr Uniatz, reclining in an abandoned attitude on the settee, had been taking advantage of being temporarily relieved of his duties to sluice his parched throat with the contents of the bottle he had brought in with him. Now, after having remained for some minutes with his head tilted back and the bottle up-ended towards the ceiling, he came reluctantly to the conclusion that no more liquid was flowing into the desert, and simultaneously returned to a sense of his responsibilities.

"Lemme give him a rub down, boss," he suggested. "He'll come t'ru fast enough."

Simon glanced at him thoughtfully.

"Do you think you could make him talk, Hoppy?"

"Sure I could, boss. I know dese tough guys. All ya gotta do is boin deir feet wit' a candle an' dey melt. Lookit, I see a box of candles in de kitchen last night—"

Mr Uniatz struggled up from the couch, fired with ambition and a lingering recollection of having seen a case of whisky in the kitchen at the same time, but the Saint put out an arm and checked him.

"Wait a minute, Hoppy."

He turned back to the driver.

"Hoppy's so impulsive," he explained apologetically, "and I don't really want to turn him loose on you. But I've got an appointment in an hour or so, and if we can't get together before then I'll have to leave Hoppy to carry on. And Hoppy has such dreadfully primitive ideas. The last time I had to leave him to ask a fellow a few questions, when I came back I found that he'd got the mincing machine screwed on to our best table, and he was feeding this guy's fingers into it. He got the right answers of course, but it made such a mess of the table."

"I'm not afraid o' you—"

"Of course you aren't, Algernon. And we don't want you to be. But you've got to change your mind about answering questions, because it's getting late."

The man watched him stubbornly, but his fists were tightening and relaxing nervously, and there was a shining dampness of perspiration breaking out on his forehead. His eyes switched around the room and returned to the Saint's face in a desperate search for escape. But there was no hope there of the kind he was looking for. The Saint's manner was light and genial, almost brotherly; it passed over unpleasant alternatives as remote and improbable contingencies that were hardly worth mentioning at all, and yet the idea of unpleasantness didn't seem to disturb it in any way. A blusterer himself, the driver would have answered bluster in its own language, but that dispassionate imperturbability chilled him with an unfamiliar sensation of fear . . .

And at that moment, with his uncanny genius for keeping his opponents in suspense, the Saint left the last word unsaid and strolled over to sit on the table, leaving the driver nothing but the threat of his own imagination.

"What's your name, Algernon?" he asked mildly.

"Jopley."

The word fell out after a tense pause, as if the man was fighting battles with himself.

"Been driving these trucks for long?"

"Wot's that got—"

"Been driving these trucks for long?"

"I bin drivin' 'em for a bit."

"Do pretty well out of it?"

The driver was silent again for a space, but this time his silence was not due to obstinacy. His frown probed at the Saint distrustfully, but Simon was blowing wisps of smoke at the ceiling.

"I don't do too bad."

"How much is that?"

"Ten quid a week."

"You know, you're quite a character, aren't you?" said the Saint. "There aren't many people who'd let Hoppy singe their tootsies for ten quid a week. How d'you work it out—a pound a toe?"

The man dragged jerkily at his cigarette, without answering. The question was hardly answerable, anyway—it was more of a gentle twitch at the driver's already overstrung nerves, a reminder of those unpleasant possibilities which were really so unthinkable.

"If I were you," said the Saint, with an air of kindly interest, "I'd be looking for another job."

"Wot sort of job?"

"I think it'd be a kind of sideline," said the Saint meditatively. "I'd look around for some nice generous bloke who wouldn't let people toast my feet or anything like that, but who'd just pay me an extra twenty quid a week for answering a few questions now and again. He might even put up fifty quid when I had anything special to tell him, and it wouldn't hurt me a bit."

"It's a waste of money, boss," said Mr Uniatz with conviction. "If de candles don't woik, I got a new one I see in de movies de udder day. You mash de guy's shins wit' a hammer—"

"You won't pay too much attention to him, will you, Algernon?" said the Saint. "He gets a lot of these ideas, you know— it's the way he was brought up. It's not my idea of a spare-time job, though."

The driver shifted himself from one foot to the other. It wasn't his idea of a spare-time job, either—or even a legitimate part of the job he had. He didn't need to have the balance of the alternatives emphasised to him. They were so clean-cut that they made the palms of his hands feel clammy. But that lazily, frighteningly impersonal voice went on:

"Anyway, you don't have to make up your mind in a hurry if you don't want to. Hoppy'll keep you company if you don't mind waiting till I come back, so you won't be lonely. It's rather a lonely place otherwise, you know. We were only saying the other day that a bloke could sit here and scream the skies down, and nobody would hear him. Not that you'd have anything to scream about, of course . . ."

"Wot is this job?" asked the man hoarsely.

Simon flicked the ash from his cigarette, and hid the sparkle of excitement in his eyes. "Just telling us some of these odd things we want to know."

The man's lips clamped and relaxed spasmodically, and his broad chest moved with the strain of his breathing. He stood with his chin drawn in, and his eyes peered up from under a ledge of sullen shadow.

"Well," he said. "Go on."

"Who was the girl friend?"

"Why don't you ask her?"

The voice was soft and musical, startlingly unlike the harsh growl that Simon's ears had been attuned to, and it came from behind him.

The Saint spun round.

She stood in the open doorway, her feet astride with a hint of boyish swagger, still in her soiled overalls, one hand in the trouser pocket, with the yellow curls tumbling around her exquisitely moulded face, a slight smile on her red lips. Her eyes, he discovered, now that he saw them open for the first time, were a dark midnight grey—almost the same shade as the automatic she held steadily levelled at his chest.

For three seconds the Saint stood rigidly spellbound. And then a slow smile touched the corners of his mouth in response.

"Well, darling," he murmured, "what *is* your name?"

5

"You ought to be a detective, Mr Templar," she said. "I don't have to ask you yours."

"But you have an advantage. We've tried checking up on your lorries, but you always send them out with fake number-plates and no other identification, so it's rather difficult. I have to suffer for being honest."

"Or for not being so careful," she said. "By the way, will you tell your friend to do something about his hands?"

Simon looked round. Mr Uniatz was still frozen as the interruption had caught him, with his mouth hanging open and his right hand arrested half-way to the armpit holster where his Betsy nestled close to his heart. His eyes welcomed the Saint with an agonised plea for guidance, and Simon took his wrist and put his hand gently down.

"Leave it alone for a minute, Hoppy," he said. "We don't want the lady to start shooting . . ." His gaze turned back to the girl. "That is, if she can shoot," he added thoughtfully.

"Don't worry," she said calmly. "I can shoot."

The Saint's glance measured the distance.

"It's about six yards," he observed. "And a lot of people have mistaken ideas about how easy it is to pot a moving target with an automatic at six yards."

"Would you like to try me?"

Simon poised his cigarette-end between his forefinger and thumb and flipped it sideways. It struck Hoppy's discarded bottle, over by the settee, with a faint *plunk!* and sent up a tiny fountain of sparks.

"Hit that," he said.

The muzzle of the gun swung away from his body, but it was only for an instant. She fired without seeming to aim, and the automatic was aligned on the Saint's breastbone again before the crash of the explosion had stopped rattling in his ears, but the bottle was spattered in fragments over the carpet.

The Saint nodded to Hoppy.

"She can shoot," he remarked. "She's been practising."

"It's not much use having a gun if you don't."

"You've been reading some good books," said the Saint, and his smile was serene but watchful. "It looks as if you have what is known as the Bulge—for the time being, anyway. So where do we go from here? Would you like us to sing and dance for you? Hoppy's just discovered that he can yodel, and he's dying for an audience."

"I'm afraid we haven't time for that. Jopley—"

The driver came out of his temporary stupor. He thrust himself forward and retrieved his gun from the Saint's pocket, and shuffled crabwise around the room in the direction of the door, keeping well clear of the girl's line of fire. Remembering the stage at which their conversation had been interrupted, the Saint could understand why he had not been so quick to seize his opportunity as might have been expected, and a malicious twinkle came into his gaze.

"What—you don't want him, do you?" he said. "We thought we'd do you a good turn and take him off your hands."

"I came back for him," she said, "so I suppose I do want him."

Simon acknowledged the argument with a slight movement of his head.

"You didn't waste much time about it, either," he said appreciatively. "How did you track him down—by smell?"

"I followed you. I pulled into a side turning in West Holme and waited to see if you'd go that way. Then I just kept behind you. It wasn't difficult."

It didn't sound very difficult, when the trick was explained. The Saint sighed ruefully at the reflection of his own thoughtlessness.

"That's the worst of lorries," he complained. "It's so hard to notice what's behind you. Something ought to be done about it . . . But I hope you'll take care of Algernon if you're borrowing him. We were just starting to get matey."

"I heard you," she said.

"Yus." Jopley's voice was loud and grating. "Goin' ter burn me feet, that's 'ow they were goin' ter get matey. I've a good mind—"

"You haven't," said the girl evenly. "We'll leave things like that to gentlemen like Mr Templar."

The Saint smiled at her.

"We've got a second-hand rack and some thumb-screws in the cellar, too," he said. "But I prefer boiling people down with onions and a dash of white wine. It makes quite a good clear soup, rather like *madrilène*."

She really did look like something out of a fairy-tale, he thought, or like a moment of musical comedy dropped miraculously into the comfortable masculine furnishings of the Old Barn, with the perfect proportions of her slender body triumphing even over that shabby suit of dungarees, and her face framed in its setting of spun gold, but there was nothing illusory about the unfaltering alertness of those dark grey eyes or the experienced handling of the gun she held. The only uncertain thing about her was the smile that lingered about her lips.

She said, "I'm glad you didn't get me here."

"But you're here now," said the Saint. "So couldn't we make up for lost time?"

His hand moved towards his breast pocket, but the two guns that covered him moved more quickly. Simon raised his eyebrows.

"Can't I have a cigarette?"

"Take them out slowly."

Simon took out his case, slowly, as he was ordered, and opened it.

"Can I offer you one?"

"We haven't got time."

"You're not going?"

"I'm afraid we've got to." Her acting was as light and polished as his own. "But you're coming with us."

The Saint was still for a moment, with the flame of his lighter burning without a quiver under the end of his cigarette. He drew the end of the cigarette to a bright red, and extinguished the flame with a measured jet of smoke.

"But what about Algernon?" he said. "Are you sure he won't be jealous?"

"You're not coming as far as that. We've got to get back to your car, and we don't want any trouble. As long as your friend stays here and doesn't interfere, we shan't have any trouble. I just want you to come down and see us off."

"You hear that, Hoppy?" said the Saint. "Any fancy work from you, and I get bumped off."

"That," said the girl grimly, "is the idea."

Simon weighed his prospects realistically. He hadn't exaggerated the solitude of their surroundings; a pitched battle with machine-guns at the Old Barn would have caused less local commotion than letting off a handful of squibs in the deepest wastes of the Sahara. There was nothing to neutralise the value of those two automatics by the door, if the ringers on their triggers chose to become dictatorial—and the experience of a lifetime had taught the Saint to be highly conservative about the chances he took in calling the bluff from the wrong side of a gun. Apart from which, he was wondering whether he wanted to make any change in the arrangements . . .

As if he were trying to find arguments for accepting the bitterness of defeat, his eyes turned a little away from the girl, to a point in space where they would include a glimpse of the face of the lorry-driver. He had sown good seed there, he knew, even if he had been balked of the quick harvest he had hoped for . . . And on the outskirts of his vision, removing all doubt, he saw Jopley's sullen features screwed up in a grotesque wink . . .

"We always see our visitors off the premises," said the Saint virtuously. "Are you sure you won't have one for the road?"

"Not tonight."

Either he was setting new records in immortal imbecility, Simon realised as he led the way down the steep, winding lane, or the threads that had baffled him for the past three weeks were on the point of coming into his reach, and some irrational instinct seemed to tell him that it was not the former. He had no inkling then of how gruesomely and from what an unexpected angle his hunch was to be vindicated.

The beam of his own torch, held in the girl's hand, shone steadily on his back as he walked and cast his elongated shadow in a long oval of light down the track. The decision was taken now—whatever he might have done to turn the tables back in the Old Barn, out there in the empty night with the torchlight against him and two guns at his back there was no trick he could play that would fall far short of attempted suicide.

They came down to the road, and he saw the lights of his car parked a little way past the turning. Jopley got in first, and took the wheel, and then the girl slipped into the seat beside him, still holding the Saint in the centre of the flashlight's ring of luminance. Simon stood by the side of the car and smiled into the light.

"You still haven't told me your name, darling," he said.

"Perhaps that's because I don't want you to know it."

"But how shall I know who it is when you call me up? You are going to call me up, aren't you? I'm in the London telephone directory, and the number here is Lyndhurst double-nine six five." He lingered imperceptibly over the figures—but that was for Jopley's benefit.

"Sometime when you're not so busy, I'd like to take you out in the moonlight and tell you how beautiful you are."

"There's no moon tonight," she said, "so you'll want the torch to get home with."

The light spun towards him, and he grabbed for it automatically. By the time he had fumbled it into his hands, the lights of the car were vanishing round the next bend in the road.

The Saint made his way slowly back up the hill. So that was that, and his wisdom or folly would be proved one way or the other before long. He grinned faintly at the thought of the expression that would come over Peter Quentin's face when he heard the news. She really would be worth a stroll in the moonlight, too, if they weren't so busy . . .

There was someone in the porch by the front door.

The Saint stopped motionless, with a flitter of impalpable hailstones sweeping up his spine. As he walked, with the torch swinging loosely in his hand, its arc of light had passed over a pair of feet, cutting them out of the darkness at the ankles. The glimpse had only been instantaneous, before the moving splash of light lost it again, but Simon knew that he had not been mistaken. He had switched out the torch instinctively before he grasped the full significance of what he had seen.

After a moment he took three soundless steps to the side and switched the light on again, holding it well away from his body. And for a second time he experienced that ghostly tingle of nerves.

For the man was sitting, not standing, on a low bench in the alcove beside the door, with his hands hanging down by his sides and his body hunched forward so that his face was buried in his knees. But although his features were hidden, there was something about the general appearance of the man that struck Simon with a sudden shock of recognition.

"Pargo !" said the Saint sharply.

The figure did not move, and Simon stepped quickly forward and raised its head. One look was enough to tell him that Ernie Pargo was dead.

6

About the manner of his dying Simon preferred not to speculate too profoundly. He had, actually, been strangled by the cord that was still knotted around his throat so tightly that it was almost buried in the flesh of his neck, but other things had happened to him before that.

"I see anudder guy like dis, once," said Mr Uniatz chattily. "He is one of Dutch Kuhlmann's mob, an' de Brooklyn mob takes him over to Bensenhoist one night to ask him who squealed on Ike Izolsky. Well, when dey get t'ru wit' him he is like hamboiger wit'out de onions—"

"You have such fascinating reminiscences, Hoppy," said the Saint.

He was laying Pargo's limp body on the settee and arranging the relaxed limbs for the rough examination which he felt had to be made. It was not a pleasant task, and for all the Saint's hardened cynicism it made his mouth set in a stony line as he went on.

In the brightness of the living-room the dead man looked even more ghastly than he had looked outside—and that had been enough to make the darkness around the house suddenly seem to be peopled with ugly shadows, and to make the soft stir of the leaves sound like cackles of ghoulish laughter. The Brooklyn mob could have learnt very little from whoever had worked on Pargo—Simon did not have to ask himself how they had known where to leave his body.

But when had it been done? There was no sign of rigor mortis, and Simon thought that he could still detect some warmth under the man's clothes. The body certainly hadn't been in the porch when they first arrived at the Old Barn. It might have been there when he went out only a few minutes ago; it would have been easy not to notice it when going out of the door and moving away from the house. It seemed impossible that it could have been placed there during the short time he had been away, but he had circled around the building for some minutes to make sure, like a prowling cat, with every nerve and sense pricked for the slightest vestige of any lurking intruder, until he had to admit that it was a hopeless quest. If it had not been done then, it could only have been done while he was talking to Jopley—or while the girl was there talking to him.

Whatever the answers were to those riddles, the happy-go-lucky irrelevance of the adventure had been brought crashing down to earth as if some vital support in it had been knocked away. There was no longer any question of coming in for the fun of the game: Simon Templar was in it now, up to the neck, and as he went further with his investigation of Pargo's mangled body the steel chilled colder in his eyes.

Hoppy Uniatz, however, having possessed himself of a bottle from the kitchen during the Saint's absence, was prepared to enjoy himself.

"Dat's a funny t'ing now, boss," he resumed brightly. "Dey is a dame wit' de Brooklyn mob what is Izolsky's moll, an' she helps de boys woik on dis guy. She tells him funny stories while dey go over him wit' an electric iron. She had class, too, just like dis dame tonight."

The Saint straightened up involuntarily as Hoppy's grisly memoirs hit a mark which he himself had been unconsciously avoiding. Now that the point was brought home to him, his first impulse was to shut it out again, and yet nagging little needle points of incontrovertible logic went on fretting at the opening that had been made.

The time-table made it impossible for her to have deliberately co-operated from the start in dumping the body where he had found it. But she might have met the dumping party on their way to the house, and come in to hold him up while they were doing their job. She might have known from the beginning that the dumping was to be done. She might have had the information that had been tortured out of Pargo to lead her there, without the necessity of following the lorry as she said she had done. She might have seen the body in the porch before she let herself in through the unlocked door, and come in unperturbed by it. In any case, as a confessed member of the gang that had done the job, was there any logical reason to presume that she knew nothing about their methods? Unsentimentally, the Saint acknowledged that golden hair and a face like a truant princess were no proof of a sensitive and lovable character. It was a pity, but the world was like that . . . The expression on his face did not change.

"She must have been a beauty," he murmured absently.

"Sure, boss, she wuz de nuts. She wuz like a real lady. But I never could make de grade wit' dese ritzy dames." Mr Uniatz sighed lugubriously in contemplation of the unappreciativeness of the female sex, and then his gaze reverted to the figure on the couch. "Dis guy," he said, gesturing with his bottle, "is he de guy we're waitin' for tonight?"

The Saint lighted a cigarette and turned away.

"That's right," he said. "Only we don't have to wait any longer."

"De guy from de goil's mob?"

"Yes."

"De guy who drives de foist truck we hijack?"

"Yes."

"De guy who gives us de wire about dat truck tonight?"

"Yes."

"De guy," said Mr, Uniatz, making sure of his identification, "what is goin' to find out who is de big shot in dis racket?"

"That was the idea," said the Saint curtly. "But I suppose he found out too much. He won't tell us anything now, I'm afraid."

Mr Uniatz wagged his head.

"Chees," he said sympathetically, "dat's too bad."

For the first time he seemed to visualise the passing of Mr Pargo as a subject for serious regret. He studied the body with a personal interest which had been lacking in him before, and reached for his bottle again to console himself.

Simon drew smoke monotonously into his lungs and breathed it out in slow trailing streamers. Pargo's death was something that was passing into his own background by then. Anger and pity would do nothing now: his troubles were over, whatever they had been. There remained revenge—and that would be taken in due time, inexorably. The Saint was grimly resolved about that . . . But that was another part of the background, an item in the unalterable facts of existence like the rising of the sun the next morning, too obvious to require dwelling on in the abstract.

Nor was he thinking of the chance that the same rising sun might find him taking no more active share in the proceedings than Pargo was. Certainly the dumping of the body was a proof that his anonymity was gone for ever, but he had taken that risk voluntarily, before he knew about Pargo, when he let the girl and Jopley go. With his almost clairvoyantly accurate understanding of the criminal mind, he wasn't expecting any further demonstrations that night: the body had been left there for an effect, and nothing more would be done until the effect had had time to sink in.

What he was thinking, with a different kind of cold-bloodedness from that of Mr Uniatz, was that the passing of Mr Pargo was a setback which it wouldn't be easy to make good. He had, now, the possible co-operation of Jopley, but that would be suspect for some time even if it materialised. The one proved spy he had had in the enemy's camp had been hideously eliminated.

The Saint sat on the edge of the table and stared abstractedly at the body on the settee.

If only Pargo could have got through to him, before that happened, with the information which he had paid for at such a price . . .

Pargo's left arm slid off the edge of the sofa, and his hand flopped on to the carpet so that his limp wrist turned over at a horribly unnatural angle.

Simon went on looking at it, with his face as impassive as a mask of bronze.

"Some guy tells me once," went on Mr Uniatz, seeking a solution, "dat if you look in a guy's eyes what's been moidered . . . "

The Saint seemed suddenly to have become very still, with his cigarette poised half an inch from his lips.

His examination of Pargo had been confined to the body itself and the contents of the pockets. The former had given nothing but confirmation to his first impressions, and the latter had been emptied of everything that might have given him any kind of information. Now, with a queer feeling of breathless incredulity, he was staring at something so obvious that he could hardly understand how he had overlooked it before, so uncannily like a direct answer from the dead that it made the blood race thunderously in his veins.

As the arm had fallen, the sleeve had been dragged back from the grimy shirt-cuff. And on the shirt-cuff itself there were dark marks too distinct and regularly patterned to be entirely grime.

Simon moved forward and lifted the lifeless hand with a sense of dizzy unreality.

He was barely able to decipher the lines of cramped and twisted writing.

"Their onto me Im done for—The stuff comes in Brandy bay
His name is Lasser—I had to tell them—if you—"

There was no more than that, and even in the way it was written the Saint could feel the agony of the man scrawling those words with broken and shaking fingers, driven by who could tell what delirious impulse of ultimate loneliness.

Simon's voice trailed away as the message trailed away, into a kind of formless silence. Hoppy Uniatz gaped at him, and then put down his bottle.

He crowded over to squint at the writing with his own eyes.

"Say, ain't dat a break?" he demanded pachydermatously. "Now if we knew who dis guy Lasser is—"

"There's one Lasser you ought to know," said the Saint acidly. "He keeps you supplied with your favourite food . . . My God!"

The immensity of the idea he had stumbled over almost rocked him on his feet, and a blaze came into his eyes as he recovered himself.

"Lasser—Lasser's Wine Stores—the biggest liquor chain in the country! It'd be perfect! . . . Wait a minute—I've just remembered. There's a picture of him somewhere—"

He picked up a copy of the *Sporting and Dramatic News* from the table and tore through it in search of the correlation of that flash of random memory; it was on a page of photographs headed *The Atlantic Yacht Club Ball at Grosvenor House*—one of those dreary collections of flashlight snapshots so dear to the peculiar snobbery of the British public. One of the pictures showed a group taken at their table, with a fat bald-headed jolly-faced man on the left. The caption under it ran,

Among Those Present: Mr Grant Lasser, Miss Brenda Marlow—

The Saint had not read any farther. His eyes were frozen on the picture of the girl next to Lasser, for it was also the picture of the girl who had been holding him up half an hour ago.

7

"Yes, I checked up on her," said Peter Quentin, sipping his whisky and soda. "She lives in Welbeck Street, and she runs one of those ultra dress shops in Bond Street. You know the kind of thing—an enormous window with nothing in it but a chromium-plated whatnot with one evening wrap hanging on it, and no price tickets."

"It all fits in," said the Saint soberly. "That load of dresses and whoosits that we knocked off a fortnight ago—that's where they would have gone. She probably took a trip to Paris herself, and spent a gorgeous week getting them together. What about Lasser?"

"Nothing that isn't public property anyway. But I found out from Lloyd's that he's the owner of a three-hundred-ton steam yacht called the *Valkyrie*. He's also the owner of a house on Gad Cliff, and if you look at the map you'll see that it overlooks Brandy Bay. It's supposed to have been unoccupied and left in charge of a caretaker for about a couple of years, but we don't have to take the caretaker too seriously."

Peter Quentin had been a rather serious young man since the Saint had told him the complete story over the telephone that morning, and curiously enough he had refrained from making any of the obvious gibes which Simon had been fully prepared for. He had arrived late in the afternoon, after what clearly could not have been an idle morning.

The Saint moved up and down the long living-room of the Old Barn for a moment with the silent restlessness and pent-up energy of a caged tiger.

"I've been going over all that we had from Pargo," he said, "and all the things we'd been trying to get sorted out before. And it all seems so simple now that it almost makes you howl."

Peter didn't interrupt him, and the Saint took another turn round the room and went on:

"What we've been up against all the time was that there seemed to be three separate gangs without any connecting link. There was one gang that brought the stuff across the Channel in some sort of ship. The stuff was brought ashore in small boats and handed over to the shore gang, and none of 'em ever saw the ship that brought it in daylight. The ship always had her lights out, and they could never even find out the first thing about her. Pargo was one of the shore gang, and I'm beginning to think now that he ought to have known where the stuff was stored, but probably he was holding out on us to get as much money as he could. Anyway, all the rest he knew was that the shore gang drove trucks to London and parked them wherever they'd been told to and went away, and somebody else came along later and picked up the truck and took it wherever it was going. That, presumably, was the third gang—the distributing gang. And none of the three gangs met anywhere except at the top, which we couldn't get near."

"Unless they all met at the same top."

"Of course, I had been thinking of that. But there was no actual proof that it was the same top, and in any case we didn't know where the top was. The point is that every lead petered out as soon as it started to get interesting. It was the perfect set-up—three separate outfits doing separate shares in the same job, and none of 'em making any contact with the others except in places that were practically leak-proof. And now they all blow up together."

"Off the same fuse," commented Peter economically. The Saint nodded.

"That's what it means. The top is the same—right the way through. This steam yacht of Lasser's—the *Valkyrie*—brings the stuff over the Channel. That's a cinch. A private yacht can go anywhere, and no questions asked. He could keep her in Southampton Water, push off for a week-end cruise, say he was going to Torquay or anywhere, scoot over the Channel, and pick up his cargo. There's probably a fourth gang on the other side, which just collects contraband for some smugglers unknown. And it's only about seventy miles straight across from Cherbourg to Brandy Bay. The *Valkyrie* comes back and sends the stuff ashore, and steams back to Southampton Water, and nobody knows where she's been or bothers to ask . . . There's a coastguard station at Worbarrow Head and another one on the far side of Kimmeridge Bay, but Brandy Bay is hidden from both of 'em, and coastguarding is pretty much of a dead letter these days."

"And the shore gang picks it up—"

"Under the same orders. It wouldn't be too hard for Lasser to organise that. And then it goes out to the great unsuspecting public, nicely mixed up with any amount of genuine duty-paid legitimate liquor, through the central warehouses of Lasser's Wine Stores, Limited—who don't know where it came from, any of the guys who handle it, but just take it as part of the day's work. What's that advertising line of theirs?—'*Butlers to the Nation.*' It's not a bad line either, from the experience I've had of butlers."

Peter lowered the level in his glass an inch further.

"Apart from what goes rustling around the limbs of the aristocracy from the salons of Brenda *et Cie*," he remarked.

"Apart from that," Simon agreed unemotionally. "But it all works out so beautifully that we ought to have been on to it months ago."

"I should have been," said Peter, "if you hadn't got in the way. And now it's all so simple. You keep on chasing the shore gang and finding bodies on the doorstep, while I sit out on Gad Cliff with a telescope every night catching pneumonia and watching for the smuggling gang, and Hoppy puts on some lipstick and ankles up and down Bond Street looking for chiffon brassières with bottles of whisky in them. I don't know what happens about this fourth gang you've invented on the French side, but I suppose you can always find somebody else to keep track of them." Peter drank deeply, and looked around for a refill. "As you said just now, it's so childishly simple that it almost makes you howl."

The Saint regarded him pityingly.

"I've always approved of these birds who want to strangle imbecile children at birth," he said. "And now I think I shall send them a donation. You ineffable fathead—what do these assorted gangs amount to? It doesn't matter if there are four of them or forty. They're only stooges, like poor old Pargo. Knock the king-pin out, and they all fall apart. Take one man in, and they all go for the same ride. All we want is Lasser, and we can call it a day."

"Just like poor old Pargo," said Peter, *sotto voce*. He looked up from manipulating the siphon. "What happened to him, by the way?"

"We took him down to Lymington and borrowed a boat while the tide was going out. If he ever gets washed up again anywhere he'll be another headache for Chief Inspector Teal, but we had to do something with him."

"Probably that's one reason why he was left here," said Peter intelligently.

Simon was kindling the latest cigarette in a chain that had already filled an ash-tray. He saw that it was burning evenly and crushed the preceding fag-end into the heap of wreckage.

"That was one obvious motive—bodies being troublesome things to get rid of," he said. "The other, of course, was *pour encourager les autres*. I've been expecting some more direct encouragement all day, but it hasn't materialised yet. I don't suppose it'll be long now, though."

Mr Uniatz, who had been silent for a long time except for intermittent glugging noises produced by the bottle beside him, stirred himself abruptly and consulted his watch with the earnest air of a martyr who realises that he is next in line for the lions. His intrusion after such a long absence seemed so portentous that both Peter and the Saint turned towards him with what must have been a disconcerting expectancy. Mr Uniatz blinked at them with his nightmare features creased in the grooves of noble self-abnegation.

"Boss," he said, with some embarrassment, "what's de next train to London?"

"Train?" said the Saint blankly.

"Yes, boss. I t'ought you an' Mr Quentin'd be busy, so ya wouldn't wanta drive me dere, an' dey ain't no udder car—"

The Saint studied him anxiously.

"You aren't feeling ill or anything, are you?" he asked. "But you don't have to worry about the ungodly giving us some more encouragement. Peter and I will hold your hand if there's any rough stuff."

"Encouragement?" repeated Mr Uniatz foggily. He shook his head, as one who was suddenly confronted with a hopelessly outlandish twist of thought. "I dunno, boss . . . But ya said I gotta go to Bond Street an' look for braseers wit' bottles in dem. Dat's okay wit' me," said Mr Uniatz, squaring his shoulders heroically, "but if any a dese dames t'ink I'm gettin' fresh—"

Simon readjusted himself hastily to the pace of a less volatile intellect.

"That's all right, Hoppy," he said reassuringly. "We're putting that idea on the shelf for the moment. You just stick around with us and keep your Betsy ready."

Mr Uniatz's eyes lighted tentatively with the dawn of hope.

"You mean I don't gotta go to London?"

"No."

"Or—"

"No."

Hoppy drew a deep breath.

"Chees, boss," he said, speaking from the heart, "dat's great!" His bottle glugged again expressively.

"We haven't any other ideas," Peter explained dishearteningly, "but that doesn't matter."

The Saint's eyes mocked him with dancing pin-points of silent laughter. During that day the Saint's cold anger of the night before seemed to have worn off, although the inexorable pith of it was still perceptible in the fine-drawn core of steel that seemed to underlie his outward languor. But now it was masked by something more vital—the mad gay recklessness that came around him like a mantle of sunlight when the hunt was up and the fanfares of adventure were sounding out in the open.

"You're wrong," he said. "We've got a much better idea. I had a telegram this afternoon—it was phoned through from Lyndhurst just before you arrived. I've been saving it up for you." He picked up the scrap of paper on which he had scribbled the message down. "It says, 'Your car will be at the Broken Sword in Tyneham at nine-fifteen tonight.' It isn't signed, and anyhow it wouldn't have mattered much who signed it. It didn't originate from any of these assorted gangs we've been talking about—otherwise why be so very accurate about the time?

It means that the Master Mind is taking a hand, just as I prophesied last night, and whatever happens he won't be far away. It's bait, of course, and we're going to bite!"

8

Simon wanted seventy-three to finish, and the babble of chaff and facetious comment died down through sporadic resurrections as he took over the darts and set his toe on the line. His first dart went in the treble 19, and the stillness lasted a couple of seconds after that before a roar of delight acknowledged the result of the mental arithmetic that had been working itself out in the heads of the onlookers. His second dart brushed the inside wire of the double 8 on the wrong side as it went in, and the hush came down again, more breathless than before. Somebody in a corner bawled a second encouraging calculation, and the Saint smiled. Quite coolly and unhurriedly, as if he had no distracting thought in his mind, he balanced the third dart in his fingers, poised it, and launched it at the board. It struck and stayed there—dead in the centre of the double 4.

A huge burst of laughter and applause crashed through the silence like a breaking wave as he turned away, and his opponent, who had been pushed forward as the local champion, grinned under his grey moustache and said, "Well, zur, the beer's on me."

The Saint shook his head.

"No, it isn't, George. Let's have a round for everybody on me, because I'm going to have to leave you."

He laid a ten-shilling note on the bar and nodded to the landlord as the patrons of the Broken Sword crowded up to moisten their parched throats. He glanced at his watch as he did so, and saw that it showed sixteen minutes after nine. Zero hour had struck while he was taking his stand for those last three darts, but it had made no difference to the steadiness of his hand or the accuracy of his eye.

Even now, it made no difference, and while he gathered up his change he was as much a part of the atmosphere of the small low-ceilinged bar as any of the rough warm-hearted local habitués . . . But his eyes were on the road outside the narrow leaded windows, where the twilight was folding soft grey veils under the trees, and while he was looking out there she arrived. His ears caught the familiar airy purr of the Hirondel through the clamour around him before it swept into view, and he saw the brightness of her golden hair behind the wheel without surprise as she slowed by. It was curious that he should have been thinking for the last hour in terms of "she," but he had been expecting nothing else, and in that at least his instinct had been faultless.

The boisterous human fellowship of the Broken Sword was swallowed up in an abyss as he closed the door of the public bar behind him. As if he had been suddenly transported a thousand miles instead of merely over the breadth of a threshold, he passed into a different world as he faced the quiet road outside—a world where strange and horrible things happened such as the men he had left behind him to their beer would never believe, a world where a man's life hung on the flicker of an eyelid and the splitting of a second, and where there was adventure of a keen corrosive kind such as the simple heroes of mythology had never lived to see. The Saint's eyes swept left and right before he stepped out of the shadow of the porch, but he saw nothing instantly threatening. Even so, he found some comfort in the knowledge that Peter Quentin and Hoppy Uniatz would be covering him from the ambush where he had posted them behind a clump of trees in the field over the way.

But none of that could have been read in his face or in the loose-limbed ease of his body as he sauntered over to the car. He smiled as he came up, and saluted her with the faint mockery that was his fighting armour.

"It's nice of you to bring the old boat back, darling. And she doesn't look as if you'd bent her at all. There aren't many women I'd trust her with, but you can borrow her again any time you want to. Just drop in and help yourself—but of course I don't have to tell you to do that."

The girl was almost as cool as he was—only a hardened campaigner like the Saint would have detected the sharp edges of strain under the delicate contours of her face. She patted the steering-wheel with one white-gloved hand.

"She's nice," she said. "The others wanted to run her over a cliff, but I said that would have been a sin. Besides, I had to see you anyway."

"It's something to know I'm worth saving a car for," he murmured.

She studied him with a kind of speculative aloofness. "I like you by daylight. I thought I should."

He returned her survey with equal frankness. She wore a white linen skirt and a cobwebby white blouse, and the lines of her figure were as delicious as he had thought they would be. It would have been easy, effortless, to surrender completely to the blood-quickening enchantment of her physical presence. But between them also was the ghostly presence of Pargo, and a chilling recollection of Pargo's livid distorted face passed before the Saint's eyes as he smiled at her.

"You look pretty good yourself, Brenda," he remarked. "Perhaps it's because that outfit looks a lot more like Bond Street than what you had on last night." Her poise was momentarily shaken.

"How did you—"

"I'm a detective too," said the Saint gravely. "Only I keep it a secret."

She unlatched the door and swung out her long slender legs. As she was doing so, a sleek black sedan swam round the nearest bend, slowing up, and turned in towards the front of the pub. The Saint's right hand stayed in his coat pocket and his eyes were chips of ice for an instant, before the driver got out unconcernedly as the car stopped and walked across to the entrance of the bar. The Saint could almost have laughed at himself, but not quite; those reactions were too solidly founded on probabilities to be wholly humorous, and he was still waiting for the purpose of their meeting to be revealed.

The girl didn't seem to have noticed anything. She straightened up as her feet touched the road, flawless as a white statue, with the same impenetrable aloofness. She said, "There's your car. Would you like to take it and drive away? A long way away—to the north of Scotland, or Timbuctoo, or anywhere. At least far enough for you to forget that any of this ever happened."

"The world is so small," Simon pointed out unhappily. "Twelve thousand miles is about the farthest you can get from anything, and that's not very far in these days of high-speed transport. Besides, I don't know that I want to forget. We've still got that date for a stroll in the moonlight—"

"I'm not joking," she said impatiently. "And I haven't got much time. The point is—I found out your name last night, but I didn't know who you were. I suppose I haven't been around enough in that kind of society. But the others knew."

"Look at the advantages of a cosmopolitan education," he observed. "There are more things in this cockeyed world than Bond Street—"

The stony earnestness of her face cut him off.

"This is serious," she said. "Can't you see that? If the others had had their way you wouldn't be here now at all. If you'd been anything else but what you are you wouldn't be here. But they've heard of you, and so it doesn't seem so easy to get rid of you in the obvious way. That's why I'm here to talk to you. If you'll leave us alone it'll be worth a hundred pounds a week to you, and you can draw the first hundred pounds this evening."

"That's interesting." said the Saint thoughtfully. "And where are these hundred travel tickets?"

"There'll be a man waiting in a car with a GB plate at the crossroads in East Lulworth at half-past ten. He'll be able to talk to you if you want to discuss it."

The Saint took her arm.

"Let's discuss it now," he suggested. "There's some very good beer inside—"

"I can't." She glanced a little to his left. "That other car's waiting for me—the one that just arrived. The man who brought it has gone out at the back of the pub, and he's only waiting a little way up the road to see that you don't keep me. It wouldn't be very sensible of you to try, because he can see us from where he is, and if I don't pick him up at once there'll be trouble." Her hand rested on his sleeve for a moment as she disengaged herself. "Why don't you go to Lulworth? It wouldn't hurt you, and it'd be so much easier. After all, what are you doing this for?"

"I might ask you what you're doing it for."

"Mostly for fun. And from what they've told me about you, you might just as easily have been on our side. It doesn't do anyone any harm—"

The Saint's smile was as bright as an arctic moon.

"In fact," he said, "you're beginning to make me believe that it really did Pargo a lot of good."

She shrugged.

"You wouldn't have expected us to keep him after we knew he was selling us out to you, would you?" she asked, and the casual way she said it almost took the Saint's breath away.

"Of course not," he answered, after a pause in which his brain whirled stupidly.

The dusk had been deepening very quickly, so that he could not be quite sure of the expression in her eyes as she looked up at him.

"Talk it over with your friends," she said in a quick low voice. "Try to go to Lulworth. I don't want anything else to happen . . . Good-bye. Here's the key of your car."

Her arm moved, and something tinkled along the road. As his eyes automatically turned to try and follow it, she slipped aside and was out of his reach. The door of the black sedan slammed, its lights went on, and it rushed smoothly past him with the wave of a white glove. By the time he had found his own ignition key in the gloom where she had thrown it, he knew that it was too late to think of trying to follow her.

The Saint's mind was working under pressure as he waited for Peter and Hoppy to join him at the corner of the inn. There was something screwy about that interview—something that made him feel as if part of the foundations of his grasp of the case were slipping away from under him. But for the present his thoughts were too chaotic and nebulous to share with anyone else.

"We've got a date to be shot up at East Lulworth at half-past ten," he said cheerfully, and gave them a literal account of the conversation.

"They're making you travel a bit before they kill you," said Peter. "Are you going on with this mad idea of yours?"

"It's the only thing to do if we're sticking to our plan of campaign. We're fish on the rise tonight, and we'll go on rising until we get a line if it—"

He broke off with his hand whipping instinctively to his pocket again as a bicycle whirred out of the shadows towards them at racing speed. The brakes grated as it shot by, and a man almost threw himself off the machine and turned back towards them. A moment later the Saint saw that it was Jopley.

"Thank Gawd I caught yer," he gasped. "I was afride it 'ud be too late. Yer mustn't go ter Lulworth tonight!"

"That's a pity," said the Saint tranquilly. "But I just made a date to go there."

"Yer carn't do it, sir! They'll be wytin' for yer wiv a machine-gun. I 'eard 'im givin' the orders, an' 'ow the lidy was ter meet yer 'ere an' tell yer the tile, an' everythink—"

Simon became suddenly alert.

"You heard who giving the orders?" he shot back.

"The boss 'imself it was—'e's at Gad Cliff 'Ouse naow!"

9

The Saint's lighter flared in the darkness, catching the exultant glint in his eyes under impudently slanted brows. When the light went out and left only the glow-worm point of his cigarette, it was as if something vital and commanding had been abruptly snatched away, leaving an irreparable void, but out of the void his voice spoke with the gay lilt of approaching climax.

"That's even better," he said. "Then we don't have to go to Lulworth . . ."

"You must be disappointed," Peter said sympathetically. "After looking forward to being shot up with a machine-gun—"

"This is easier," said the Saint. "This is the fish sneaking out of the river a little way downstream and wriggling along the bank to bite the fisherman in the pants. Peter, I have a feeling that this is going to be Comrade Lasser's unlucky day."

"It might just as well have been any other day," Peter objected. "He isn't any unknown quantity. He's in the telephone book. Probably he's in *Who's Who* as well. You could find out everything about him and all his habits, and choose your own time—"

"You couldn't choose any time like this! Just because he is supposed to be such a respectable citizen, his pants would be a tough proposition to bite. Can you imagine us trying to hold him up in his own baronial halls, or taking him for a ride from the Athenaeum Club? Why, he could call on the whole of Scotland Yard, including Chief Inspector Teal, not to mention the Salvation Army and the Brigade of Guards, to rally round and look after him if we tried anything. But this is different. Now he isn't a pillar of Society and Industry, surrounded by bishops and barons. He's in bad company, with a machine-gun party waiting for us at East Lulworth—and while he's waiting for news from them he's sitting up at Gad Cliff House, on top of the biggest store of contraband that the Revenue never set eyes on. We've got him with the goods on him, and this is where we take our chance!"

Peter Quentin shrugged.

"All right," he said philosophically. "I'd just as soon take my chance at this house as take it with a machine-gun. Lead on, damn you."

Mr Uniatz cleared his throat, producing a sound like the eruption of a small volcano. The anxiety that was vexing his system could be felt even if it could not be seen. Ever a stickler for detail once he had assimilated it, Mr Uniatz felt that one important item was being overlooked in the flood of ideas that had recently been passing over his head."

"Boss," said Mr Uniatz lucidly, "de skoit."

"What about her?" asked the Saint.

"She didn't look to me like she had no bottles in her braseer."

"She hadn't."

"Den why—"

"We're giving her a rest, Hoppy. This is another guy we're going to see."

"Oh, a guy," said Mr Uniatz darkly. "Den how come he's wearin' a—"

"He's funny that way," said the Saint hastily. "Now let's have a look at the lie of the land. He led the way over to the Hirondel and spread out a large-scale ordnance map under the dashboard light. Gad Cliff House was plainly marked on it, standing in about three acres of ground bordered on one side by the cliff itself, and approached by a narrow lane from the road that ran over the high ground parallel with the coast.

"That's plain enough," said the Saint, after a brief examination of the plan. "But what are the snags?"

He looked round and found Jopley's face at his shoulder, seeming even more sullen and evil in the dim greenish glow of the light. The man shook his head.

"It's 'opeless, that's wot the snag is," he said bluntly. "There's alarms orl rahnd the plice—them invisible rye things. A rabbit couldn't get in wivout settin' 'em orf."

"But you were able to get out."

"Yus, I got aht."

"Well, how did you manage it?"

"I said I 'ad ter go aht an' buy some fags."

"I mean," said the Saint, with the almost supernatural self-control developed through long association with Hoppy Uniatz, "how did you get out through these alarms?"

Jopley said slowly, "I got aht fru the gates."

"And how will you get back?"

"I'll git back the sime wye. The man ooze watchin' there, 'e knows me, an' 'e phones up to the 'ouse an' ses 'oo it is, an' they ses it's orl right, an' 'e opens the gates an' lets me in."

The Saint folded his map.

"Well," he said deliberately, "suppose when this bird had the gates open to let you in, some other blokes who were waiting outside rushed the pair of you, laid him out, and let themselves in—would anyone at the house know what had happened?"

The man thought it out laboriously. "Not till 'e came to an' told 'em."

"Then—"

"But yer carn't git in that wye," Jopley stated flatly. "Not letting me in for it, yer carn't. Wot 'appens when they find aht I done it? Jer fink I wanter git meself bashed over the 'ead an' frown to the muckin' lobsters?"

Simon smiled.

"You don't have to get thrown to the lobsters, Algernon," he said. "I'm rather fond of lobsters, and I wouldn't have that happen for anything. You don't even have to get bashed over the head, except in a friendly way for the sake of appearances. And 'they' don't have to find out anything about it—although I don't think they'll be in a position to do you much damage anyway, when I'm through with them. But if it'll make you any happier, you don't have to be compromised at all. You just happened to be there when we rushed in, and nobody could prove anything different. And it'd be worth a hundred pounds to you—on the nail."

Jopley looked from one face to the other while the idea seemed to establish itself in his mind. For a few seconds the Saint was afraid that fear would still make him refuse, and wondered what other arguments would carry conviction. In mentioning a hundred pounds he had gone to the limits of bribery, and it was more or less an accident that he had as much money as that in his pockets . . . He held his breath until Jopley answered.

"When do I get this 'undred quid?"

Simon opened his wallet and took out a folded wad of banknotes. Jopley took them in his thick fingers and glanced through them. His heavy sulky eyes turned up again to the Saint's face.

"I won't do nothing else, mind. Yer can rush me along o' the other bloke, an' if yer can git inside that's orl right. But I didn't 'ave nothink ter do wiv it, see?"

"We'll take care of that," said the Saint confidently. "All we want is to know when you're going back, so that we can be ready. And it had better be soon, because the time's getting on. I want to be in that house before the machine-gun squad gets back from Lulworth."

"I can start back naow," said the other grudgingly. "If you drive there in yer car, yer'll'ave ten minutes before I git there on me bike." The Saint nodded.

"Okay," he said peacefully. "Then let's go!"

The steady drone of the Hirondel sank through his mind into silence as the long shining car swept up the winding road towards the crest of the downs. Instead of it, as if the words were being spoken again beside his ears, he heard Brenda Marlow's clear unfaltering voice saying, *"You wouldn't have expected us to keep him after we knew he was selling us out to you, would you?"* Lasser, Pargo, what had been done to Pargo, and what might be done at Gad Cliff House that night—those other thoughts were a vague jumble that was almost blotted out by the clearness of the words which he was hearing over again in memory. And he could feel again the chill of downright horror that had struck him like an icy wind when he heard them first.

Simon Templar had travelled too far on the iron highways of outlawry to be afflicted with empty sentimentality, and he had been flippant enough about death in his time—even about such ugly death as Pargo's. But about such an utter unrelenting callousness, coming without the flicker of an eyelash from a face like the one he had seen when it was being spoken, there was a quality of epic inhumanity to which even the Saint could not adjust himself. It made her look like something beside which a blend of Messalina and Lucrezia Borgia would have seemed like a playful schoolgirl—and yet he could recall just as clearly the edged contempt in her voice, after she had overheard the lurid bluff he had encouraged Hoppy to put over on Jopley, when she said, "We'll leave things like that to gentlemen like Mr Templar." The contradiction fretted at the smooth surface of his reasoning with maddening persistence, and yet the one and only apparent way of reconciling it raised another question which it was too late now to track down to its possible conclusions . . .

A dull kind of tightness settled over the Saint's nerves as he brought the Hirondel to a stop just beyond the opening of the lane that led to the entrance of Gad Cliff House. He switched off the engine and climbed out without any visible sign of it, but his right hand felt instinctively for the hilt of the sharp throwing-knife strapped to his left forearm under the sleeve, and found it with an odd sense of comfort. At other times when he had made mistakes, that hidden and unlooked-for weapon had brought rescue out of defeat, and the touch of it reassured him. He turned to meet the others without a change in his blithe serenity.

"You know what you have to do, boys and girls," he said. "Follow me, and let's make it snappy."

Mr Uniatz coughed, peering at him through the darkness with troubled intensity.

"I dunno, boss," he said anxiously. "I never hoid of dis invisible rye. Is dat what de guy has in de bottles in his—"

"Yes, that's it," said the Saint, with magnificent presence of mind. "You go on an invisible jag on it, and end up by seeing invisible pink elephants. It saves any amount of trouble. Now get hold of your Betsy and shut up, because there may be invisible ears."

The lane ran between almost vertical grass banks topped by stiff thorn hedges, and it was so narrow that a car driven down it would have had no more than a few inches clearance on either side. The car that came up it from the road must have been driven by someone who knew his margins with the accuracy of long experience, for it swooped out of the night so swiftly and suddenly that the Saint's hearing had scarcely made him aware of its approach when it was almost on top of them, its headlights turning the lane into a trench of blinding light. Simon had an instant of desperate indecision while he reckoned their chance of scaling the steep hedge-topped banks and realised that they could never do it in time, and then he wheeled to face the danger with his hand leaping to his gun. Hoppy's movement was even quicker, but it was still too late. Another light sprang up dazzlingly from behind the gates just ahead of them; they were trapped between the two opposing broadsides of eye-searing brilliance and the two high walls of the lane as if they had been caught in a box, and Simon knew without any possibility of self-deception that they were helplessly at the mercy of the men behind the lights.

"Put up your hands," ordered a new voice from the car, and the Saint acknowledged to himself how completely and beautifully he had been had.

10

"I might have known you'd be a great organiser, brother," murmured the Saint, as he led the way obediently into the library of Gad Cliff House with his hands held high in the air. "But you were certainly in form tonight."

The compliment was perfectly sincere. When Simon Templar fell into traps he liked them to be good ones, for the sake of his own self-esteem, and the one he had just walked into so docilely struck him as being a highly satisfactory specimen from every point of view.

It was all so neat and simple and psychologically watertight, once you were let into the secret. He had kept his first appointment with Brenda Marlow, as anyone would have known he would. He had been duly suspicious of the second appointment at the cross-roads in East Lulworth, as he was meant to be. He had accepted it merely as a confirmation of those suspicions when Jopley arrived with the warning of the machine-gun party—exactly as he was meant to do. And with the memory of the proposition he had made to Jopley the night before still fresh in his mind, the rest of the machinery had run like clockwork. He had been so completely disarmed that even Jopley's well-simulated reluctance to lead him into the very trap he was meant to be led into was almost a superfluous finishing touch. A good trap was something that the Saint could always appreciate with professional interest, but a trap within a trap was a refinement to remember. He had announced himself as being in the market for bait, and verily he had swallowed everything that was offered him.

Simon admitted the fact, and went on from there. They were in the soup, but even if it was good soup it was no place to stay in. He reckoned the odds dispassionately. Their guns had been taken away from them, but his knife had escaped the search. That was the only asset he could find on his own side—that, and whatever his own quickness of thought was worth, which on its recent showing didn't seem to be very much. And yet no one who looked at him would have seen a trace of the grim concentration that was driving his brain on a fierce, defiant search for the inspiration that would turn the tables again.

He smiled at Lasser with all the carefree and unruffled ease that only reached its airiest perfection with him when the corner was tightest and the odds were too astronomical to be worth brooding over.

"What does it feel like to be a Master Mind?" he inquired interestedly.

Lasser beamed back at him, with his rich, jolly face shining as if it had been freshly scrubbed.

"I've read a lot about you," he said, "so I knew I should have to make a special effort. In fact, I'm not too proud to admit that I've picked up a few tips from the stories I've heard of you. Naturally, when I knew who our distinguished opponent was, I tried not to disappoint him."

"You haven't," said the Saint cordially. "Except that I may have expected a larger deputation of welcome."

His gaze drifted over the assembly with the mildest and most apologetic hint of criticism. Besides Lasser, there was only Jopley and one other man, presumably the gatekeeper—a short, thick-set individual with a cast in one eye and an unshaven chin that gave him a vicious and sinister aspect which was almost too conventional to be true. There was also Brenda Marlow, who came into the room last and sat on the arm of a chair near the door, watching from the background with an expression that the Saint couldn't quite analyse.

"I think there are enough of us," said Lasser blandly. He turned to Jopley. "You searched them all thoroughly?"

The man grunted an affirmative, and Lasser's glance passed fleetingly over Peter Quentin and Hoppy and glowed on the Saint again.

"You can put your hands down," he said. "It will be more comfortable for you. And sit down, if you want to." He tugged at the lobe of his ear absent-mindedly while the Saint turned a chair round and relaxed in it, crossing his legs. "Ah—about this deputation of welcome. Yes. I had thought of giving you more of a show, but I decided not to. You see, I brought you here to talk over some more or less private business, and I thought the fewer people who knew about it the better. You have rather a persuasive way with you, Mr Templar, so Jopley tells me, and I shouldn't want you to tempt any more of my employees. Will you have a drink?"

"I'd love one," said the Saint graciously, and Lasser turned to the villainous specimen with the unshaven chin.

"Some drinks, Borieff."

Simon took out his cigarette-case while Borieff slouched over to a cupboard under one of the bookshelves and brought out a bottle and a siphon.

"You know, this makes me feel quite guilty," he said. "I've had so many drinks with you before, and yet I've never bought you one."

"Two van-loads, isn't it?" Lasser agreed, with his fat, bright smile. "And the other van with—um—silks and things in it. Yes, yes. That's what I brought you here to talk to you about. We shall have to have those vans back, of course, what you haven't actually used of them."

"Hoppy certainly has rather improved the shining hour," Simon admitted. "But there's quite a lot left. What sort of an offer were you thinking of making?" Lasser shook his head.

"No," he said judiciously. "No, I wasn't thinking of making an offer. I just want them back. I'm afraid you're going to have to tell us where to find them. That's why I arranged for you to come here."

"What's all this," Brenda Marlow asked quietly, "about bringing them here?"

She had been so much in the background that the others seemed to have forgotten her, and when she spoke it was as startling an intrusion as if she had not been there before and had just walked in. Lasser looked round at her, blinking.

"Eh?"

"What's all this," she repeated, in exactly the same quiet voice, "about bringing them here?"

Lasser rubbed his chin.

"Oh, of course," he said. "Bringing them here. Yes. I didn't tell you—I didn't really mean them to meet me at Lulworth. That was just to get them ready for the story Jopley had to tell them. It was all arranged so that they'd be sure to come here, so I suppose I can say we brought them."

"I see," she said innocently. "So you were just using me as a sort of stuffed decoy." Lasser's broad smile did not waver.

"I shouldn't say that, my dear. No. Not at all. You couldn't have played your part nearly so well if you hadn't believed in it. I was just making it easier for you." He tugged at his ear again for a moment, and then pulled out his watch, consulted it, stuffed it back in his pocket, and rubbed his hands briskly together with an air of breezy decision. "Now, Brenda, it's time you were off. As a matter of fact, I thought you'd have started by this time. Remember you're due in London at one o'clock."

Her shoulders moved slightly.

"I can make it in three hours easily in the new Lagonda," she said slowly. "And since I'm here I'd like to see how you get on."

"But you've got to allow for accidents. If you had a puncture—"

"Do you mean you don't want me to stay?"

The Saint felt an odd thrill of breathlessness. There was a subtle tension in the room that had not been there before, even in spite of the display of artillery which was still in evidence. To the Saint's preternaturally sharpened senses it was perceptible in the darkened sullenness of Jopley, in the harsh rigidity of Borieff, even in the frozen fixity of Lasser's expansive smile.

And there could only be one explanation for it. It meant that he must have been right in the one wild theory which had come to him on the way there when it was too late to probe into it—that Brenda Marlow and her contradictions were accounted for, and that it was no longer necessary to look to Messalina and Lucrezia Borgia for her prototype. It gave the Saint a curious sense of lightness and relief, even though it did nothing to improve his own position. There were worse things than to be at the mercy of men like Lasser and Jopley and Borieff, and in Simon Templar's own inconsequential philosophy to have to think of a girl as he had been thinking of her was one of them.

"I don't mean that at all," Lasser was saying jovially. "No. Of course not. But that—um—envelope has got to be delivered, and this is rather a private matter—"

"Doesn't it concern all of us?"

The Saint raised his glass and drank with a certain deep satisfaction.

"Comrade Lasser has his own views about who's concerned with one thing and another, darling," he explained. "For instance, there was that business about Pargo. I'll bet he didn't tell you that Pargo was tortured to death and dumped on my—"

Borieff's lunging fist thudded against the side of the Saint's head and sent the glass he was holding spinning away to splinter itself on the edge of a table.

Simon's muscles gathered themselves in spontaneous reaction. And then, as he gazed squarely into the muzzle of Borieff's automatic, they slowly loosened again. Just as slowly, he took out a handkerchief and wiped a few drops of spilt liquid from his coat.

After the sudden crash of shattering glass there was a brief interval of intense silence. And then Lasser spoke, with his eyes creased up to slits in his plump jolly face.

"Tie them up," he said, and as Jopley and Borieff moved to obey the order, the smile that had been only temporarily shaken came back to his wide, elastic mouth. "I'm sorry, Templar, but you must have some respect for the position you're in. I can't have you saying things like that. Now for the rest of this interview you'd better confine yourself to speaking when you're spoken to, or I may have to do something you won't like."

Simon looked at the girl.

"You see how touchy he is?" he drawled recklessly. "I don't know how well you know the signs of a guilty conscience—"

Out of the corner of his eye he could see Lasser's forefinger tightening on the trigger of his levelled gun, but there were provocations that could bring the Saint's contempt for such things to the verge of sheer insanity. What might have happened if he had been allowed to go on was something that he could hardly have refused to bow to in cold blood, but before he could say any more the girl stepped forward.

"Leave him alone, Lasser," she said. "I'm interested in this. What did happen to Pargo?"

"We sent him to Canada, of course, as I told you," Lasser replied brusquely. "You surely don't believe any of this fellow's wild accusations?"

Her dark grey eyes went over him with an unexpectedly mature kind of thoughtfulness.

"I believe what I see," she said. "And I saw Borieff hit him. I think that was a better answer than yours—"

She was opening her bag as she spoke, and Lasser went to meet her suddenly, with a swiftness that was surprising and somehow horrible in a man of his build. His downward-sinking fist knocked the bag through her hands, and then he was holding her by the wrists.

"You mustn't interfere in things like this," he said, still smiling. "Of course I don't tell you everything—you wouldn't like it if I did. But we've got to put a stop to Templar's interference, and that isn't your business unless you want to make it so." He looked at the Saint over his shoulder. "You're going to tell me what happened to those three vans—and do you know why you'll tell me the truth? Because I'm going to take each one of you separately into the next room and ask you questions in my own way, and when you all tell me the same thing I'll know you aren't lying!"

11

There were bands of adhesive tape around the Saint's wrists and ankles, and Peter Quentin had been quickly strapped up in the same way at the same time. Now they were working on Hoppy Uniatz, after first depriving him of the whisky bottle which by some irresistible magnetism had gravitated into his hands.

Lasser held the girl until they had finished, and then he pushed her back into an armchair and signed to Borieff to take charge of her. He straightened his coat and picked up her bag and tossed it into her lap, but not before he had transferred a heavy sealed envelope from it to his pocket.

"This is really very tiresome of you, my dear," he said heartily. "Now I shall have to make some other arrangements."

"You certainly will," she retorted. "I wouldn't have any more to do with this business of yours for all the money in the world."

He stood manipulating his ear meditatively for a little while.

"No," he said. "No, of course not. No, but it's your own fault. You didn't have to know any more than was good for you. Naturally you would be—um—sentimental, but you ought to have realised that there are serious things in this business. Well, we'll talk about that presently. Now that you're here, you'll have to be quiet and behave yourself, because we can't waste any more time."

"Be quiet and behave myself while you torture them, I suppose," she said with bitter directness.

"No. Not necessarily. But they've got to answer my questions. It'll only be their own fault if they're obstinate." He shrugged. "Anyhow, you've no choice. If you don't behave yourself, Borieff will have to keep you quiet."

He beamed at her in his stout, avuncular way, as if he were insisting on giving her an especially extravagant birthday present.

She looked at Simon with a white face.

"I apologise for what I said to you last night," she said huskily. "If I'd known why you were going to burn Jopley's feet, I'd have stayed and helped you."

"The joke is that we didn't really mean to do it," Simon answered regretfully. "But next time—"

"There won't be no muckin' next time," Jopley stated with savage complacency. "Come on." He grasped the Saint's arm, but Simon was still looking at the girl.

"Maybe you made a mistake about me," he said. "And I'm glad I was wrong about you. Remind me to make up for it when we take that stroll in the moonlight."

His gaze rested on her a moment longer with all the steadying courage he could send her, and then he turned to Peter.

"I ought to have come alone," he said. "But since we're all here we might as well tell Comrade Lasser what he wants to know."

"What for?" Peter demanded indignantly, as Simon might have known he would. "If you think we give a damn for that fat slob—"

Lasser pointed at the Saint.

"Take him in, Jopley," he said, like a genial host arranging the procession of guests to a dining-room.

With an evil grin, Jopley pushed the Saint off his balance and half dragged and half carried him through a door at one end of the room. The room that it opened into was almost bare of furniture and smelt strongly of paraffin—even at that moment the Saint's brow wrinkled with puzzlement as he met the rank, powerful odour.

Jopley heaved him up and shoved him roughly into the only chair as Lasser followed them in. The door closed softly behind him—an ancient and massive door of solid oak that settled into place with a faint *fuff* of perfectly fitting joints, seeming to shut out every sound and contact with the outside world. He stood there, smiling benevolently at the Saint, smoothing his large hands one over the other.

"I hope we shan't have to hurt you very much," he said. "If you would like to tell me at once what happened to those vans, we needn't go any further. But of course I shall take care that your two friends don't have a chance to find out what you've told me, so if they don't tell the same story we shall have to hurt them until they do."

The Saint looked at him and then at Jopley. And as he did so he felt the blood run faster in his veins. For Jopley was sliding his gun away into his pocket.

A flood of strength seemed to surge through the Saint's body like a tidal wave. He could feel the race of it through his muscles, the galvanic awakening of his nerves, the sudden clearing of his brain to crystal brilliance. It was as if his whole being was lifted up in a sublime ecstasy of renewed life. And yet otherwise everything was the same. The corner was just as tight, the prospects just as deadly, but that one action had altered a balance in which the difference between life and death would be weighed. Lasser had already put away his gun. Jopley's gun was going—had gone. It was in his pocket, and his hands were hanging empty at his sides. In that room, with the two of them together against one man bound hand and foot, they had done what any other two men would have done in the confidence of their obvious superiority. And the astronomical hopelessness of the odds had been lessened by the fraction of time that it would take a man to draw a gun from his pocket . . .

Only the Saint's face betrayed nothing of the fanfares of exultation that were pouring magnificent music through his soul. He moved slightly in his chair, twisting his right hand as far as he could, and his fingertips touched the hilt of his knife under the sleeve with a thrill that added new harmonies of its own.

"And what happens after we've told you all this?" he asked. Lasser pursed his lips.

"Well, I'm afraid we shall still have to get rid of you. You know too much, Templar, and we can't risk your being tempted to interfere with us again."

"Do we get sent to Canada too?"

"No, not to Canada. No. I think we shall just leave you here. This place is being burnt down tonight," Lasser explained calmly. "You may have noticed the smell of paraffin. Yes. It's rather antiquated and I want to rebuild it—something modern, you know. It's quite well insured, so I thought it would be a good idea to have a fire. Yes, we'll just have to leave you here with a lighted candle on the floor, and kill two birds with one stone, if you know what I mean."

Simon had his knife in his hand and he was working the point of it under the tapes on his wrists, but for a moment he almost stopped.

"You mean you'd leave us here to be burnt alive?" he said slowly.

"I'm afraid we'd have to. The place is supposed to be unoccupied, you know, and I sent the caretaker away this morning. It'd look as if you were tramps who'd broken in to sleep for the night, and you might have set fire to the house yourselves by accident. So it wouldn't look right if they found bullets in you or anything like that."

Lasser seemed to ponder over his reasoning again, and shook his head with refreshed conviction.

"No, that would never do," he said, and then his sunny smile dawned again. "But don't let's meet our troubles half-way. After all, I've heard that in a real fire people are often suffocated by the smoke before they get burnt at all. But we could hurt you a lot first if you didn't tell us what happened to those vans."

The Saint's hands were free—behind his back, he could move his wrists apart. But even so, he felt as if his stomach was emptied with a kind of sick revulsion. There was no doubt in his mind that Lasser would have done everything he spoke of with such a genial matter-of-factness—would still do it, if the Saint failed in the only gamble he had left. That rich, unchangingly beaming smile was a better guarantee of it even than Jopley's lowering vindictiveness. And now the Saint seemed to read through it for the first time into something that explained it, something monstrous and gloating, something that smoothed Lasser's bald, glistening forehead into a horrible vacantness of bland anticipation . . .

"Where are those vans, Templar?" he asked in a silky whisper. Simon met his gaze with eyes of frosted sapphire.

"They're where you'll never find them," he said deliberately, "you greasy grinning bladder of lard."

Lasser turned his head as if he was pleased. "Light the candle, Jopley," he said.

He took three steps forward and squatted down in front of the Saint like a great glossy toad. With leisured care he began to unlace the Saint's shoes.

"You shouldn't say things like that," he muttered protestingly. "You're only making it worse for yourself. Now we shall have to hurt you anyway. But of course you'll tell me about the vans. It's only a question of time, you know. Pargo didn't want to talk to me either, but he had to before Borieff had finished."

The Saint looked sideways. Jopley was at the table, fumbling with a box of matches. He was half turned away, intent on a short length of candle stuck in a saucer. The match he had extracted sizzled and flamed suddenly, and at the same moment Simon felt one of his shoes being pulled off.

If anything was to be done it had to be done now—now, while Jopley was concentrating on dabbing the match at the candle wick, and while Lasser's head was bent as he tugged at the other shoe.

The Saint breathed a silent prayer to whatever gods he acknowledged, and brought his hands from behind him.

His clenched right fist drove down like a hammer at the exposed nape of Lasser's bent neck. On that blow hung the unthinkable issue of the adventure and the fate of more lives than his own, and the Saint stocked it with all the pent-up strength that was in him. For Peter Quentin, and Hoppy Uniatz, and Pargo, and the girl whose life might be worth no more than theirs now that she also knew too much, the Saint struck like a blacksmith, knowing that if he failed to connect completely with one punch he would have no chance to throw in a second. He felt his fist plug achingly into the resisting flesh, and Lasser grunted once and lurched limply forward.

Simon caught him with one hand as he slumped on to his knees, and his other hand dived like a striking snake for the pocket that sagged with the weight of Lasser's gun.

Jopley looked round, with the candle burning, as the sudden whirl of movement caught his ear. An almost comically incredulous expression transfixed his face as he grasped the import of the scene, but the shock only stopped him for a moment. In the next instant he was grabbing for his own gun and plunging towards the Saint at the same time.

Only for an instant. And then he was brought up again, rocking, as if he had run into an invisible wall, before the round black muzzle of the automatic in the Saint's hand.

The Saint's smile was seraphically gentle.

"If I have to shoot you, Algernon," he said, "I shall be terribly disappointed."

The man stared at him in silence, while Lasser's unconscious body, released from the Saint's grasp, slid down and rolled over on the floor.

"You can put your hand in your other pocket," Simon went on, in that soft and terrible voice. "I want the rest of that sticking plaster. And then we will talk a little more about this Guy Fawkes party."

12

Standing in the shadows outside the library windows, the Saint studied the scene within. The chairs where Peter and Hoppy and Brenda Marlow sat were ranged roughly at the three corners of a square; approximately at the fourth corner stood Borieff, leaning against the back of an armchair and watching them, with his gun in his hand and a cigarette drooping from the corner of his mouth. Simon could easily have dropped him where he stood, but that was not what he wanted. He saw that Borieff's back was directly turned to the door through which they had first entered the library, and spent a few seconds more printing the estimated distances and angles on his memory. Then he returned silently along the path to the room he had just left.

Jopley, taped hand and foot exactly as the Saint had been a little while ago, glared up at him malevolently from the floor, and in another corner Lasser groaned and stirred uneasily as if he was rousing from a troubled sleep, but that was very near the limit of their power of self-expression. The Saint smiled encouragingly at Jopley as he went by.

"I don't mind if you yell, Algernon," he said kindly. "I should say that door was almost sound-proof, but in any case it'd be quite good local colour."

The other seemed to consider whether he should accept the invitation, but while he was still making up his mind the Saint crossed the room to the door opposite the French windows and let himself out into the dark, bare hall.

His fingers closed on the knob of the library door and turned it slowly, without the faintest rattle. His only fear then was that the door itself might creak as it opened, but it swung back with ghostly smoothness as far as he needed to step into the room.

Peter Quentin saw him with an instant's delirious amazement, and quickly averted his eyes. The girl saw him, and her face went white with the clutch of wild, half-believing hope before she also looked away. She sat with her head bent and her eyes riveted on the toe of one shoe, her fingers locked together in intolerable suspense. The crudely assembled features of Mr Uniatz contracted in a sudden awful spasm that seemed to squeeze his eyes half-way out of their sockets: if he had been anyone else, the observer would have said that he looked as if he had a stomach-ache, but on Mr Uniatz it only looked as if the normal frightfulness of his countenance had been lightly stirred by the ripple of a passing thought. And the Saint moved forward like a stalking leopard until he was so close behind Borieff that he could have bitten him in the neck.

The actual state of Borieff's neck removed the temptation to do this. Instead, his right hand whipped around Borieff's gun wrist like a ring of steel, and he spoke into the man's ear.

"Boo," he said.

The man gasped and whirled round convulsively as if he had been touched with a live wire, but the Saint's grip on his wrist controlled the movement and kept the gun twisted harmlessly up towards the ceiling.

At the same time, Simon's left hand pushed the automatic he had taken from Lasser forward until he met Borieff's ribs.

"I should drop that little toy if I were you," he said. "Otherwise I might get nervous."

He increased the torque on Borieff's wrist to emphasise his point, and the man yelped and let go the gun. Simon kicked it towards the girl.

"Just keep him in order for a minute, will you?" he murmured. "If he does anything foolish, mind you hit him in the stomach—it's more painful there."

As she picked up the gun, he pushed Borieff away and took out his knife. With a few quick strokes he had Peter free, and then he turned to Hoppy.

Peter stood up, peeling off the remains of the adhesive tape.

"I'm getting discouraged," he said. "All these years we've been trying to get rid of you, and every time we think you're nicely settled you come back. Won't you ever learn when to die a hero's death and give somebody else a chance with the heroine?"

"I will when I find someone else who'd have a chance," Simon assured him generously.

He straightened up from releasing Mr Uniatz's ankles, and held out the remains of the roll of plaster.

"Make a parcel of Comrade Borieff, will you, Hoppy?" he said. "We don't want him to get restive and hurt himself."

"Okay, boss," said Mr Uniatz willingly. "All I need is just one drink—"

"I'll have mine first," said Peter Quentin, swooping hastily on the bottle, "or else there mightn't be enough to go round."

Simon took the glass away from him as he filled it, and strolled over to the girl.

"Was that date in London very important?" he said. "Or will you come along with us and make it a party?"

She shook her head.

"I was only going for Lasser—I had to meet the Frenchman who supplies him and give him his money."

"My God," said the Saint. "I'd almost forgotten—"

He left her standing there, and disappeared through the communicating door into the next room. In another moment he was back, with the sealed envelope that Lasser had taken from her bag.

"Is this it?"

"Yes."

"I thought it was worth something the first time I saw it," said the Saint, and slit it open with his thumbnail.

When he had counted the thick wad of banknotes that came out of it, his eyebrows were lifted and his eyes were laughing. He added it to the hundred pounds which he had recovered from Jopley, and put it carefully away in his pocket.

"I can see we staged the showdown on the right evening," he said. "This will be some consolation to all of us when we divide it up." His eyes sobered on her again. "Lasser must have trusted you a good deal."

"I suppose he knew I was that sort of fool," she said bitterly.

"How did you get in with him?"

"I met him through some friends I used to go sailing with, and he seemed to be an awfully good egg. I'd known him for quite some time when he told me what he was doing and said that he needed some help. I knew it was against the law, but I didn't feel as if I was a criminal. You know how it is—we've all smuggled small things through the customs when we've had the chance, and we don't feel as if we'd done anything wicked. I just thought it'd be great fun with a bit of danger to make it more exciting."

"I've wangled things through the customs myself," said the Saint. "But there's a difference between that and making a business of it."

"Oh, I know," she said helplessly. "I was a damn fool, that's all. But I didn't realise . . . I didn't have anything to do with the organisation. I went out in the yacht once or twice, and another boat met us in the Channel and we took things on board, and then we came back here and unloaded it and went away. I went to Paris and bought those dresses and things, but Lasser gave me the money and he was to take half the profits. And I used to meet people and take them messages and things when he didn't want them to know who they were dealing with. I'd never been on one of the lorries before last night, but Lasser wanted two people to go for safety because of the lorries that had disappeared, and there was nobody else available. I know why, now—because Lasser wanted Borieff to help him, and Pargo was being tortured."

"You didn't happen to think that Jopley and Borieff were retired churchwardens, did you?"

"No—I hated them. But Lasser said you had to employ anyone you could get for jobs like theirs, and I didn't think even they could go so far." She shrugged, and her eyes were dark with pain. "Well, it's my own fault. I suppose you'll be handing them over to the police, and you'd better take me with you. I shan't give you any trouble. Whatever happens, I'm glad you beat them."

He shook his head.

"I'm afraid it wouldn't be any good handing them over to the police," he said. "You see, the Law has such pettifogging rules about evidence."

"But—"

"Oh yes, you could convict them of smuggling, and get them about six months each. But that's all."

"Then—"

He smiled.

"Don't worry about it, darling," he said. "Just stay here for a minute, will you?" He turned to Peter and Hoppy, and indicated Borieff with a faint nod.

"Bring him in," he said, and led the way into the next room.

Jopley was cursing and fighting against his bonds, and Lasser had recovered enough to be writhing too. Simon dragged them over to the fireplace, and went back to tear down the heavy silk cords that drew the long window hangings. He roped the two men expertly together, and when Borieff arrived he added him to the collection. The other end of the rope he knotted to a bar of the iron grate that set solidly in the brickwork.

Then he closed the door and looked at Peter and Hoppy, and the smile had gone altogether from his face.

"There's just one thing more which you didn't know," he said quietly. "Comrade Lasser told me about it in here. There's supposed to be a fire here tonight—the place is all prepared for it. And after we'd all been worked over like Pargo was—Borieff was the assistant in that, by the way—whatever else happened, however much we told, the idea was to leave us tied up here with a lighted candle burning down to the floor. We were to be got rid of anyway, and according to Lasser we had to be burnt alive so that it would look like an accident."

The Saint's eyes were as cold and passionless as the eyes of a recording angel. "We are the only jury here," he said. "What is our justice?"

The Hirondel thundered down into the valley and soared up the slope on the other side. Somewhere near the first crest of the Purbeck Hills, Simon stopped the car to take out a cigarette, and through the hushing of the engine his ears caught a familiar gurgling sound that made him look round.

In the back seat, Mr Uniatz detached the bottle from his lips and beamed at him ingratiatingly.

"I find it in de cabinet where dey keep de liquor, boss," he explained. "So I t'ought it'd keep us warm on de way home."

"At least you won't freeze to death," said the Saint philosophically.

He turned the other way as he struck his lighter, and gazed out into the darkness where the hills rose again at the edge of the sea. Somewhere in the black silhouette of them there was a dull red glow, pulsing and brightening, like a palely luminous cloud. The eyes of the girl beside him turned in the same direction.

"It looks like a fire," she said interestedly.

"So it does," said the Saint, and drove on without another backward glance, eastwards, towards Lyndhurst.

THE BEAUTY SPECIALIST

1

The fact that Simon Templar had never heard of the "Z-Man" was merely a tremendous proof that the Z-Man himself, his victims, and the police authorities had joined forces in a monumental conspiracy of silence. For the Saint invariably had a zephyr finger on the pulse of the underworld, and the various forms of fun and frolic that went on in the ranks of the ungodly without his knowledge were so few that for all practical purposes they might have been regarded as non-existent.

He was lunching alone at the Dorchester Grill when the first ripple of new adventure irrigated the dusty dryness of a particularly arid spell. He had been ruminating on the perfidious dullness of the cloudy day when the grill-room was suddenly supplied with its own sunshine. A girl had entered.

She was alone. She was tall and trim-waisted and as graceful as a dancer, and the soft waves of her fair golden hair rippled in the gentle stir of air caused by her own motion. Exquisitely dressed, devastatingly sure of herself, she was escorted to a vacant table in a sudden hush of awed admiration that enveloped a world-famous film producer, two visiting bishops, three cosmopolitan millionaires, a music-hall comedian, a couple of ancient marquises, and about fifty other minor celebrities in a simultaneous speechlessness of homage. Simon Templar, who had as many human instincts as any of the aforesaid, would have stared at her anyway, but somehow he found himself watching her with even more than that natural curiosity and interest. And a faint tentative tingle went through him as he realised why.

For an instant, when he had first raised his eyes and seen her, he had wondered if Patricia Holm had missed an appointment of her own and had come to join him. This girl was surprisingly like Pat: the same height, the same fair grace, the same radiant charm. There was something vaguely familiar about her face, too, and now the Saint was no longer reminded of Pat. He wondered who she was, and he was not the kind of man to be satisfied with wondering. "Tell me, Alphonse," he murmured to the waiter who was hovering about him like a ministering angel, "who is the vision in smoke-blue at that table over there?" The waiter looked across the room.

"That, sir," he said, with a certain visible contempt for such ignorance, "is Miss Beatrice Avery."

Simon wrinkled his brow.

"The name strikes a chord, but fails to connect."

"Miss Avery is a film star, sir."

"So she is. I've seen photographs of her here and there."

"Her latest picture, *Love, the Swindler*, is the best thing she's done," volunteered the waiter dreamily. "Have you seen it, sir?"

"Fortunately, no," answered the Saint, glancing with some pain at the waiter's enraptured face, and then averting his own. "Swindlers have never interested me—much."

The waiter departed hurt, and Simon continued to watch the girl at the other table. It was only a transient interest which held him, his inevitable interest in any exceptionally beautiful girl, coupled with the additional fact, perhaps, that Beatrice Avery was certainly a great deal like Pat . . . And then, in an instant, as if an invisible magic wand had been waved, his interest became concrete and vital. He flipped out his cigarette-case and put a smoke between his lips. Nobody could have guessed that his attention was more than casually attracted as he lighted the cigarette and inhaled deeply; the sudden lambent glint that came into his blue eyes was masked behind their lazy lids and the filmy curtain of smoke that trickled from his nostrils. But in that instant he knew, with the blissful certainty of experience, that the syncopated clarions of adventure had sounded in the room, even if no other ears were tuned to hear them.

As the girl had seated herself, a waiter had deftly removed the "reserved" card which had been conspicuously displayed on the table, and the cloud of obsequiously fluttering *chefs de restaurant, maîtres d'hôtel,* waiters, *commis,* and miscellaneous bus-boys had faded away. Evidently, she had intimated that she was not yet ready to order. The girl had then given the grillroom a thoughtful once-over as she removed her gloves and lighted a cigarette. These trifling details Simon had noticed while his own waiter was burbling about *Love, the Swindler.* All very proper and correct—and commonplace. But that which followed was not commonplace at all. Beatrice Avery's cigarette suddenly dropped from her fingers to the floor, and the colour drained out of her face until the patches of rouge on her cheeks and bright-tinted lips stood out in vivid contrast to the deathly pallor of her skin. Her eyes grew wide and glazed with terror, and she stared at the table as though a snake had suddenly appeared through a hole in the snowy cloth.

Simon hadn't the remotest idea what it was all about. That was the common factor of most adventures—you usually didn't, until you were well into them. The difference between the Saint and most other men was that most other men were satisfied to wonder and let it go at that; whereas the Saint had to find out. And Simon Templar had discovered, after some years of experiment, that the most direct way of finding anything out was to go and ask somebody who knew. Characteristically, he didn't hesitate for a second. Almost without any conscious decision on his part, his seventy-four inches of lean debonair immaculacy had unfolded from their chair and were sauntering across to Beatrice Avery's table, and he was smiling down at her with sapphire lights twinkling in gay blue eyes that few women had ever been able to resist.

"Could you use an unemployed knight-errant?" he murmured.

The girl seemed to shrink back. Some of the colour had returned to her face, but her eyes were more terrified than ever. He could see, at close quarters, that her resemblance to Pat was purely superficial. She had none of that calm ethereal tranquillity that was Pat's very own. She opened her bag as if she was too dazed and desperate to have grasped what he was saying.

"I didn't expect you so soon," she said breathlessly.

He was a bit slow on the repartee for two reasons. First, he was wondering why she had expected him at all, and secondly he was searching the square of snowy whiteness with its gleaming glass and silver for some explanation of the frozen horror that he had seen in her face. Everything was in order except for the fact that a knife and two forks were out of their correct places and laid in a peculiar zigzag. Even the most fastidious stickler for table ceremony would hardly have registered quite so much horror at that displacement of feeding tools, and Beatrice Avery looked like the healthily unceremonious kind of girl who wouldn't have cared a hoot if all the knives and forks and spoons were end-up in a flower-pot in the middle of the table.

"I came over as soon as you sent out the distress signals," Simon began, and then he stopped short out of sheer incredulous startlement.

The girl had taken something from her bag, and she was looking at him with such an expression that the words died a natural death on his lips. She had conquered her fear, and instead of the terror that had been there before, her eyes were charged with so much loathing and hatred and disgust that Simon Templar knew just what it felt like to be one of those wriggly things with too many legs that make their abode under flat stones. The reaction was so amazing and unexpected that for once in his life the Saint was at a loss for words. He invariably had such a totally different effect on beauteous damsels in distress that his self-esteem felt as though it had been hit by a coal truck.

"I have nothing whatever to say to you." The girl suddenly thrust a bulky envelope into his hand, and rose. "But if you have any regard at all for my feelings please return at once to your own table."

Her voice was low and musical, but it had in it the bitter chill of an arctic night. She didn't even look at him again, or she would have seen the utter bewilderment in his eyes. She closed her red mouth very tightly and walked with a steady tread and long exquisitely graceful legs towards the exit. Simon was convinced that she had never done anything half so fine before the camera.

He stood and watched her out of sight, and then returned slowly to his own table in a kind of seething fog. The Manhattan he had ordered earlier had arrived, and he drank it quickly. He felt that he needed it. And then, in a hazy quest for enlightenment, he took another look at the envelope which she had left in his paralysed hands. It was not sealed, and the numbed feeling in the pit of his stomach tightened as he glanced into it.

"Well, well, *well!*" he murmured softly.

His tanned face hardened into bronze lines of puzzled concentration, with his eyes steadied into fragments of blued steel against the sunburned background: for the envelope was stuffed full with Bank of England notes for one hundred pounds apiece.

He withdrew the ends and flicked his thumb over them.

Without careful counting he calculated that the wad contained about a hundred bills— ten thousand genuine and indisputable pounds. After his recent experience, and in spite of the Manhattan, he was in no condition to resist shocks of that kind. Boodle he had seen in his time, boodle in liberal quantities and many different forms, but he had always worked for it. He had never seen it come winging into his hands, when he wasn't even looking for it, like pigeons going home to roost. At any other time he would have been inclined to accept it as one of the many inexplicable beneficences of his devoted guardian angel, but he didn't feel like that now.

He couldn't get that look of hers out of his mind. It hurt his pride that she could have mistaken him for the common and vulgar agent of some equally common and vulgar blackmailer. It seemed obvious enough that that was what had happened . . . But was it? Simon didn't know exactly how many dazzling figures it took to write down Beatrice Avery's annual income, but he knew that film stars were burdened with hardly less colossal living expenses, for they have to scintillate off the screen as well as on or else risk submersion in the fathomless swamps of public forgetfulness. And the Saint doubted very much if Beatrice Avery, for all her fabulous salary, could afford to whack out ten thousand pounds as if it were chicken feed. A sum like that spoke for a grade of blackmail that could hardly be called common or vulgar: it hinted at something so dark and ugly that his imagination instinctively tried to turn away from it. He didn't like to believe that such a golden goddess could have anything in her past that she would pay so much to keep secret. It made him feel queerly grim and angry.

He finished his lunch, paid his bill, and then looked up the name of Beatrice Avery in the telephone directory. Her address appeared as 21 Parkside Court, Marble Arch. Simon made a mental note of it, paid a call in Piccadilly, and then strolled along to his own apartment in Cornwall House.

"Anybody called, Sam?" he inquired of the wooden-faced janitor, and Sam Outrell detected a faintly thoughtful note in the Saint's voice.

"Were you expecting somebody, sir?"

"I'm always expecting somebody. But this afternoon, in particular, I shall expect a lady, gloriously fair and graceful, with wavy golden hair—"

"I know, sir. You mean Miss Holm."

"No, I don't mean Miss Holm," said Simon, as he strolled to the elevator. "The lady's name, Sam, is Miss Avery. If she appears before you with my name on her rosebud lips, shoot her straight up."

He was whisked to his floor, and as he let himself in to his apartment he found Hoppy Uniatz in the living-room's best easy chair with his feet on the table. Mr Uniatz was chewing the ragged end of a cigar, and there was an expression on his battle-scarred face which indicated that all was right with the world. The empty whisky bottle on the table may have contributed its own modest quota to this happy state of affairs.

"Hi, boss," said Mr Uniatz cordially. "Where ya bin?" Simon spun his hat across the room.

"Lunching at the Dorchester."

"I got no time for dem fancy places," said Mr Uniatz disparagingly. "Dose pansy dishes ain't nut'n to eat. Now, yesterday I find a swell jernt where a guy can get a kosher hamboiger wit' fried onions an' all de fixin's—"

"I wondered why that cigar was so overpowering," said the Saint, moving carefully out of range of Mr Uniatz's breathing. "I'm not sure yet, Hoppy, but there are indications that fun and games hover in the middle distance."

"Who's dat, boss?" asked Mr Uniatz, struggling valiantly to get his grey matter flowing.

This was no small effort, for nature had only provided him with a very small quantity, and even this was of a glue-like consistency.

"You may be right about the Dorchester," said the Saint sourly, as he eased himself into a chair. "Anyway, it didn't do me much good. A charming young lady gave me ten thousand quid and the dirtiest look of the century. Tell me, Hoppy, has anything happened to my face to make it look as if I'd blackmail charming young ladies?"

"You look okay to me, boss," said Mr Uniatz blankly. "Who is dis dame?"

Remembering Mr Uniatz's mental disadvantages, Simon told his story in simple one-syllable words that would have sent the Director of Children's Hour programmes delirious with delight. He had had so much practice in that difficult exercise that Mr Uniatz, in spite of the limitations of his cerebral system, finally grasped the basic facts.

"De goil t'inks you are some udder guy," he said brightly.

"You put it in a nutshell, Hoppy," said the Saint admiringly.

"De guy who puts de black on her."

"Precisely."

"De guy," persisted Hoppy, working nobly to get all his facts in order, "who is playing games in de distance."

The Saint sighed, and was bracing himself to go into further laborious explanations when the sound of the telephone bell spared him the ordeal. He went to the instrument.

"Two visitors for you, sir, but they ain't ladies," said Sam Outrell hurriedly.

"Give me two guesses."

"You ain't got time for guessin', sir," interrupted the janitor. "It's Mr Teal, and he's lookin' madasell, and he went straight up without letting me call you first. He'll be there any minute—"

"Don't worry, Sam," said the Saint imperturbably. "I'm not leaving. Go out and get Mr Teal some chewing-gum, and we'll have a party."

The doorbell rang violently, and Simon Templar hung up the telephone and went out to admit his favourite visitor. And the absolute truth is that he hadn't a cloud on his conscience or any suspicion that the visit would be more than a routine call.

2

Chief Inspector Claud Eustace Teal thrust his large regulation foot into the opening as soon as the Saint unlatched the door. It was an unnecessary precaution, for Simon flung the door wide and stood aside invitingly, with a smile on his lips and the light of irrepressible amusement in his eyes.

"Come in, souls," he said genially. "Make yourselves at home. And what can I do for you today?"

The invitation was somewhat superfluous; for Mr Teal and the man with him, whom Simon recognised as Sergeant Barrow, were already in. They hadn't waited to be asked. They came in practically abreast, and Barrow kicked the door to with his foot. The Saint was compelled to back into the living-room in face of that determined entry. There was an unusual aggressiveness about Mr Teal; his plump body seemed taller and broader; the phlegmatic dourness of his round pink face under its shabby derby was increased by the hard lines of his mouth. He looked like a man who was haunted by the memory of many such calls on this smiling young buccaneer—calls which had only lengthened the apparently hopeless duel which he had been waging for years against the most stupendous outlaw of his day. And yet he looked like a man who had a certain foreknowledge that this time he would emerge the victor, and a kind of creepy puzzlement wormed itself into the Saint's consciousness as the meaning of those symptoms forced itself upon him.

"Hi, Claud," said Mr Uniatz, in friendly greeting. Chief Inspector Teal ignored him.

"I want you, Templar," he said, turning his sleepy eyes on the Saint.

"Of course you do, Claud," said the Saint slowly. "Somebody has sold an onion after closing-time, and you want me to track him down for you. A gang of lemonade smugglers who have eluded Scotland Yard for years have been—"

"I mean," Teal said immovably, "that I'm taking you into custody on a charge of—"

"Wait!" said the Saint tragically. "Think what you'd be losing if you really pulled me in. What would you do with your afternoons if you couldn't come round here for these charming little *conversaziones*?"

"All the talking in the world won't save you this time, Templar," said Mr Teal in a hard voice. "Do you want to see the warrants I've got? One for your arrest, and another to search this flat."

The Saint shrugged watchfully.

"Well, Claud," he said resignedly, "if you want to make a fool of yourself again, it's your funeral. What's the charge this time?"

"Demanding money with menaces," said the detective flatly. For a moment his eyes lost their sham of perpetual boredom; they looked oddly hurt and at the same time contemptuous. "You know how much I've wanted to get you, Templar, but now that the time's come I'd just as soon not have the job. I never thought I shouldn't even want to touch you."

Simon glanced down at his brown hands, and in his mind was a vivid memory of Beatrice Avery's look of unutterable loathing. Teal's voice contained that very look, transmuted into sound. His pulses, which up to that moment had been ticking over as steadily as clockwork, throbbed a shade faster.

"Is there something the matter with me?" he asked curiously.

"Have I suddenly taken on a resemblance to Boris Karloff, or is it only a touch of leprosy?"

"You're the Z-man," retorted Mr Teal, and stopped chewing his cud of tasteless chicle.

There was a silence that pressed down on the four men like a tangible substance. It was as though the air had become a mass of ectoplasm. Hoppy Uniatz broke the suffocating spell by shuffling his feet. It is doubtful if more than a dozen words of the conversation had infiltrated through the bony mass which protected the sponge-like organisation of nerve-endings which served him in lieu of a brain, but the impression was growing on him that Mr Teal was making himself unpleasant.

"What was dat crack again?" he said, his unmusical voice crashing into the silence like a bombshell.

"Yes, Claud," said the Saint gently. "What was it?"

"You heard me the first time," Teal said crunchily. "You're the Z-Man, and if I couldn't prove it I wouldn't have believed it myself. It's something new to know that you've sunk as low as that."

Simon moved across to the mantelpiece and leaned an elegant elbow on it. He pulled hard at his cigarette until the end glowed red, and the smoke stayed down in his lungs. A dim light was breaking in the darkness through which he had been groping his way: he saw, in his mind's eye, the disarranged knives and forks on Beatrice Avery's table in the Dorchester Grill, and he knew the meaning of that queer zigzag formation. They had shaped the letter Z, and it was the sudden sight of this that had caused the girl's terror.

But the light was still not enough . . . The Saint's eyes switched over to Mr Teal, and their clear blue glinted like the sheen of polar waters under the sun.

"My poor old blundering fathead," he said kindly. "I'm afraid you're off the rails again, for the umpteenth time. I don't know what the hell you're talking about."

"Dat goes for me too, boss," contributed Mr Uniatz, who had clearly understood every word of the Saint's last terse sentence.

Mr Teal's lips thinned out.

"Oh, you don't know what the hell I'm talking about?" he barked. "Are you going to deny that you were in the Dorchester Grill an hour ago?"

"Why should I deny it? I lunched there."

"And you spoke to Miss Beatrice Avery?"

"We had a few brief words, yes. Of course, I suppose that was very wicked of me, because we hadn't been introduced—"

"You took a package from her."

"No."

"You deny taking a package from her?" shouted Mr Teal.

"I do. She thrust the package into my hand and breezed off before I could even examine it—"

Teal's face turned a shade redder.

"You're not going to save yourself by quibbling like that," he snarled. "It's no good, Templar. You can try it on the jury. You're under arrest."

He took his right hand out of his pocket for the first time in that interview, and a pair of handcuffs clinked in it.

Simon glanced at them without moving.

"Hadn't you better think again, old dear?" he suggested quietly. "I don't know why I should go out of my way to save your hide, but I suppose I'm funny that way. Perhaps it's because life wouldn't be the same if you got chucked out of Scotland Yard on your ear and couldn't bring your tummy round to see me anymore. Perhaps it's because I object to being marched into Piccadilly with bracelets over my wrists. But somehow or other I've got to save you from yourself."

"You don't have to worry—"

"But I do, Claud. I can't help it. It'd keep me awake at night, thinking of you sleeping out in the cold gutters with no one even to buy you a piece of spearmint. And it's all so obvious. The whole trouble is that you're jumping to too many conclusions. Just because I'm the Saint, and you never found any other criminals, you think I must be all of them. Then you hear of some guy called the Z-Man, so you think I must be him too. Well, who the hell is this Z-Man, and why haven't I heard of him before?"

Chief Inspector Teal bit on his gum in a supercharged effort of self-control that threatened to boil over at any moment. It was only by straining his will-power to the limit that he succeeded in recovering the pose of mountainous boredom that he usually struggled in vain to maintain in the Saint's maddeningly nonchalant presence.

"I don't know what you hope to gain by all this Templar, but you're wasting your breath," he said, shifting his lump of worn-out spearmint from one side of his mouth to the other.

"I'm acting on facts that even you can't get away from. You may as well know that Sergeant Barrow was in the Dorchester at the time."

"Keeping a fatherly eye on me?"

"No; he was looking for someone else that we're interested in. But that's neither here nor there. Barrow happened to see Miss Avery, and for reasons which I'm not going to explain he kept his eye on her."

"I only hope his thoughts were pure," said the Saint piously.

"Barrow saw you take a package from Miss Avery, and immediately afterwards he saw her leave the restaurant," continued Mr Teal coldly. "He accosted her in the foyer—"

"Disgusting, I call it," said the Saint. "What these policemen get away with—"

"He showed her his authority—"

"She must have been thrilled," murmured Simon.

"She refused to say anything, and Barrow rang me up," went on Teal, his self-control gradually slipping and his voice taking on its old familiar blare. "I got hold of these warrants, but I went to Miss Avery's flat first. She denied knowing anything about the Z-Man, but I'd been expecting that. What I did make her admit was that the package she handed you contained a large sum of money."

"Ten thousand pounds," said the Saint lazily. "I counted it." Teal glowered at him, pop-eyed.

"I want that package—"

"Sorry, old dear," said the Saint regretfully. "I haven't got it"

"You haven't got it!" brayed Mr Teal.

"Calm yourself, sweetheart," drawled the Saint. "Much as I hate parting with perfectly good boodle when it's pushed right into my hand, I realised that a mistake had been made. Always the perfect gentleman, I immediately took steps to correct the error. On my way home I stopped at a District Messenger office and bunged the package back to Miss Avery, with contents intact. So you see, Claud, old thing, you'll have to tear those warrants up and go back to the Assistant Commissioner and let him flay you alive. And now that that's all cleared up, what about a smoke and a drink?"

He flicked open his cigarette-case with one hand, and indicated the whisky decanter with the other. Hoppy Uniatz, aware of the decanter's presence for the first time, moved mechanically towards it, licking his dry lips. Mr Teal, who had been unravelling his tonsils from his epiglottis, lumbered forward like a migrating volcano.

"You're not getting away like that this time, Templar," he said thickly. "You're coming with me! We've been after the Z-Man for a long time now, and now we've got him. Are you coming quietly?"

"About as quietly as a brass band," answered the Saint, succinctly. "But you needn't blow your whistles and bring in a troop of rozzers. I'm not going to pull a gun on you or start any rough-house. I know it's a serious thing to interfere with an officer of the law in the execution of his duty—even when he's a mahogany-headed dope with barnacles all over his brain like you are. You say you're armed to the molars with warrants, or else I'd just bounce you out on your fat stomach and call it a day." His blue eyes rested on Mr Teal like twinkling icicles. "So instead of that I'll give you a chance to save your bacon. Before you commit the unmitigated asininity of arresting me, and thereby get yourself slung out of a perfectly good job, don't you think you'd better take the one obvious step?"

Nothing was obvious to Mr Teal except that he had got Simon Templar where he wanted him at last. But there was a mocking buccaneering challenge in the Saint's voice that could not go unanswered.

"What obvious step?" he asked scorchingly. "I've got all the evidence I need—"

"I'm sorry; I forgot for the moment that you're only a detective," Simon apologised. "Let me put it into simple words. My answer to you is that Miss Avery gave me the ten thousand quid by mistake, and I rectified the mistake by immediately sending the money back to her. She's bound to have received it by now—and I know she's on the telephone. Since she seems to be the only important witness against me, wouldn't it be rather a good idea to make quite certain that all this beautiful evidence of yours is really in the bag?"

He indicated his own instrument and his meaning was clear enough. But Chief Inspector Teal merely grunted and opened the handcuffs.

"That's an old one, isn't it?" he said contemptuously. "While I'm fooling about with the telephone you make your getaway. I'm surprised that you should suggest such a whiskery—"

He was interrupted by the shrill ringing of the twin bells of the telephone, and the Saint automatically reached for the instrument.

"No, you don't!" barked Mr Teal. "I'll take it."

Simon couldn't help smiling, for the detective was doing the very thing he had just been sneering at. But the Saint had no desire to make a getaway. He had a hunch that he knew where that call was coming from.

"Hullo!" said Mr Teal, in a carefully controlled Saintly voice.

"Is that Mr Simon Templar?"

"Yes," replied Mr Teal untruthfully, and he experienced a sudden awful feeling as though somebody had removed his stomach in one piece, leaving a wide open space; for the voice at the other end of the wire belonged unmistakably to Beatrice Avery. Mr Teal went to the movies often enough to know that.

"I owe you a humble apology, Mr Templar, for making such a stupid mistake," said Beatrice Avery, and Mr Teal heard the words through a kind of infernal tantara, in which the Assistant Commissioner's eloquent sniff was the most easily recognisable sound. "Thank you a thousand times for sending the money back so promptly. It was all a silly joke. Please forgive me."

3

If there was any joke in sight, it was beyond the range of Mr Teal's sense of humour. He stood clinging to the telephone like a drowning man attached to a water-logged straw. However it had been managed, somehow it had been done again: the Saint had been right in his hands, and had slipped through them like a trickle of water. It was impossible, incredible, inhuman, unfair, unjust—but it had happened. Teal's head buzzed with the petrifying impact of the blow. He swallowed voicelessly, trying to think of something to say or do, but his brain seemed to be taking a temporary siesta. All he could think of was that he wanted to find some peaceful place in which to die. And at the same time he was bitterly aware that the Saint would probably still be capable of making him turn in his grave.

The Saint had enough confirmation of his hunch in the expression on Mr Teal's stricken face. He took the receiver gently out of the detective's hand and placed it to his own ear.

"I was half expecting you to ring, fair lady," he said easily. "If ever we meet again I hope you will make full compensation for that look you gave me—"

"I just told you, Mr Templar, that it was only a silly joke," interrupted the girl's breathless voice. "Please forget all about it."

"That's not so easy. If there's anything I could do to help—"

"Help?" The girl forced a laugh, and to the Saint it sounded almost hysterical. "Why should I want any help? It was just an idiotic practical joke, and it went wrong. That's all, Mr Templar. I'm afraid I made a dreadful little fool of myself, and I shall be eternally grateful if you'll forget the whole thing."

"Is it as bad as that, darling?" Simon asked softly. "Because—"

"Thank you so much, Mr Templar. Good-bye."

Simon slid a cigarette into his mouth as he turned away from the instrument. In the fuliginous silence that followed, as the Saint lighted his smoke, Chief Inspector Teal's pudgy fingers slowly and laboriously unwrapped a fresh wafer of spearmint. Mr Teal was making a game effort to recover his composure, and it was brutally hard going. He was tied in a knot, and he knew it. It was an old, old knot, and he was familiar with every twist of it. Once again he had believed that triumph was within his grasp, and once again that debonair outlaw had cheated him. And it would happen again, and again, and again, and for ever. The knowledge percolated into Mr Teal's interior like a liquid cannon-ball, solidifying into its original shape in the lower region of his stomach. He thrust the wafer of gum into his mouth and glared murderously at the unemotional Sergeant Barrow.

"Well?" he demanded sulphurously. "What are we waiting for?"

"Don't take it so much to heart, Claud, old dear," said the Saint, his voice surprisingly innocent of raillery. "Don't be in a hurry to dash off, either. You're not bursting with anxiety to have that chat with the Assistant Commissioner, are you? I'm not going to prod you in the waistcoat—"

"You'd better not try!" said Mr Teal hoarsely, as he shifted his ample paunch well out of range of the Saint's questing forefinger.

"Have a drink, and let's get together," pleaded the Saint. "The mistake you made was natural enough—and, if the worst comes to the worst, you can always shove the blame on to Sergeant Barrow. You probably will, anyhow. But that doesn't make it up to me. The thing which pains me is that you should have mistaken me for this bird of prey who calls himself the Z-Man. A bloke who can cause a girl full of charm and glamour and a hardboiled detective to frizzle me with a couple of looks like the interior of a sewage incinerator must be pretty epizootic. Tell me, Claud, who is this descendant of Dracula?"

But something else had settled upon Mr Teal's tortured presence—something oddly stubborn and impenetrable that didn't fit in with his earlier demonstrations any more than it belonged to the stunned paralysis which had since overcome him. It was as if he had drawn back inside himself and locked a door.

"Forget it," he said stonily.

"I can't forget something I don't know. Be reasonable, dear old nitwit. It's only fair to me—"

"I don't know anything about the Z-Man, and nobody else knows anything about the Z-Man," Teal said deliberately. "I was just trying to be funny. Understand?"

He nodded sleepily, jerked his head towards Sergeant Barrow, and they both left. As the front door gave a vicious slam, Hoppy Uniatz reached for the whisky decanter and thrust the neck of it into his capacious mouth.

"Boss," he said, coming to the surface, "I don't get nut'n."

"Except the whisky," murmured the Saint, rescuing the decanter. "For once, Hoppy, I'm right in your street. I don't get nut'n, either."

"Why ja let dem bums get away wit' it?" asked Mr Uniatz discontentedly. "Dey got a noive, bustin' in like dat. Say, if we knew some politicians we could have dose mugs walkin' a beat again so fast—"

Simon was not listening. He was pacing up and down like a tiger, inhaling deeply from his cigarette, and as Mr Uniatz watched him a slow smile of appreciation illuminated his homely face. He could see that his boss was thinking, and knowing from his own experience what a painful ordeal this was, he relapsed into a sympathetic and respectful silence.

It was clear enough to the Saint that Mr Teal had been disturbed by certain dimensions of his blunder which hadn't been apparent at first sight. The very existence of the Z-Man, it seemed, had been a closely guarded secret—until Teal had let the cat peep out of the bag and wink at Simon Templar, of all people. Unable to undo the damage which he had done in his first excess of confidence, the detective had taken the only remedy he had left and had escaped from the Saint's magnetic presence before he could be lured into any more mistakes. But as far as the Saint was concerned, he had still left plenty of interesting ideas behind him.

A key turned in the front door, and a moment later Patricia Holm walked into the living-room. She looked at the Saint accusingly.

"I met Teal downstairs," she said. "What are we going to be arrested for now?"

"Nothing," answered the Saint peacefully. "Claud Eustace thought I was, though, until I showed him the error of his ways. Sit down, lass, and listen to the tale of how a perfectly respectable buccaneer was mistaken for the ungodliest of the ungodly."

Patricia sat down, with the patience that she had learned through years of testing it.

She had known the Saint too long to be surprised by any story he had to tell, and she knew him too well to be deceived by the transparency of his present calm. There was the unmistakable hell-for-leather lilt in his voice, hinting at battle, murder, and sudden death, and when that lilt was there it was as useless to oppose him as it would have been useless to argue with a cyclone.

"We're going after the Z-Man," he said dreamily.

"Who's the Z-Man?"

"I don't know."

"That ought to give us a flying start, then," said Patricia kindly. "Do you know what it's all about, Hoppy?"

"I don't know nut'n," answered Mr Uniatz, as though he were a phonograph record with a crack in it.

It didn't take the Saint long to give a full and vivid recital of what he knew. He was always fond of his own voice, but this time there wasn't much for him to tell. The girl listened with growing interest, but at the finish, when he asked for her opinion, she had none to offer.

"You still don't really know anything," she objected.

"Exactly," agreed the Saint unabashed. "It was only by chance that I heard anything about the Z-Man at all—and that was mostly because Claud dropped a brick. It's just another proof, Pat, old cherub, that my guardian angel never falls down on the job. Something tells me that this game is Big, and I should be lacking in formal duty if I didn't sit in on it. Observe the reactions of Beatrice Avery and Claud Eustace Teal—two people who have just about as much in common as a gazelle and a hippopotamus. Both of them closed up as enthusiastically as a couple of lively clams. Both of them refused to discuss the subject of the Z-Man. Both of them told me it was all a joke." The Saint rose to his feet and lighted another cigarette. His eyes were mere slits of steel.

"A joke!" he repeated. "If you'd seen the look in Beatrice Avery's eyes, Pat, you'd know how much of a joke the Z-Man is! Teal, too. He was fool enough to think I was the Z-Man, and he didn't want to put the bracelets on me because he'd have to touch me! By God, this bird must be something that'd make Jack the Ripper look like a Salvation Army drummer-boy."

"You still don't know anything useful," Patricia said practically. "What are you going to do—advertise for him?"

"I don't know . . . There's a hell of a lot I don't know," answered the Saint, scowling. "I don't even know what the Z-Man's racket is—excepting that it must be damned profitable. It's no good asking Teal for information; he's in trouble enough already. I can't go to Beatrice Avery—or, at least, if I did, she wouldn't see me or tell me anything."

"She might see me."

"She won't see anybody," said the Saint. "After what has happened today, she'll be scared as stiff as a corpse. Don't you get it, darling? She had an appointment with the Z-Man, or one of his agents, and she knows she failed to keep it. The Z-Man won't know that she actually *did* keep it, and he'll start turning on the heat. This girl will have extra locks and bolts on her doors—"

"Didn't you say that she and I look a bit alike?"

"Only in height and build and fair-headedness and general beauty and all that sort of thing," replied Simon. "You're both the same type, that's all."

"Then leave it to me," said Patricia calmly. "I'll show you what a real detective can do."

It was the conventional tea hour when she entered the handsome new apartment house in the neighbourhood of Marble Arch known as Parkside Court. Number 21 was on the sixth floor, and Patricia went up in the elevator in spite of the fact that the porter had warned her that Miss Avery had given instructions that she was not at home to anybody. The porter had put it more broadly than this; he had declared that Miss Avery had gone down to Cornwall for a holiday—or up into Aberdeenshire, he wasn't sure which. But Patricia had looked at him with her sapphire blue eyes, so remarkably like the Saint's, and her bewitching smile, and the unfortunate man had dried completely up.

In the carpeted corridor outside the door of Number 21 a man was repairing a vacuum cleaner. Patricia was sorry for him. He had taken the vacuum cleaner apart into so many pieces that it was very doubtful whether it could ever be put together again. Notwithstanding his workmanlike overalls, Patricia had no difficulty in recognising him as an employee of some private detective agency. He had "ex-policeman" stamped all over him in embossed lettering.

"No good you ringing that bell, Miss," he said gruffly, as Patricia placed her finger on the button. "There's nobody at home. Miss Avery's gone into the country."

He had looked at her very hard at first, with a somewhat startled expression on his face. Patricia knew why. She went on smiling at him.

"Is there any special way of ringing?" she inquired sweetly. "I don't think she'll refuse to see her own sister."

The man suddenly grinned.

"Well, of course, that's different, Miss," he said hastily. "I thought there was a likeness. Why, when you came round the corner I took you for Miss Avery herself."

He gave three short tings, a long one, and three more short. The door was almost immediately opened by a nervous-looking maid.

"Okay, Bessie; it's Miss Avery's sister."

Patricia walked straight in, just as the Saint might have done, and her complete assurance gave the maid no chance to reply. A moment later, in the artistically lighted living-room, she was face to face with Beatrice Avery.

"I'm quite harmless, and I hope you'll forgive me for getting in by a trick, Miss Avery, " she said directly. She opened her bag and produced a card. "This will tell you who I am—and perhaps you'll guess why I'm here."

The film-star's frightened eyes looked up from the card.

"Yes, I've heard your name," she whispered. "You work with the Saint, don't you? Sit down, please, Miss Holm. I don't know why you've come. I told Mr Templar over the phone that it was all a silly joke—"

"And I'm here because the Saint didn't believe you," Patricia interrupted gently. "If you've heard of him, you must know that you can trust him. Simon thinks that something ought to be done about the Z-Man, and he's the one man in all the world to do it."

Beatrice Avery's breasts stirred shakily under her clinging satin negligée, and her grey eyes grew obstinate—with the dreadful obstinacy of utter fear.

"It's all very absurd, Miss Holm," she said, trying to speak carelessly. "There's no such person as the Z-Man. How did Mr Templar know . . . I mean, there's nothing I can tell you."

"You'd rather pay ten thousand pounds—"

"There's nothing I can tell you," repeated the girl, rising to her feet. "Nothing! Nothing at all! Please leave me alone!"

Her voice was almost shrill, and Patricia saw at a glance that it would be hopeless to prolong the interview. Beatrice Avery was a great deal more frightened than even the Saint had realised or Patricia had expected. Patricia was shrewd and understanding, and she knew when she was wasting her time. Anybody less clever would have persisted and only hardened Beatrice Avery's obstinacy. All Patricia did was to point to her card on the table.

"If you change your mind," she said, "there's the phone number. We'll do anything we can to help you—and we keep secrets."

She was not feeling very satisfied with herself as she rode down in the elevator. It wouldn't be pleasant to go back to the Saint and report failure, after the boast she had made. But it couldn't be helped. It was just one of those things. The Saint would think of some other approach . . .

The hall was deserted when she reached it, and she walked out into the evening dusk and paused uncertainly on the sidewalk, in the glow of the red and green neon lights that decorated the entrance. A taxi crawled by, and she signalled. The driver swung round in the road and pulled in.

"Cornwall House, Piccadilly," said Patricia.

"Yes, Miss," answered the driver, reaching round and opening the door.

She got in, and the cab was off before she had fairly closed the door. Something hard and round pressed into her side, and she looked quickly into the shadows. A smallish man with ferret-like eyes was sitting beside her.

"One scream, sister, and you're for it," said the man, in a flat, matter-of-fact voice. "This thing in your side is a gun, and I'm not afraid to use it."

"Oh!" said Patricia faintly, and she sagged into limpness.

She had done it so well that Ferret Eyes was completely taken in. Patricia, her brain working like oiled machinery, did not blame herself for having fallen into such a simple trap. She had no reason to be on the alert for one, and she knew that it had not been laid for her at all. The ungodly had mistaken her for Beatrice Avery! And why shouldn't they? She was the same height and colouring, close enough to have deceived even the Saint at a distance, and she had emerged from the apartment house where Beatrice Avery lived. With the added help of the dim light, she might have deceived anyone—and might go on deceiving him for a while, so long as she kept her mouth shut. It was to avoid being forced to talk too much that she had feigned that rapid faint, to give herself a chance to think over her next move.

She was aware of a throb of excitement within her. There was no fear in her—the Saint had taught her to forget such things. Instead, he had bequeathed her so much of his own blithe recklessness that she saw in a flash that while she had failed with Beatrice Avery, she might yet succeed in this new and unexpected quarter. It amused her to think that while the enemy wouldn't have dared to use the taxicab trick with her, they had thought it good enough for the film star, who was naturally unversed in the ways of the ungodly. And yet it was she, Patricia Holm, who had fallen for it! It was a twist that might provide the Saint with the scent he was looking for.

She was preparing to come naturally out of her faint when the taxi bumped heavily and swung giddily round in a sharp arc. Then it came to a jerky stop, and Pat heard some doors closing. She sat half forward with a dazed look on her face.

"Take it easy, sister," said Ferret Eyes gratingly. "Nobody's going to hurt that lovely face of yours—yet."

"Where am I? What are you going to do to me?" she gasped, her voice faltering. "I'll pay!" she went on hysterically. "I tried to pay at the Dorchester. You didn't come. I had the money—"

"Tell it to somebody else," he said callously.

He forced her to get out, and she saw that the cab had been driven into an ancient garage and the doors closed on it. There was a ramshackle door at the rear, just against the cab's radiator, and he gripped her by the arm and hustled her through it and down a steep flight of stairs into a low, malodorous cellar. The taxi driver followed. An electric torchlight flashed on her out of the black darkness as she stumbled down to the bottom—and a man who was already down there behind the light drew his breath through his teeth in a long, sibilant hiss.

"Who's the damn fool responsible for this?" His harsh voice came from behind the blaze. "This girl is not Beatrice Avery!"

The taxi driver lurched forward.

"You're crazy!" he growled. "I recognised 'er as soon as she came out . . ." He swung Patricia round and stared into her face with the light full on it, and then he swore savagely. "God, it isn't! But it's just like 'er. I never sore 'er in a light like this—"

Ferret Eyes stiffened, and swore also, more fluently. His grip on the girl's arm tightened.

"Well, who is she?" he rasped. "She knows what it's about— she was gabbing about the money as if she knew everything!"

The man behind the torch reached out a claw-like hand and seized Patricia's bag. He opened it. The card she had given to Beatrice Avery was not the only one. She could feel him staring from the card to her face in the silence that followed.

"Patricia Holm!" said the man in the darkness, with a dry sandy grit in his voice. "That's who she is. A fine pair of saps you've turned out to be!" His voice quivered with rising fury. "No wonder she fooled you! Don't you know who she is? Haven't you ever heard of the Saint?"

There was a silence that descended like a fog. It seemed to throb and vibrate through the cellar, filling it with a choking stillness broken only by the heavy breathing of the three men. It was something, Patricia reflected wryly, to know that the Saint's name alone was capable of creating such panic. At the moment it was about the only asset she had.

"You know what he'll say when he finds out that your blasted blundering has brought the Saint down on us!" snapped the man behind the torch. "You'd better do something about it. I'll hold this girl here. You two get straight out and go after Templar. And get him before he gets you. Understand? Don't come back until you've got him!"

"Why bother?" drawled a voice that cut through the air like the thrust of a rapier blade.

"I've already invited myself. And just which of you is planning to be the hero?"

Three gasps sounded in unison, and the beam of the electric flashlight jerked round as if it had been snatched by an invisible wire. On the mouldering stairs stood the Saint, immaculate and deadly.

4

The gun in Simon Templar's hand circled leisurely over the three male occupants of the cellar in a generous expansiveness of invitation. The man who had been doing the talking was still only a vague shape behind the dazzling bulb of his electric torch, but the Saint's uncanny eyes pierced the screen of light enough to see the unoccupied hand which reached round towards a hip pocket.

"That's only one of the many ways of dying, brother," said the Saint instructively. "But of course, you can make your own choice . . ."

The hipwards movement of the hand was arrested, and at the same moment the man switched off his torch. He was disappointed, however, in assuming that this would result in a decrease in the cellar's illumination. The general lighting effect was not only doubled, but he himself stood in the direct glare of a miniature searchlight. The Saint had decided that it was time to take full stock of the situation, and his own flashlight was even better than the one that had gone out.

The man who had stood concealed behind the light was a disappointment. His appearance, after the crisp and authoritative tone of his voice, came as a considerable shock. He was a small, skinny bird of about forty, extraordinarily neatly dressed, his ornamentations including a waisted overcoat and fawn spats. His face was small-featured, with sandy eyebrows just visible over the tops of his highly respectable gold-rimmed pince-nez. His nose and mouth were small, and his chin, after a half-hearted attempt to establish itself, drifted away to hide itself shyly in his neck.

"You ought to be more careful, Andy," Simon admonished him. "Take that gun out of your pocket if you like, but spread it out on the floor where we can all feast our eyes on it."

"My name is not Andy," said the chinless man.

"No? Except for the eye-gear and the spats, you look exactly like Andy Gump," answered the Saint. "Pat, old darling, if you can spare a moment you might build up our collection of artillery."

Not one of the men attempted to move. They knew the Saint's reputation, and they had an earnest and unanimous desire to continue living. Behind the bantering cadence of the Saint's voice there was a glacial chill that converted the cellar into a refrigerator. His gun was extremely visible, too, and the lean brown fingers that held it had a lively quality that made them look as if they would just as soon start squeezing as keep still.

Patricia relieved the clerkly-looking Mr Gump of his gun, and Ferret Eyes threw his own weapon on the floor before she could even turn to him.

"I ain't got no pistol, Miss, swelp me I ain't," swore the taxi driver hoarsely.

She believed him, but she patted his pockets just the same. And Simon descended the stairs.

"Now, boys, you can line yourselves up against that wall over there," he said, with an indicative flick of his gun muzzle.

"And don't forget where you are . . . Pat, you take this heater and stand well to the side. Here's the torch, too, and keep the light nicely steady . . . It will interest you birds to know," he added, for the benefit of the obedient trio, "that the lady can hit a microbe's eye at fifty yards. If you don't believe me, you only have to bring on your microbes."

He took Mr Gump's gun from Patricia and picked up Ferret Eyes's weapon from the floor; then he swiftly examined both and thrust them into his pocket. From another pocket he produced a second automatic of his own. He never trusted strange weapons. Holding his gun with careless ease, he briefly inspected the taxi driver and Ferret Eyes; he was not particularly interested in either of them, since they definitely came within the dull category of small fry. Mr Gump, however, was probably very close to the Z-Man. Mr Gump needed careful investigation. He looked very meek and inoffensive as the Saint started going through his pockets—except, perhaps, for the snake-like glitter in his eyes behind the gold-rimmed pince-nez—a glitter which belied the disarming weakness of his chin.

And suddenly Mr Gump gave a demonstration which proved him to be either a very rash fool or a very brave man. As Simon Templar was in the act of insinuating a brown hand into Mr Gump's breast pocket, a knee shot up and dug itself into the lower region of his stomach. With a simultaneous cohesion of movement, Mr Gump grabbed at the Saint's gun and tore it out of Simon's relaxed fingers. In another instant the muzzle was jammed hard against Simon's chest with Mr Gump's finger on the trigger.

"Drop that gun, Miss Holm, or your friend becomes an angel instead of a Saint," said Mr Gump.

Patricia made no movement. Nobody made any movement. And the Saint chuckled.

"That was careless of me, brother—but not so careless as you think," he murmured. "That gun's the one I didn't load."

He raised his hand almost casually and took hold of Mr Gump's small nose. He gripped it very hard between his finger and thumb, and twisted it.

Click!

Mr Gump pulled the trigger in a flurry of blind fury and extreme anguish. And that empty *click!* was the only result. He pulled again, and nothing happened. Nothing, that is, except that the agonising torque on his sensitive nose increased. He let out a strangled squeal and dropped his useless weapon, and at the same time the Saint released his grip.

"I told you it wasn't loaded," said the Saint, picking up the automatic by the trigger-guard and dropping it into his pocket. "I think I'd better use your gun, Andy. But don't try any more tricks like that, or I might really have to hurt you."

Mr Gump did not reply; except for the baleful glitter in his streaming eyes he seemed unmoved. Patricia, who knew the Saint's twisted sense of humour better than anybody, wondered why he had wasted time by amusing himself so childishly at Mr Gump's expense. There must have been a reason somewhere; for Simon Templar never did strange things without a reason, and it was invariably a good one. It was noticeable that he held the new gun, which was loaded with death, in such a way that Mr Gump would never have a chance of grabbing it.

"So we collect pretty pictures, do we?"

The Saint's voice held nothing but tolerant amusement as he inspected four glossy photographs of feminine pulchritude which he had abstracted from Mr Gump's breast pocket.

"Why not?" said the other defensively. "I'm a film fan."

"Brother, you certainly know how to pick winners," commented the Saint. "This young lady in the voluminous mid-Victorian attire, complete with bustle, is undoubtedly Miss Beatrice Avery, shining star of Triumph Film Productions Limited. Very charming. Of course, it's her you thought you were snatching tonight. Number Two, in the exotic Eastern outfit, is the lovely Irene Cromwell, under contract with Pyramid Pictures. We could use her, Andy. Number Three, in the dinky, abbreviated beach-suit, is no less a person than Sheila Ireland, now starring with Summit Picture Corporation. I can see I shall have to get out my old water-wings. And Number Four—" He paused, and his eyes hardened. "Very sad about Number Four, don't you think, Andy? A couple of months ago Miss Mercia Landon was doing the final scenes of her new film for Atlantic Studios. A couple of months ago . . . And now?"

"I don't know what you're getting at," said Mr Gump woodenly.

"If you don't, the Z-Man is very careless in choosing his assistants," answered the Saint.

"What the hell do you mean?" stammered the chinless man, his inward alarm crashing suddenly through the veneer of calm which he had tried to preserve. "There's no harm in my carrying those photographs. Anybody can get them. I'm a film fan—"

"So you told me," agreed the Saint, slipping the photographs into his own pocket. "And a kidnapper in your spare time, too, by the looks of it," he added casually. "Well, I may as well see what the rest of your hobbies are, although I'm not likely to find anything half so interesting as your favourite film stars."

He put a cigarette into his mouth, lighted it with a match which he sprung into flame with his thumb-nail, and set it at a rakish angle. If the men before him had known him better they would have sweated with fear; for that rakish slant was an infallible sign that something was going to happen and that he was personally going to start it. Patricia felt her heart beating a shade faster. Except for that one danger signal there was nothing to give her a clue to what was in his mind.

He completed the search, finding cigarettes, matches, money, keys, and all the usual contents of an average man's pockets, but nothing to reveal Mr Gump's real identity, and nothing to connect him with the mysterious Z-Man. Even the tailor's label inside his breast pocket had been removed.

"Well, gents, we can call it an evening." The Saint waved his gun muzzle gently over the three men. "Pat, old thing, sling me the torch and then get up to the garage. We've finished here."

She obeyed at once, and a moment later Simon himself was backing up the stairs, keeping his flashlight flooding downwards. As soon as he reached the top he swung the door to and fastened it. It was not a good door. There were cracks in it, the hinges were old and rusted, and the lock had long since ceased to function, but the Saint overcame these trifling drawbacks by the simple expedient of propping three or four heavy wooden stakes against the door. Since it opened outwards, the three musketeers would have to work for some time before they could make their escape.

"We have been having a lot of luck lately, haven't we?" Patricia remarked philosophically.

"Have I grumbled?" asked the Saint, making no attempt to lower his voice—and, indeed, speaking quite close to the barricaded cellar door. "We're going to shoot off to Parkside Court now, old dear, and warn Beatrice Avery that she'd better be packing. After what happened to you, it's pretty obvious that the ungodly are likely to put in some fast work, and we're going to be just one move ahead of them. If necessary we'll take the fair Beatrice away by force."

"Why didn't you question those fellows about the Z-Man?"

"They wouldn't have come through with a syllable unless I'd beaten it out of them, and I'm not in one of my torturing moods this evening," answered Simon. "Don't worry about the Three Little Pigs—it'll take them about an hour to get out, and I doubt if they'll go after Beatrice again tonight, anyway. Ready, darling?"

While he spoke he had been flashing his torch about the garage. There was a telephone in one corner, and this interested him for a moment, but a few odd potatoes lying on the floor against one of the walls interested him almost as much. He picked up the biggest he could find, and bent down at the rear of the taxi to jam the providential tuber firmly over the end of the exhaust pipe.

"All set, keed," he murmured, and his eyes were bright with mischief.

5

The men in the cellar heard the main garage door creak open and then close. After that there was a large silence, broken at last by Ferret Eyes. Exactly what he said is immaterial. Ninety per cent of it would have burned holes through any printed page, and the subject matter in between the frankly irrelevant patches cast grievous aspersions on Simon Templar's parentage, his physical characteristics, and his purely personal habits. The air of the cellar was rapidly turning a deep blue when the chinless man cut in.

"It's no good cursing the Saint," he said sharply. "The mistake was yours, Welmont, and you know it. Why don't you try cursing yourself?"

"What's Z going to say?" asked Welmont, a frightened note coming into his voice. "It wasn't my fault, Raddon. Damn it, you can't blame me. From the other side of the road the girl looked exactly like Beatrice Avery. How the hell was I to know? She came out of Parkside Court—"

"Save it until later," Raddon cut him off impatiently. "The first thing we've got to do is to get out of here. See what you can do with the door, Tyler. You know more about this damn place than I do."

The taxi driver mounted the stairs and heaved against the door. It creaked and groaned, but gave no sign of opening.

"It's jammed," he reported unnecessarily. "The lock's no good and there ain't any bolts. That ruddy perisher must have done somethink." He swore comprehensively. "Now we're in a ruddy mess, ain't we? I told yer not to bring that ruddy jane to my garridge."

It was not the best of all places for applying force. The stairs were narrow and steep and slippery, and there was no possible way of exerting leverage, or even making a shoulder charge. It was equally impossible for two men to stand side by side; Raddon himself went up and examined the door, holding the torch to the cracks so that the beam of light passed through.

"There's only one way to get out," he said. "If we cut away the lower part of the door we can use a plank to shift the props. There are two or three planks lying in the cellar against the wall. You'd better start, Tyler."

The taxi driver cursed and grumbled, but set to work. The door was old and misshapen, but it was tough. Tyler and Welmont, working in turn while Raddon held the light, took the better part of half an hour to break through. They had only penknives for tools, and they had to split and chip away the wood in fragments. Finally, Tyler forced one of his heavy boots through the opening with a vicious kick. A plank was then thrust through and the props dislodged.

"S'pose 'e sends the rozzers?" asked the driver anxiously.

"I'll lose my licence, that's wot I'll do. I was a ruddy fool to let you use my garridge."

"If Templar had sent the police they'd have been here twenty minutes ago," Raddon answered promptly. "The Saint doesn't want the police in this any more than we do. But he's an interfering swine and we've got to get after him. Start up the cab, Tyler."

"Give me a charnce, will yer?" protested Tyler, climbing into his seat. "I'll 'ave it out in a jiffy."

He was an optimist. They gave him a chance, but the self-starter, which usually had the engine firing after the first whirr, whirred in vain. Tyler's cursing only added to the ear-aching sounds which filled the garage.

"You'll have no batteries left," Raddon said helpfully. The taxi man climbed down from his seat.

"Funny bloomin' thing." he rumbled. "She don't usually play tricks like this 'ere. 'Tain't as if she was stone cold, neither."

"Perhaps you forgot to turn the petrol on," ventured Welmont.

"P'raps there ain't any blinkin' engine," snarled Tyler. "Wot the 'ell d'yer take me for?" He uncovered the engine and addressed a few scorching remarks to it. "Can't nobody show me a light?" he said bitterly. "Think I'm a blarsted cat? Nothink wrong with the jooce." The carburettor flooded at his touch. "Ignition looks all right, too. 'E didn't take out the plugs. Nothink loose nowhere . . ."

He tried again, with the same result. The engine, for some inexplicable reason, amused itself by turning over, but it simply refused to fire. Tyler had been a taxi driver for years, and before that he had worked as a motor mechanic. The cab was his own property, and he always did his own repairs. He tried everything he could think of, but he never thought of taking a look at the rear end of the exhaust pipe.

"We've wasted enough time," said Raddon angrily. "I've got to get in touch with Z—"

He broke off as he caught sight of the telephone in the corner. It was only by chance that he had seen it at all, for it was almost hidden behind a number of ancient and ragged tyres which hung on the wall, and Welmont's torchlight had swung in that direction quite casually and without any intentional objective. Raddon's eyes narrowed behind the gold-rimmed pince-nez and he flashed his own torch into the corner.

"Is this phone connected?" he asked sharply.

"Wot the 'ell d'yer mean?" Tyler demanded, looking round indignantly. "Think I ain't paid the rent for it? Of course it's connected."

"Why didn't you tell me it was here?" Raddon retorted. "I could have used it long ago. Now it may be too late . . . You heard what Templar said to the Holm girl before they left?"

He went to the instrument, held his light steadily on it, and dialled Scotland Yard. As soon as the switchboard operator answered he spoke in a deep voice with a forced foreign inflection.

"Take this down garefully," he said distinctly. "Simon Templar, alias the Saint, alias the Z-Man, is at this moment gidnabbing Beatrice Avery, the film star, from her apartment in Barkside Gourt. That's all."

He hung up before the operator could answer.

"'Ere, wot abaht me?" demanded Tyler frantically. "You got a ruddy nerve, usin' my phone for that job. They can trace that call. Think I want the cops round 'ere arskin' questions?"

"You know nothing about it," said Raddon calmly. "You left the garage unlocked, and somebody used your phone. What does it matter, you fool? They can't pin anything on you. I had to get through to the Yard at once. If they pull Templar in he'll spend the next two weeks trying to explain his movements. The Yard's been trying to get him for years, and if they catch him red-handed snatching the Avery girl they'll send him up for a ten-year stretch."

He turned to the instrument again and flashed his light on the dial. Placing his body between the telephone and the other two men, so that they could not watch the movements of his finger, he quickly dialled another number and waited. He listened to the steady "*burr-burr*" for a few moments, and then a voice answered.

"Raddon here," he said in a rapid, subdued voice. "Something has gone wrong. Can't do anything more this evening. Better turn our attention to the next proposition . . ." He broke off and listened. "All right. Usual place tomorrow, as early as possible."

He hung up at once, and found Welmont looking curiously at him out of his ferret eyes. "Was that Z?" Welmont asked.

"It was Gandhi," answered Raddon curtly. "If you're ready we'll go. There's nothing more for tonight. Too dangerous to move until we know more about Templar."

They departed—none too soon for Tyler, who was jumpy and worried—leaving one of the big double doors slightly ajar.

Simon Templar stroked the cog of his lighter and inhaled deeply and luxuriously from a much-needed cigarette. He heard the three men walking over the cobbles outside, and then silence. With the lithe ease of a panther he lowered himself from the overhead beam on which he had been lying at full length, dropped to the roof of the taxi, and thence descended to the ground.

There was a smile on his lips as he dusted himself down. That beam, so easily reached from the roof of the taxi, had positively asked him to make its acquaintance when he had first glanced up at it. Patricia, he knew, could handle her end of the job with smooth efficiency; he had had a couple of minutes' earnest talk with her before they parted. For Simon Templar, even before he left the cellar, had put in some of that characteristic quick thinking which was the everlasting despair of the law and the ungodly alike. His restless brain, working at supercharged pressure, had looked into the immediate future with a clarity that was little short of clairvoyant; he had formulated a plan of action out of a situation that had not even acquired a definite geography. But that power of thinking ahead, into the most remote possibilities, was the gift which had so often left his enemies breathless in the background, hopelessly outpaced by the hurricane speed of the Saint's imagination . . .

Which satisfactorily explains why he was still in Mr Tyler's garage, dusting the well-creased knees of his impeccable Anderson & Sheppard trousers, and by no means dissatisfied with the results of his roosting. He grinned helplessly as he realised how easily the departed trio could have seen him if they had only looked up into the dusty rafters. Not that it would have mattered much: he was armed, and they weren't. However, it was just as well that he had remained undiscovered. His ears hadn't told him much more than he knew already, but his eyes had served him well.

Raddon's phone call to Scotland Yard had given him nothing to worry about. If he knew anything of Patricia, she would be through with Beatrice Avery long before the padded shoulders of the law could darken the portals of Parkside Court.

His eyes had served him on the second phone call. Lying along the overhead beam, he had looked straight down upon the telephone . . . He chuckled as he thought of Raddon's precautions. Raddon would never have used the Instrument at all for his second call if it had been one of the old-fashioned non-dialling type. He couldn't have given his number to the exchange without giving it to Welmont and Tyler at the same time. Dialling was different: he had only to obtrude his body between his companions and the telephone, and they couldn't possibly know what number he had called.

But the Saint, with a perfect bird's-eye view, had watched every movement of Raddon's fingers on the dial; his super-sensitive ears had listened to every click of the returning disc; he had memorised the number and rucked it securely away in a corner of his retentive brain. Raddon's finger had first jabbed into the PRS hole; then into the ABC; then into the PRS again. This could only mean one exchange—PAR, otherwise PARliament. The numbers were easy. Raddon had called PARliament 5577.

The Z-Man's telephone number. Or, at least, a number he was in the practice of using. There were ways and means of discovering to whom that number had been allocated.

Searching through the London Telephone Directory was one of them, but the Saint had never been able to rave about that particularly tedious occupation. There were easier methods. One of them he tried at once. He dialled PARliament 5577 himself, and blew smoke-rings at the mouthpiece while he waited. His connection came quickly, and a thick voice said,

"Vell?"

"The same to you, comrade," said the Saint fraternally. "Kindly put me through to Mr Thistlethwaite—"

"Vot? Der iss nobody named that," said the thick voice.

"You'll pardon me, but there's a very large somebody named that," said the Saint firmly. "Senior partner of the firm of Thistlethwaite and Abernethy—"

"This iss not the firm you say."

"No? Then who is it?" asked the Saint obstinately. "What's the idea of using Thistlethwaite and Abernethy's telephone number? Aren't you Parliament 5577?"

"Yes."

"Then don't be silly. You're Thistlethwaite. Or are you Abernethy?"

"Ve are not dose names," shouted the thick voice. The line became dead, but Simon Templar was not discouraged. He had not expected to click at the first attempt. He dialled the number a second time and waited.

"Vell?"

"Oh, it's you again, is it?" said the Saint cheerfully. "Vell— I mean, well, that proves that you *must* be Thistlethwaite. Or else you're Abernethy. I damn well know I dialled the right number."

"Ve are *not* Thistle-votyousay und somebody," roared the thick voice, its owner clearly under the impression that he was dealing with a genial half-wit. "You got the wrong number again, you fool!"

"If you're Parliament 5577 you're Thistlethwaite and Abernethy," insisted the Saint. "Think I don't know?"

"Ve are Zeidelmann und Co.," bellowed the angry voice, "und ve know nothing of the peoples you say."

"Well I'm damned!" said Simon, in surprise. "Then am I the bloke who's been making the mistake? A thousand apologies, dear old frankfurter. And the same to Co."

He hung up, and with his cigarette slanting dangerously out of the corner of his mouth he turned over the last few pages of Vol. II of the London Telephone Directory, which lay on a shelf. There was only one Zeidelmann & Co., and the address was Bryerby House, Victoria.

The Saint paused for a moment to remove the potato from the taxicab's exhaust pipe, and as he strode silently down a long narrow yard, with high walls on either side, he reflected on the absurdity of a mere humble potato rendering impotent one of man's greatest mechanical wonders. And at the same time he reflected on his own remarkable good fortune. Beyond any shadow of doubt, his guardian angel was having a busy day . . .

6

He was somewhere in the Cricklewood district, and he found his great cream and red Hirondel parked where he had left it. His opportune arrival in the garage cellar a little earlier had been no coincidence. He had allowed Patricia Holm to go to Parkside Court alone, but he had hovered cautiously in the offing himself, and it had been a simple matter to follow the taxi which had started off with such suspicious abruptness.

"The Z-Man—Zeidelmann & Co.," he said to himself, as he drove swiftly towards Victoria. "Significant—and yet rather too easy. There's a catch in it somewhere."

Bryerby House stood in a quiet road off Victoria Street. Simon parked his car nearby and walked to the office building. He had formulated no plan of action, but doubtless something would occur to him when it was necessary. Direct action, the straightforward and devastatingly simple approach which had always appealed to him, continued to offer tempting possibilities. It looked as if Zeidelmann & Co. had something to do with the Z-Man. Therefore he wanted to feast his eyes on Zeidelmann & Co. The logic of the proposition seemed incontrovertible, and as for its consequences, Simon was cheerfully prepared to let the Lord provide.

There was a wicked glimmer of anticipation in his eyes as he inspected the grubby board in the hall on which was painted a list of the occupants and their various callings. Zeidelmann & Co. apparently did nothing for a living, for beyond stating that their office was situated on the ground floor, the board was completely dumb. The Saint wandered down a shabby, bare-boarded passage, scanning the names on the doors as he passed them. He met nobody, for Bryerby House was one of those janitor-less office buildings in which one could wander unhindered and unchallenged at any hour of the day, and although the evening was still quite young it was still old enough for most business men to have paddled off to the discomfort of their suburban homes. The passage took a turn at the end, and Simon Templar found himself facing a glass-topped door. There was a light within, and painted on the glass were the illuminating words:

ZEIDELMANN & CO.
Curios

Simon cocked his hat at the sign.

"And indeed they are," he drawled, and knocked on the door. "Vell?" came a familiar thick voice.

"So our old pal Mr Vell is here," murmured the Saint, turning the door handle and entering. "Good evening, Z-Man," he added affably, as he closed the door and lounged elegantly against it. "This is the Saint calling. And how's the trade in old pots and pans?"

One hand rested carelessly in his pocket, and the other flicked a cigarette into his mouth and then snapped a match head into flame. His languidly mocking eyes had missed nothing in the first quick survey of the room. The office was small and barren. It contained nothing but a shabby flat-topped desk, a couple of chairs, a table-lamp, and a telephone. At the desk sat a big, shadowy man—the Saint could only see him indistinctly, for the lampshade was tilted over so that the light shone towards the door and left the man at the desk in semi-gloom. It seemed to be a popular lighting system among the clan.

"*Himmel!* You are the crazy fool who telephoned, yes?"

"Well, I did telephone," Simon admitted. "But I don't know if I'd answer to the rest of it." His gaze swept coolly over the room again. "You must do a thriving business here," he drawled. "I see your stock's pretty well sold out. Or do you mostly keep it in old cellars?"

"Vot you vant mit me?" demanded the other. "Vot iss tiss 'Saint' nonsense? I am Mr Otto Zeidelmann und you I do not know."

"That's a condition which will be remedied from now onwards, brother," said the Saint pleasantly. "You'll get to know me better every minute. I dropped in this evening to have a look at you, and I must say you're not very obliging. That lamp-shade—excuse me."

Thud!

Something like a streak of silver lightning hissed across the desk and buried its point in the arm of the chair a fraction of an inch from Mr Zeidelmann's hand, which had been edging towards the centre drawer of the desk.

"I'm getting out of practice," said the Saint regretfully. "I meant that knife to pin your sleeve to the chair."

Mr Zeidelmann looked down at the still quivering ivory hilt and sat as still as a mummified corpse.

"God!" he muttered shakily. "Are you a lunatic?"

"No," said the Saint mildly. "But I'm afraid you'll look like one if you waste any time denying that you're the Z-Man. By the way, did you notice that in your perturbation you said 'God' just now instead of 'Gott'? You want to watch little details like that when you disguise yourself. Respectable manufacturers' agents don't keep guns in their desk drawers, either—or any other kind of drawers, if it comes to that. Besides, I heard Mr Gump—Mr Raddon to you— talking to you over the phone. He made an appointment for tomorrow. That's why I'm here this evening."

The Z-Man stared at him without speaking, rolling a pencil monotonously between his fingers. The sudden shattering discovery that the notorious Saint knew so much must have hit him like a blow in the stomach. Recovery was not easy. Meanwhile, Simon had leisure to inspect his victim with greater care. His sight had accommodated itself to the unequal lighting, and he was able to form a fair picture of Mr Zeidelmann's appearance.

He had to acknowledge that if he had set out to feast his eyes, he was doomed to be disappointed again. Mr Zeidelmann was no feast, except in sheer quantity. He was grossly fat, with a great swelling belly which occupied all the space between his chair and the desk. A thick woollen muffler was bundled round his neck, and above it the Saint could catch only a glimpse of the dark beard which camouflaged the shape of his chin. Big horn-rimmed spectacles with clumsily thick rims covered his eyes, and a wide-brimmed soft hat was pulled well down over his forehead.

"You know, brother, if you're one of the curios, I wouldn't want you on my mantelpiece," observed the Saint critically. "You remind me of a great fat, overgrown slug. Only in appearance, of course; for slugs are highly moral and inoffensive creatures, and their only crime is to sneak up on your lettuces at night and test their succulency. By the way, I wonder if you leave a visible trail of slime behind you wherever you go?"

"You make the mistake!" Zeidelmann said gutturally. "I nodding vot you say understand. I am not this man you say. You come here, und you insult me—"

"And call you a slug—"

"Und say I am a Z-Man, votever that iss," proceeded Mr Zeidelmann wrathfully. "I tell you, you make the mistake. You are one pig fool."

"You can't get away with it, *Agriolimax Agrestis*—which, believe it or not, is what Mamma Slug calls Papa Slug when she wants to cut a dash," said the Saint imperturbably. "You didn't know I was such a walking encyclopedia, did you? There's no mystery about it really. You see, Slug, I always make a point of knowing everything there is to be known about obnoxious vermin and pernicious germ life."

"Vill you go avay?" thundered Mr Zeidelmann.

"In a way," said the Saint, "you puzzle me. You're not particularly good, and I'm wondering where you got your Frankenstein reputation. I'm beginning to think that you're just an amateur. Blackmailers often are. But your racket isn't exactly common-or-garden black, is it? You seem to mix it with kidnapping on the side. You've hit a new angle of the game, and you've got me guessing."

"Me, too," fumed the big man in the chair. "I, too, guess! Vot you mean I do not know."

"Oh, yes you do, and you'd better know what I mean when I tell you that Beatrice Avery is now out of your reptilian reach," said the Saint coldly. "She's safely hidden away—and so are your other intended victims."

"You are crazy mad. I haf no victims."

"You also have a large sackful of boodle tucked away somewhere, Mr Vell, and when the right time comes I'm going to dig my shovel into it." The Saint was missing none of the Z-Man's many reactions. He watched his victim's hands, his heaving stomach, and his dark, vicious eyes, just visible behind the big lenses. "As far as I can see you've been running your show too long, so I'm going to close it down." He pulled himself off the door and shifted closer towards the desk. "And now, if you don't mind, we're going to have a much more intimate look at you, as the bishop said to the actress. Take off the fur and the windows and give your face an airing."

He made a suggestive move of the hand which still rested in his pocket, and then his ears caught a faint whisper of sound behind him. He started to turn, but he was a shade too late. The door behind him was already open, and something round and hard jabbed accurately into his spine. The toneless voice of Mr Raddon spoke behind him.

"Take your hand out of your pocket and keep still." The Saint kept still.

"This is a dirty trick, Andy," he complained. "I distinctly heard you tell Comrade Vell that you'd meet him tomorrow at the usual place. Why can't you keep your word instead of butting in like this and spoiling everything?"

He continued to keep studiously still, but he did not move his hand from his pocket. The bantering serenity of his voice had not changed in the slightest degree, and the smile on his lips was unaltered. The Z-Man, who had struggled cumbersomely to his feet, did not know that behind that blandly unruffled smile the Saint's brain was turning over like a high-speed turbine.

"Shut the door, Raddon," he said tensely. "Your gun in his back keep, and if he a muscle moves, shoot."

"Well done, Slug," approved the Saint. "You sound exactly like Dennis the Dachshund."

"So, Mr Saint, your cleverness iss not so hot, yes?" Zeidelmann's voice came in a throaty purr. "There are things that even you do not know—you who know so much about slugs. You do not know that I haf a code with Raddon, for use on the telephone. 'Tomorrow' means 'today,' und 'today' means 'tomorrow.' 'Yes' means 'no,' und 'no' means 'yes.' Ve are careful, yes?"

"No," said the Saint. "Or should that be 'yes?' It sounds like a silly game to me. Don't you ever get muddled?"

The pressure on his spine increased.

"You talk too much," Raddon said curtly. "Take your gun out of your pocket and put it on the desk."

The Saint's eyes were twinkling blue icicles.

"Talking about guns, where did you get this one from?" he inquired. "I took one rod from you and I've got it in my pocket at this very moment. Guns aren't so easy to pick up in London. I believe you're bluffing, Andy."

"You drivelling fool!" grated Raddon. "Do as I tell you."

There was more than impatience and exasperation in his voice. It was just a little too sharp to be convincing. Simon Templar laughed almost inaudibly, and took the chance that he had to take.

"You haven't got a gun, brother," he said softly. "Have you?"

Without warning, his right heel swung back in a kick that any mule in the full bloom of robust health would have boasted about for weeks. Mr Raddon collected it on his shin, and as he reeled back with a shriek of agony the Saint spun round like a human flywheel, his arm slamming vimfully into the other's wrist. His precaution was unnecessary, for the object which clattered to the floor from Raddon's hand was a harmless piece of iron piping.

"Your ideas are too juvenile," said the Saint sadly. "I read detective stories myself. Instead of fooling about with that chunk of gas barrel you ought to have whacked me on the back of the head with it."

Several other things happened immediately afterwards, one of them quite unrehearsed and unexpected. As Raddon bumped into the wall and clawed wildly at it to keep his balance, his hand dragged over the electric light switch, to which the standard lamp was connected. Instantly the room was plunged into inky darkness, for there was no light out in the passage near enough to penetrate the glass top of the door. The Saint leaped towards the switch, his gun now snug in his fist, and as he did so a splintering crash of glass came from the other side of the room, and he looked round and saw an uneven patch of grey light in the blackness. He knew just what had happened. The Z-Man, fearing that the tables were to be turned again, had left his lieutenant to his fate and charged desperately into the window, taking blind and glass and broken frame with him. Mr Zeidelmann was nothing if not thorough.

The Saint dashed for the window, and one of his feet got caught in the flex of the table-lamp and almost tripped him. It was only a brief delay, but that was all the Z-Man needed. When Simon dived through the window into the narrow alley which ran along the rear of the building, he caught a glimpse of a bulky, lumbering figure streaking away beneath a solitary lamp at the far corner. Considering Mr Zeidelmann's load of superfluous flesh, he certainly knew how to sprint. The Saint ran to the end of the alley and found himself in a dingy side street. A little way from this was a main road, with buses and other heavy traffic. The Z-Man had vanished into the anonymity of London's millions.

Simon was not surprised to find Mr Otto Zeidelmann's office empty when he got back. Nobody seemed to have noticed the crash of glass, if there was anyone left in the building to notice it, and Mr Raddon had clearly wasted no time in taking advantage of his opportunity. The Saint was not disturbed about that—he had already had all that he wanted from Comrade Raddon in a business way, and an extension of their acquaintance along social lines was something that the Saint could hardly see as a pleasure without which life would be merely a succession of empty hours.

He retrieved his knife from the arm of the chair, and made a quick search of the office. As he had anticipated, every drawer of the desk was empty except the middle one, which contained a loaded revolver of ancient design. It was obvious that the Z-Man used the office only for a base of communications when his assistants were on the job. He was too clever to have any hand in the actual operations, but he could be reached by telephone if necessary. And after this, Simon reflected ruefully, he would certainly find himself a new address and telephone number . . . The visit hadn't been anything like as profitable as he hoped it would be, but it had been fun while it lasted. And at least, in spite of disguises, he would have some slight chance of recognising Mr Zeidelmann when they met again. The Saint's mind always turned optimistically towards the boundless possibilities of the future. He wondered how Patricia was getting on with her share of the campaign.

7

Patricia Holm had had little or no difficulty in inducing Beatrice Avery to leave her apartment and go down to the big limousine with Hoppy Uniatz at the wheel which waited outside. With that calm realism which was peculiarly her own, she had described her recent adventure, and the film actress had come to the obvious conclusion that Parkside Court was the unhealthiest spot in London. Perhaps she had been close to that conclusion even before that, for since Patricia's last visit she had had time to reconsider the Saint's offer.

"I asked for it, in a way," said Patricia, as the car raced towards Piccadilly. "I took advantage of my superficial resemblance to you to gain admission to your flat, and when the Z-Man's agents saw me come out, they made the same mistake as your bodyguard."

"Supposing it had really been me?" said Beatrice Avery with a shudder. "I shouldn't have had the Saint to help me."

"Well, you've got him now," said Patricia. "So you can stop worrying. The Saint's after the Z-Man, and that means that the Z-Man will have so much on his mind that he won't have time to think about you."

"But why are we going to Scotland?"

"We're not going to Scotland."

"When we were on our way out you said you always preferred to motor to Scotland at night because the roads were clearer—"

"That was just for the benefit of the commissionaire," Patricia explained.

The car stopped outside a handsome new apartment house in Berkeley Square. Patricia went up to Irene Cromwell's extravagant flat. The exotic star of Pyramid Pictures was not in.

"I think she had better be," said Patricia to the scared-looking maid who had answered the door. "Tell her that Miss Holm, of the Special Branch, Scotland Yard, wishes to see her on a matter which affects her personal safety."

The maid, duly impressed, discovered that her mistress was in after all. She left Patricia in the little hall for only a minute, and then ushered her into a gorgeous boudoir which only a £500-a-week film star could dream of maintaining. Irene Cromwell looked surprisingly frail and timid, wrapped in a trailing feather-trimmed chiffon negligée.

"You are from Scotland Yard?" she asked, her eyes round and big.

"I don't want to beat about the bush," replied Patricia, her manner brisk and efficient. "It has come to our knowledge at Scotland Yard that the Z-Man is active again . . ."

"The Z-Man!" breathed the other girl, turning deathly pale.

"Oh yes, we know all about him, and we think it would be wise to transfer you to a place of safety," continued Patricia imperturbably. "I have an official car waiting outside. Miss Beatrice Avery, whom you probably know, is in the car already. You will also be accompanied, I hope, by Miss Sheila Ireland."

The startled actress opened her eyes even wider.

"But where are we going? I've got a dinner engagement—"

"Ireland," answered Patricia, without batting an eyelid. "We have everything arranged with the Free State authorities. Ireland is within a comparatively few hours, and yet sufficiently remote for our purpose. You see, Miss Cromwell, it is of vital importance that Scotland Yard should be left with a clear field. While this organisation is being cleaned up you are in grave danger."

Irene Cromwell took less than a minute to make up her mind. In fact, she regarded Patricia's suggestion as a police order, and so thoroughly had the urgency of the matter impressed itself on her mind that she was ready, with two packed suitcases, within the incredible space of twenty minutes.

Beatrice Avery had been given her cue, and she kept up the deception as the limousine rolled smoothly off towards Kensington. But very little was said. Irene Cromwell sat back in her corner, huddled in her furs, apparently fascinated by the very official-looking cap which reposed on the unprepossessing head of Mr Uniatz.

Exactly the same procedure was followed in Sheila Ireland's dainty home—and again Patricia got away with it. The blonde Venus of Summit Pictures was successfully lured out into the waiting car, and any doubts she might have entertained were dispelled when she saw Beatrice Avery and Irene Cromwell. An impression was left behind that Miss Ireland was bound for a remote spot in the Welsh mountains.

At Patricia's request, further discussion of the subject that was uppermost in all their minds was tacitly postponed. The limousine now started off in real earnest, leaving London behind and speeding through the night in the direction of Kingston. Their actual destination was Weybridge, less than twenty miles to the south-west.

Simon Templar's house on St. George's Hill was not easily found at night, but Hoppy Uniatz knew every inch of that aristocratic neighbourhood, with its nameless roads and its discreetly hidden residences which were far too exclusive to be demeaned by ordinary numbers. The passengers in the car caught vague glimpses of pine trees and silver birches which rose from rolling banks of rhododendrons and bracken.

There were bright lights in the windows as the limousine came to a standstill outside the front door, and a man with a loose walrus moustache and a curious strutting limp came out on the step.

"Here we are, Orace," said Patricia, as she got out.

"Yer lyte," replied Orace unemotionally.

He took charge of the suitcases, and showed no surprise at seeing three of the prettiest girls in England follow Patricia out of the car. If they had been three performing kangaroos he wouldn't even have blinked. Years of employment in Simon Templar's service had deprived him of any quality of surprise he might have once possessed.

"Dinner narf a minnit," he said, when they were in the hall, and stumped off to his own quarters.

"He means it, too," smiled Patricia. "But for once Orace and the dinner must be kept waiting."

She led them into the living-room, and looked from Irene Cromwell to Sheila Ireland with quiet calmness. Mr Uniatz, who had helped to carry the bags in, licked his lips and gazed longingly at the cocktail cabinet, where liquor was always to be found in plenty and in great variety. But he caught Patricia's warning eye, and he knew that the time for refreshment had not yet come. His impersonation of a police officer was no longer important, but Patricia Holm felt that the sudden shock of Mr Uniatz's speech would be lessened if she explained certain other things to her guests beforehand.

"You'll forgive me, I hope, for practising a small deception," she said in her forthright way. "Miss Avery knows that I'm not really connected with Scotland Yard: I am Patricia Holm, and this house belongs to Simon Templar."

"You mean—the Saint?" asked Irene, with a little quiver of excitement and incredulity.

"The Saint is out to get the Z-Man, and before he could let himself go he had to be sure that he wouldn't be placing any of you in danger," Patricia went on. "I took the risk of lying to you in London because it was too urgent to go into explanations. But before we go any further I want to tell you that you're free to go whenever you please. This very minute, if you like. Any one of you, or all three of you, can go if you want to. You haven't been kidnapped. The car is ready to take you back to London. But if you're wise you'll stay here. I'll tell you why."

Irene and Sheila, bewildered at first, began to understand as she went on, and Beatrice Avery contributed some heartfelt persuasions of her own. And while they talked, the subtle atmosphere of peace and security with which the Saint had invested the house began to add its charm to the other arguments. The girls looked at each other, and then at the less comforting dark outside . . .

"Well, you've been very frank about it, Miss Holm," said Irene Cromwell at length. "I'm willing to stay if you think it would help. But the studio—"

"You can phone them in the morning and say you've been taken ill."

"But why are we safer here than in London?" asked Sheila.

Patricia smiled.

"With Orace and Hoppy Uniatz to look after us, we can make faces at a dozen Z-Men," she replied confidently. "Also, nobody except yourselves knows where you are. And this house isn't quite as innocent as it looks. It has all sorts of surprises for people who try to crash the gate. Now suppose we have a cocktail."

Mr Uniatz drew a deep breath.

"Say, ain't dat an idea?" he asked of the assembled company, with the enthusiasm of an alchemist who has just heard of the elixir of life. "Dat'll make everyt'ing okay."

Orace was serving the second course of dinner when he cocked his head on one side and listened. Patricia, too, had heard the familiar drone of the Hirondel.

"It's 'im," remarked Orace ominously. "And abaht time, too. 'E'll get some cold soup."

8

Chief Inspector Teal was out of his office when Raddon's telephone call came through to Scotland Yard. Consequently, another officer went to Parkside Court, purely as a matter of routine, to make a few discreet inquiries. All he learned was that Beatrice Avery had left for Scotland, and she had been accompanied by her sister. It seemed, therefore, that the telephone call was true to type—in other words, merely another of those pointless practical jokes which regularly add to the tribulations of the C.I.D.

Mr Teal, when he heard about it, was not so sure.

It is a matter of record that he set off to Parkside Court without a minute's delay to make some inquiries of his own, and they were not so discreet. He cross-examined the hall porter and the commissionaire and the elevator boy until they were in momentary expectation of being dumped into a Black Maria and shot off to the cells. Mr Teal was definitely suspicious because when he interviewed Beatrice Avery that afternoon she had definitely assured him that she had no intention of leaving London. And now, apparently, she had gone off to Scotland.

"Why Scotland?" demanded Mr Teal, turning his baby blue eyes smoulderingly on the commissionaire.

"She didn't tell me she was going to Scotland," said the man. "But I heard her sister saying that they'd have a nice clear run—"

"How do you know it was her sister?"

"That private detective chap who was here told me so," said the commissionaire. "As soon as they'd gone, he went off duty. Miss Avery's maid went home, too. The flat's empty."

From the description supplied by the commissionaire and the elevator boy, Mr Teal had no difficulty in recognising Patricia Holm. His worst suspicions were strengthened when the commissionaire proffered the additional information that the limousine which had waited outside had been driven by a large man with a face which had the appearance of having once been run over by a traction engine, and afterwards left in the hands of an amateur face-lifter.

"The Holm girl and Uniatz!" raged Mr Teal, champing viciously on his flavourless spearmint. "It's as clear as daylight! They came here as openly as a couple of innocent schoolchildren and got her away with some fairy tale. I'll bet it was the Saint himself who rang up the Yard—just to get my goat!"

These remarks he addressed to himself as he paced up and down the luxuriously carpeted foyer. The monumental conviction was growing within him, and rapidly assuming the size of the Arc de Triomphe, that the Saint had made every variety of fool of him in the early afternoon.

Simon Templar was the Z-Man. Mr Teal's grey matter was flowing like molten lava. The Saint had spotted Sergeant Barrow at the Dorchester, and on the off-chance that Barrow had spotted him, he had thought it advisable to shoot back the package of money to Beatrice Avery, so that he could clear himself. Whatever hold he had on her had been enough to force her to lie on the telephone. Then, to keep her quiet, he had kidnapped her . . . It was like the Saint's devilish sense of humour to ring up . . . There wasn't any real proof . . . But if he could find Beatrice Avery in the Saint's hands, there would be enough evidence to put him away for keeps, the detective told himself, to the accompaniment of an imaginary fanfare of triumphal trumpets. It would be the last time that the Saint would pull a long nose at the majesty of the law . . ."

Seething and sizzling like a firework about to go off, Mr Teal realised that he was wasting time at Parkside Court. He plunged into the police car which had brought him, and was driven to Cornwall House. He guessed that this would be a further waste of time, but the visit had to be made. He was right. Not only did Sam Outrell coldly inform him that the Saint was away, but he used a pass key to show him the empty flat. Fuming, and expectorating a devitalised lump of chicle on to the sidewalk for the unwary to step on, he climbed into his car again and this time told the driver to go to Abbot's Yard, in Chelsea. It was well known that the Saint owned a studio in this modernised slum.

"We might as well try it," Teal said grimly. "Ten to one they've taken the girl out of London, but it would be just like the Saint's blasted nerve to hold her here, right under our very noses."

Again his fears were confirmed. Twenty-six Abbot's Yard was in the same condition as Mother Hubbard's cupboard, and inquiries among the near-artist neighbours elicited the information that the Saint had not been seen for weeks.

Mr Teal was so exasperated that he nearly inserted the next slice of spearmint into his mouth without removing the pink wrapper, but on the intellectual side his grey matter was not quite so white hot now, and therefore was slightly more efficient. He was certain of one thing: the Saint had not taken Beatrice Avery to Scotland. After years of experience of Simon Templar's methods, Mr Teal easily guessed that Patricia Holm's reference to Scotland had very much the fishy smell of a red herring.

"Not much good looking for him, is it, sir?" asked the driver of the police car depressingly.

"No; let's sit down on the kerb and play shove-ha'penny," retorted Teal, with searing sarcasm.

"I mean, sir, the Saint's got all sorts of hideouts," said the man. "There's no telling—"

"I've long since come to the conclusion that most of these stories of the Saint are pure legend," said Mr Teal, with a real flash of intelligence. "In nine cases out of ten he remains in full view, and just dares us to do our worst. One of these days he's going to dare us once too often. Perhaps this is the day," he added hopefully. "Anyhow, let's get going."

"Where to, sir?"

"We know he's got a place at Weybridge, so we might as well run down and have a look at it," replied Mr Teal, climbing into the car. "We'll try every place we know until we find him."

The more he thought of his recent interview with the Saint, the more he reviewed the subsequent happenings, the higher became his dudgeon. In everything except outward appearance Chief Inspector Teal was exactly like a fire-breathing dragon as he sat in the back of the car, asking the driver why he had left the engine behind and what was the blank-blank idea of driving with the brakes full on.

However, in spite of his unsympathetic comments, the journey was accomplished in remarkably good time, and a gleam of hope appeared in Mr Teal's overheated blue eyes when he saw lights gleaming from the windows of Simon Templar's house on St. George's Hill. In answer to his thunderous knock and insistent ringing the door was opened by Orace, who inspected him with undisguised disfavour.

"Oh, it's you, is it?" said Orace witheringly.

"Is Templar here?" roared Mr Teal.

"Is 'oo 'ere? If you mean Mister Templar—"

"I mean Mr Templar!" said the detective chokingly. "Is Mr Templar here?"

"'Oo wants ter know?"

"I want to know!" bellowed Mr Teal, his spleen surging out of him like a discharge of poison gas. "Stand out of the way, my man. I'm coming in—"

"Like 'ell you are," Orace said stolidly. "Back door fer you, my man. The idear!"

At this point of the proceedings Simon Templar, resplendent in Tuxedo and soft silk shirt, materialised into the picture. The living-room door was half open, and the Saint had an idea that the dialogue would soon become blue around the edge, and unfit for the shell-like ears of his guests.

"All right, Orace," he said breezily. "Walk right in, Claud Eustace. What brings you into the wilds this evening? Not that I wasn't expecting you—"

"Oh, you were expecting me, were you?" broke in Mr Teal, forcing the words past his strained throttle with some difficulty. "Well, I hope you're glad to be right. You've been just a little too smart since I saw you this afternoon. Now I know damned well you *are* the Z-Man!"

"In that case, dear heart, there must be two Z-Men," answered the Saint accommodatingly. "Isn't it amazing how the little fellows breed? I'm glad you're here, Claud. There's something I want you to do. It'll interest you to know that I had quite a chat with the original Z-Man this evening—"

"When I want to listen to any more of that, I'll let you know," Teal said massively. "Just now I'm going to be busy. I have reason to believe that you kidnapped Miss Beatrice Avery from her apartment in Parkside Court this evening, and I'm not going to leave this house until I've searched it—and you might as well know that I haven't got a warrant."

"But why search the house, dear old fungus?" Simon protested reasonably. "Kidnapping is a hard word, and I resent it. But I'm willing to make allowances for your blood pressure. At the rate the red corpuscles are being pumped through that lump of petrified wood you wear your hat on, the poor thing must be feeling the strain. Have I denied that Miss Avery is under this roof? She came down with Patricia a little more than an hour ago, and we're just having our coffee."

Mr Teal gulped, and his chewing-gum slithered to the back of his mouth, played hide-and-seek with his tonsils, and finally slid into his gullet before he could recover it.

"What!" His voice was like a pin-pricked carnival balloon. "You admit you've got her here? You admit you're the Z-Man? Then by God—"

"My poor boob," said the Saint sympathetically. "I haven't admitted anything of the sort. I merely said that Miss Avery was having dinner with me. If that makes me the Z-Man, it makes you the Grand Lama of Tibet. Miss Avery is a friend of Pat's, and we've got a couple of other good-looking girls here, too. We're making a collection of them. If you'll promise to behave yourself I'll take you in and let you look at them."

He turned back into the living-room, and Mr Teal followed him with the beginnings of a new vacuum pumping itself out from under his belt. Somehow it was going to be done again—the awful certainty of it made Mr Teal feel physically sick. He had a wild desire to turn back to his car and drive away to the end of the earth and forget that he had ever seen Scotland Yard, but he had to drag himself on, like a condemned man walking to the scaffold.

He stood in the doorway, with his hands clasped tightly on his belt, and stared around at the four eye-filling sirens who reclined in arm-chairs around the fire. Patricia Holm and Beatrice Avery he knew, but his heavy eyelids nearly disappeared into the back of his head when he heard the names of Irene Cromwell and Sheila Ireland. And the worst of it was that they all looked perfectly happy. They didn't leap up with shrill cries of joy and greet him as their deliverer. They studied him with the detached curiosity of surgeons inspecting a new kind of tumour revealed by an operation.

Mr Teal grunted his acknowledgment of the introductions, and stood glaring desperately at Beatrice Avery.

"I've got one thing to ask you, Miss Avery," he said, with a hideous presentiment of what the answer would be. "Did you come here entirely of your own free will?"

"I think that's a very unkind thing to ask, Mr Teal," she answered sweetly. "It's unkind to me, since it implies that I'm weak-minded, and it's unkind to Mr Templar—"

"I want to be unkind to Mr Templar!" Teal stated homicidally. "If there is any kind of threat being held over you, Miss Avery, I give you my word that so long as I'm here—"

"Of course there isn't any threat," she said. "How ridiculous! What do you think Mr Templar is—a sort of Bluebeard?"

Mr Teal didn't dare to say what he thought Mr Templar was. But he knew that Beatrice Avery would give him no help. There was nothing about her that gave the slightest hint of fear or anxiety. However accomplished an actress she might be, he knew that she could never have acted like that under compulsion. What other supernatural means the Saint had taken to silence her, Mr Teal couldn't imagine, but he knew that it was hopeless to fight them.

He pulled himself miserably together.

"I don't think I need bother you with any more questions, Miss Avery," he said brusquely.

He went out of the room very much like a beaten dog, and if he had had a tail it would have been hanging between his legs. The Saint followed him out, closed the door, and lighted a fresh cigarette.

"Cheer up, Claud," he said kindly. "You've got over these things before, and you'll get over it again. Look me squarely in the eye and tell me you're sorry I'm not the Z-Man, and I'll spread you all over the hall in a mass of squashy pulp."

The detective looked at him for a long time.

"Damn it, Saint, you've got me," he growled sheepishly. "You know how much I want to get my hands on you, but I'd still be glad if you weren't the Z-Man."

"Then why not be glad?"

"I think I'm getting some more ideas now," Teal went on, flashing the Saint a glance which was very far from sleepy. "Miss Avery—Miss Cromwell—Miss Ireland, top-line film stars, every one. Let me make another guess. Those girls are the Z-Man's intended victims, and if you aren't the Z-Man yourself, you've brought them here so that they'll be safe while you go after him."

"You must have been eating a lot of fish and spinach," said the Saint respectfully. "Your ideas are improving every minute—except for one minor detail. I've been out after the Z-Man already, I've met him, and we had quite an interesting five minutes."

Mr Teal, who had just rolled up a fresh slice of spearmint with his tongue like a miniature piece of music, shook his head sceptically.

"Just because I'll believe you up to a point—"

"Would I lie to you, Claud?" asked the Saint. "Have I ever told you anything but the truth? Listen, brother. I don't know much about the Z-Man, but I can tell you this. Until this evening he has been known as Mr Otto Zeidelmann, and he's large and fat and has a black beard and wears horn-rimmed glasses and speaks with a phoney German accent. He has been using an office in Bryerby House, Victoria, for his business address, but you needn't trouble to look for him there, because I don't think he likes the place so much now. And I doubt if his appearance in ordinary life is anything like my description. But that's where I saw him, and that's what he looked like to me."

Mr Teal opened his mouth, but words failed him.

"And here's a gun," Simon went on, taking something wrapped in a silk handkerchief from his pocket. "It's one of my own, but I fooled a gentleman who goes by the name of Raddon into making a grab for it, and you ought to find a fair sample of his fingerprints. Get Records to look them up, will you? I have an idea it's what you professionals call a Clue. I'll drop into your office in the morning and get your report. Has that percolated?"

"Yes," replied Mr Teal, taking the gun and putting it carefully away. "But I'm damned if I get the rest. Is this another of your tricks, or are you playing the game for once? We've been trying to get a line on the Z-Man for months—"

"And I heard of him for the first time today," murmured the Saint, with a smile. "You can call it luck if you like, but most of it's due to the fact that I'm not festooned with red tape until I look like a Bolshevik Egyptian mummy. Having a free and unfettered hand is a great help. It might even help you to solve a mystery sometimes—but I'm not so sure about that."

"Well, what are you getting out of it?" asked Mr Teal with reasonable curiosity. "If you think I'm going to believe that you're doing this for fun—"

"Maybe I might persuade the Z-Man to contribute towards my old-age pension," Simon admitted meditatively, as though the idea had just occurred to him. "But it's still a lot of fun. And if you get his body, dead or alive, you ought to be satisfied. Don't you think you're asking rather a lot of questions?"

Mr Teal did, but he couldn't help it. His mind would never be at ease about anything so long as he knew that the Saint was busy. He stared resentfully at the smiling man in front of him, and wondered if he was still only being hoodwinked again.

"I've got to get back to town," he said curtly. "I'm sorry about the misunderstanding. But who the devil did phone that message through to the Yard?"

"That was Comrade Raddon, whose fingerprints are carefully preserved on that gun in your pocket," Simon replied. "I expect he thought it was a bright idea. Now run along home and play with your toys."

Mr Teal hitched his coat round.

"I'm going," he said, fighting a losing battle with the new crop of gnawing suspicions that were springing up all over the well-fertilised tracts of his unhappy mind. "But get this. If you still think you're putting anything over on me—"

"I know," said the Saint. "I needn't think I can get away with it. How empty the days would be if I couldn't hear that dear old litany! I think I could recite it in my sleep. Come again, Claud, and we'll have some new grey hairs for you." He opened the front door, and steered the detective affectionately down the steps. "Take care of Mr Teal, George," he said to the police driver who still sat at the wheel of the car. "He isn't feeling very strong just now."

He patted the detective's bowler hat well down over his ears, and went back into the house.

9

Back in the living-room, the Saint's air of leisured badinage fell off him like a cloak. He draped himself on the mantelpiece with a cigarette tilting from his mouth and a drink in his hand, and started to ask questions. He had a lot to ask.

They were not easy questions, and the answers were mostly vague and unsatisfactory. The subject of the Z-Man was not one that seemed to encourage conversation, but Simon Templar had a knack of his own of making people talk, and what he did learn was significant enough. Two or three months earlier, Mercia Landon, dancing and singing star of Atlantic Studios, had been working in the final sequences of a new supermusical when for no apparent reason she had had a breakdown. All work on the production was held up, the overhead mounted perilously, and finally the picture had to be shelved. It was rumoured that Mercia was being threatened by a blackmailer, but nobody knew anything for certain. And then, one morning, she was found dead in her apartment from the conventional overdose of Veronal.

"Accidental death," said the coroner's jury, since there was no evidence to show that the overdose had been deliberately taken, but those "in the know"—people on the inside of the screen world—knew perfectly well that Mercia Landon had taken her own life. And for a good and sufficient reason. Although she was only twenty-two and in perfect health, she had known that her screen career was finished. For when her maid found her, there was a deep arid jagged cut on her face in the rough zigzag shape of a Z. The upper line crossed her eyebrows, the diagonal crossed her nose, and the lower horizontal gashed her mouth almost from ear to ear. No amount of plastic surgery, no miracles of skin grafting could ever have restored the famous modelling of her face, or made it possible for her to smile again that quick sunny smile that had been reflected from a million screens.

"Nobody ever knew who Mercia met that night, or even where she went," said Sheila Ireland, her slim white fingers nervously twisting her empty cigarette-holder. "I suppose they took her away like—like they thought they were taking Beatrice. Nobody could have blackmailed Mercia. She never had any affairs, and everybody loved her. And she just laughed at the idea of being kidnapped—here in England. When they started demanding money, she just laughed at it. She wouldn't even go to the police. All anybody knows about this is that she once said to her maid, 'That idiotic Z-Man who keeps phoning must be an escaped lunatic.' And then—" She shivered. "Since then we've all been terrified."

"It's an old racket with a new twist," said the Saint. "The ordinary blackmailer has something on his victim. The Z-Man has nothing—except the threat that he'll disfigure them and ruin their screen careers if they don't come across. I seem to remember that some other actress recently had a nervous breakdown, exactly like Mercia Landon. The picture she was in was shelved, too, and it's still shelved. She went to Italy to recuperate. I take it that she was Victim No. 2. She was threatened, she lost her nerve, and she paid. She saved her good looks, but her bank balance wasn't big enough to go on paying. So Beatrice is probably Victim No. 3."

The girl shuddered.

"I know I am," she said. "During the last three weeks I've had three telephone calls— always in a thick guttural foreign sort of voice, asking me for ten thousand pounds. I was told to lunch at the Dorchester, and if I saw that the knives and forks formed the letter Z, I was to have my lunch and then leave the package of money under my napkin. And he said if I went to the police, or anything, they'd know about it, and they'd do the same to me as they did to Mercia, without giving me another chance to pay . . . Today was my last chance, and when I saw the knives and forks in the shape of a Z, I think I lost my nerve. When you came to my table, Mr Templar, I thought you must be the man who was to take the money. I hardly knew what I was doing—"

"Take a look at that cunning, will you, Pat?" said the Saint. "It's a million to one that his victim won't go to the police, but he's even ready for that millionth chance. He's ready to pick up the money as soon as the girl has left the table; disguised as a gentleman, he's sitting there all the time, and as he walks past the table he collars the package. And he's got his alibi if the police should be watching and pick him up. He happened to see the young lady had left something, and he was going to hand it over to the manager. No proof at all that he's the man they're really after. It also implies that he must be somebody with a name and reputation as clean as an unsettled snowflake, and as far above suspicion as the stratosphere . . . But who was it? There was a whole raft of people at the Dorchester, and I can't remember all of them—unless it was good old Sergeant Barrow."

"If the Z-Man was in the Dorchester today he must have seen your knightly behaviour," said Patricia thoughtfully. "And he must have seen you pocket Beatrice's last week's salary."

"But he didn't know who I was, and I expect he beetled off as soon as he saw that something had come ungummed," said the Saint, stubbing the end of his cigarette into an ash-tray and lighting a fresh one. He turned. "What about the picture you're working on now, Beatrice? I'll make a guess that it's nearly finished, and if anything happened to you now the whole schedule would be shot to hell."

She nodded.

"It would be—and so should I. My contract doesn't entitle me to a penny if I don't complete the picture. That's why—"

She broke off helplessly.

Simon went to bed with plenty to think about. The Z-Man's plan of campaign was practically fool-proof. Film stars are able to command colossal salaries for their good looks as well as their ability to act—sometimes even more so. All three of his guests were in the £20,000-a-year class; they were young, with the hope of many more years of stardom ahead of them. Obviously it would be better for them to pay half a year's salary to the Z-Man rather than suffer the ghastly disfigurement that had been inflicted on Mercia Landon; for then they would lose not only half a year's salary, but all their salaries for all the years to come.

The film world still didn't really know what was happening. Beatrice Avery had been afraid to tell even her employers about the threats she had received, for fear that the Z-Man would promptly carry out his hideous promise. Irene Cromwell and Sheila Ireland had each received one message from the Z-Man, and had been similarly terrorised to silence. Only Patricia's blunt statement that the Saint had found their photographs in Raddon's pocket had made them unseal their lips after she had got them to St. George's Hill.

Simon could well understand why he had never heard of the Z-Man before. Even in the film world the name was only rumoured, and then rumoured with scepticism. These three girls were the only ones who knew it, apart from Mercia Landon, who was dead, and the actress who had fled to Italy.

For once in his life he spent a restless night, impatient for the chance of further developments the next day, and he walked into Chief Inspector Teal's office at what for him was the fantastic hour of eleven o'clock in the morning.

"I thought you never got up before the streets were aired," said the detective.

"I put on some woolly underwear this morning and chanced it," said the Saint briefly. "What do you know?"

Mr Teal drew a memorandum towards him.

"We've checked up on that address you gave me. I think you're right, Saint. There's no such person as Otto Zeidelmann. It's just a name. He's had the office about three or four months."

"His occupation dates from about the time Mercia Landon died," said Simon, nodding. "Anything else?"

"He never went there in the daytime, apparently," answered the detective. "Always after dark. Hardly anybody can remember seeing him. The postman can't remember delivering any letters, and we didn't find a fingerprint anywhere."

"You wouldn't," said the Saint. "A wily bird like him would be just as likely to walk about naked as go out without his gloves. But talking about fingerprints, what's the report on that gun—which, by the way, is mine."

Mr Teal opened a drawer, produced the automatic, and pushed it across the desk. Chewing rhythmically, he also handed the Saint a card on which were full-face and profile photographs of one Nathan Everill.

"Know him?"

"My old college chum, Andy Gump—otherwise known as Mr Raddon," said the Saint at once. "So he has got a police record. I thought as much. What do we know about him?"

"Not very much. He's not one of the regulars." Teal consulted his memorandum, although he probably knew it by heart already. "He's only been through our hands once, and that was in 1933. From 1928 to 1933 he was private secretary to Hubert Sentinel, the film producer, and then he started making copies of Mr Sentinel's signature and writing them on Mr Sentinel's cheques. One day Mr Sentinel noticed something wrong with his bank balance, and when he went to ask his secretary about it, his secretary was on his way to Dover. He was sent up for three years."

"What's he been doing since he came out?"

"He reported in the usual way, and as far as we knew he was going quite straight," replied Mr Teal. "He was doing some freelance writing, I think. We've lost track of him during the last five or six months—"

"He's got a new job—as the Z-Man's assistant," said the Saint. "And, by the Lord, he's the very man for it! He knows the inside of the film business, and he must hate every kind of screen personality, from producers downwards, like nobody's business. It's a perfect set-up . . . Have you seen Sentinel?"

"I'm seeing him this afternoon—he probably knows a lot more about Everill than we do. But you aren't usually interested in the small fry, are you?"

"When the small fry is in the shape of a sprat, yes," answered the Saint, rising elegantly to his feet. "You see, Claud, old dear, there might be a mackerel cruising about in the neighbouring waters . . . That's a good idea of yours. I think I'll push along and see Comrade Sentinel myself."

The detective's jaw dropped.

"Hey, wait a minute!" he yapped. "You can't—"

"Can't I?" drawled the Saint, with his head round the door. "And what sort of a crime is it to go and have a chat with a film producer? Maybe my face is the face the world has been waiting for."

He was gone before Teal could think of a reply.

Mr Hubert Sentinel, the grand panjandrum of Sentinel Films, was not an aristocrat by birth, or even a Conservative by conviction, but even he might have been slightly upset if he had heard himself referred to as "Comrade Sentinel." For he was considered a coming man in the British film industry, and obtaining an entry into his Presence was about as easy as getting into Hitler's mountain chalet with one fist clenched and a red flag in the other.

But the Saint accomplished the apparently impossible at the first attempt. He simply enclosed his card in a sealed envelope with a request that it should be immediately delivered to Mr Sentinel, and he waited exactly two minutes.

Mr Sentinel was in conference. He took one look at the card, and during the next half-minute one matinée idol, one prominent author, two script writers, a famous director, and a covey of yes-men were swept out of the office like leaves before an autumn gale. When Simon Templar was admitted, Mr Hubert Sentinel was alone, and Mr Sentinel was looking at the back of the Saint's card. On it were pencilled the words: Re the Z-Man.

"Take a pew, Mr Templar," he said, pushing forward a cigar-box and inspecting his visitor out of bright and observant eyes. "I've heard about you, of course."

"Who hasn't?" murmured the Saint modestly.

He accepted a cigar, carefully clipped the end, lighted it, and emitted a fragrant cloud of blue smoke. It was merely an example of that theatrical timing which so pleased the Saint's heart. Sentinel waited restively, turning a pencil between his fingers. He was a thin, bald-headed man with a bird-like face and an air of inexhaustible nervous vitality.

"If it had been anyone else, I should have thought it was some crank with a bee in his bonnet," he said. "We get a lot of them around here. But you—are you going to tell me that there's anything in these rumours?"

"There's everything in them," said the Saint deliberately. "They happen to be true. The Z-Man is as real a person as you are."

The producer stared at him. "But why do you come to me?"

"For the very important reason that you once employed a man named Nathan Everill," answered the Saint directly. "I'm hoping you'll be able to tell me something useful about him."

"Good God, you're not suggesting that Everill is the Z-Man, are you?" asked the other incredulously. "He's such a poor specimen—a chinless, weak-minded fool—"

"But you employed him as your secretary for five years."

"That's true," confessed Sentinel hesitantly. "He was efficient enough—too damned efficient, as a matter of fact. But he always had a weak streak in him, and it came out in the end. He forged my name to some cheques—perhaps you know about that . . . But Everill! It doesn't seem possible—"

The Saint shook his head.

"I didn't say he was the Z-Man. But I know that he's very closely connected with him. So if you can help me to locate Everill, you'll probably help me to get to close quarters with the Z-Man himself. And he interests me a lot."

"If you can get him, Templar, you'll not only earn my gratitude, but the gratitude of the whole film business," said Hubert Sentinel, rising to his feet and pacing up and down with undisguised agitation. "If he's a real person, at least that gives us something to fight. Up to now, he's just been a name that people have tried to stick on to something they couldn't explain any other way. But when we see our stars having mysterious breakdowns just when pictures are in their last scenes—getting hysterical over something you can't make them talk about— well, we have to put it down to something."

"Then you've had trouble yourself?"

"I don't know whether it's a coincidence or not," replied Sentinel carefully. "I'll only say that my production of Vanity Fair is held up while Mary Donne is recovering from a slight indisposition. She has said nothing to me, and I have said nothing to her. But that doesn't prevent me from thinking. As for the rest, Mr Templar, I believe I can tell you a great deal about Everill." He sat down again and rubbed his chin in earnest concentration. "You know, I've got some ideas of my own about the Z-Man. Can you tell me just what your interest in him is?"

"I have various interests," said the Saint, leaning back and making a series of perfect smoke-rings. "The Z-Man must have collected a fair amount of boodle already, and that's always interesting. I take it that if 1 got rid of him, nobody would mind me helping myself to a reward. And then, I don't like his line of business. I think it would be rather a good idea if he was put out of the way—for keeps."

"Unless he puts you out of the way first," suggested the producer grimly. "If he's the sort of man he seems to be—"

The Saint shrugged.

"That's all in the game."

The other smiled appreciatively.

"I sincerely hope it won't be in your game," he said. "As for Everill—what do you want to know?"

"Anything you can remember. Anything that might give me a lead. What his tastes are, his amusements—his favourite haunts—his habits—why he started forging cheques—"

"Well, I suppose he's an extravagant little devil—wants to live like a rich playboy, and so on. I suppose that's why he had to increase his income. He was trying to run one of my actresses, and he couldn't keep pace with her. She had a big future ahead of her, and she knew it—"

It was as if the Saint's ears had closed up suddenly, so that he scarcely heard any more. All his senses seemed to have been arrested except the sense of sight, and that one filled his brain to the exclusion of everything else. He was staring at Hubert Sentinel's hands, watching the thin, nervous fingers twiddling the pencil they held—and remembering another pair of hands . . .

The astounding import of it drummed through his head like the thunder of mighty waterfalls. It jeered at his credulity, and yet he knew that he must be right. It all fitted in—even if the revelation made him feel as if his mind had been hauled loose from its moorings. He sat in a kind of daze, until a knock on the door brought him back to life.

Sentinel's secretary put her head in the door.

"Chief Inspector Teal is here, Mr Sentinel," she said.

"Oh yes." Sentinel stopped in the middle of a sentence. He explained, "Mr Teal made an appointment with me—is he interested in Everill too?"

"Very much," said the Saint. "In fact, I was stealing a march on him. If there's another way I can go out—"

Sentinel stood up.

"Of course—my secretary will show you. I wish we could have a longer talk, Mr Templar. The police are admirable in their way, but in a situation like this—" He seemed to come to a snap decision. "Look here, could you dine with me tonight?"

"I'd be delighted," said the Saint thoughtfully.

"That's splendid. And then we can go into this thoroughly without any interruptions." Sentinel held out his hand. "Will you come back here at six? I'll drive you out myself—I live out at Bushey Park."

Simon nodded.

"I'll be here," he said.

He went back to Cornwall House with his head still buzzing, and for a long time he paced up and down the living-room, smoking an interminable chain of cigarettes and scattering a trail of ash behind him on the carpet. At lunch-time he called Patricia.

"I've met a bird called Hubert Sentinel, and I think I know who the Z-Man is," he said. "I'm having dinner with him tonight."

He heard her gasp of amazement. "But, boy, you can't—"

"Listen," he said. "You and Hoppy are going to be busy. I've got a lot more for you."

He talked for ten minutes that left her stunned, and gave her comprehensive instructions.

Six o'clock was striking when he re-entered Sentinel's office, and the producer took down his hat at once. A large Rolls-Royce was parked outside the studio, and Sentinel himself took the wheel.

"How did you get on with Scotland Yard?" Simon inquired, as they purred through the gates.

Sentinel shifted his cigar.

"I had to give him a certain amount of information, but I didn't say anything about your visit. I noticed that he kept looking at the cigarettes in the ash-tray, though, so perhaps he was trying to spot your brand."

"Poor old Claud," said the Saint. "He still keeps on reading Sherlock Holmes!"

Little more was said on the swift, northward run, but the Saint was not ungrateful for the silence. He had plenty to keep his mind occupied. He sat smoking, busy with his own thoughts.

The evening was cold and pitch black by the time they had left the outer suburbs behind and the Rolls turned its long nose into a private driveway. There were thick trees on either side, and after a hundred yards, before there was any sign of the house, Sentinel slowed down to take a sharp curve. As though they had materialised out of the fourth dimension, two figures jumped on the car's running-boards, one on either side. The Saint could see, dimly in the reflection of the headlights, the bloated figure and bespectacled, bearded face of the man who had swung open the driving door.

"You vill stop der car, please."

"Vell, vell, vell!" said the Saint mildly. "This is certainly great stuff."

His hand was reaching round for his automatic, but by this time his own door had opened, and the car had jerked to a standstill, for both Mr Sentinel's feet had instinctively trodden hard on the pedals. The cold rim of an automatic inserted itself affectionately into the back of Simon Templar's neck.

"Move one finger and you're dead," said Mr Raddon unimaginatively.

"Brother, unless you're very careful you'll drive that thing out through my Adam's apple." Simon complained.

"What the devil does this mean?" spluttered Sentinel angrily, and he suddenly revved up the engine. "Look out, Templar!" he shouted. "I'm going to drive on."

The automatic that was held only a foot from Sentinel's head thudded down, and the film magnate slumped over the wheel.

"Step out, Saint," ordered Raddon.

The Saint stepped. He always knew instinctively when to resist and when not to resist. As his feet trod on hard gravel the gross figure came round the back of the car like some evil monster of the night, and gloved hands went rapidly over the Saint and deprived him of his gun. Then he was told to walk forward. Almost at once he was brought to a halt against the rear of a small delivery van parked in the darkness under a tree with its doors open. A sudden violent shove from behind sent him pitching headlong into it, and the doors slammed behind him with a heavy crash. In another moment the engine roared to life, and the truck lurched forward.

10

Simon had one compensation. The opposition had not waited to search him thoroughly or to bind his wrists and ankles in the approved style. The truck was evidently considered to be secure enough as a temporary prison. Which, in fact, it was. When the Saint heaved against the closed doors he soon came to the conclusion that they were sufficiently strong to hold him in for some time. Wherefore, with his characteristic philosophy, he made himself as comfortable as he could and set out to relieve the tedium of the journey with a cigarette. At least he had gone into the trap with his eyes open, so he had no valid grounds for whining.

He judged that the truck had driven through a hidden path between the trees and had then bumped across a field. After that it had gained a road, and now it was bowling along more smoothly. The journey proved to be comparatively short. Within ten or fifteen minutes there was no longer any sound of other traffic, and the road surface over which the truck was travelling became more rutty and uneven. Then, with a giddy swing to the near side, the truck left the road again, and ran evenly for a few seconds on a level drive before it stopped. For a little while it backed and manoeuvred, and then the sound of the engine died away. There was a slight delay, in which he heard occasional murmurs of voices without being able to detect any recognisable words. It was just possible that a red carpet was being laid down for him, but somehow he doubted it. Then there was a rattle at the doors, and they were flung open. Three powerful electric flashlights blazed on him.

"If I make the slightest resistance, I suppose I shall be converted into a colander?" Simon remarked calmly. "I'm just trying to save you the trouble of giving the customary warnings—"

"Get out," Raddon's voice ordered shortly.

Simon obeyed. He was unable to see much of his surroundings, for the truck had been backed up against a crumbling stone doorway, and the torchlights were so concentrated on him that practically everything else was in black shadow.

Two of the men closed in on him as his feet touched the ground, ramming their guns into his sides. He was thrust on through the doorway into what seemed to be a bare and damp and uninhabited hall, and halted with his face to one bleak stone wall. Then, while a gun was still held against his spine, swift and efficient hands went over him again. His pockets were completely emptied, even to his cigarette-case, his automatic lighter, and his loose change, and one of the investigating hands felt along his sleeve and removed the knife strapped to his forearm. After the demonstration he had given in Bryerby House, thought the Saint, that was only to be expected, but he would have been happier if it had been overlooked as it had been so many times before.

"So!" came the Z-Man's sneering voice. "The knife, it voss somewhere, und it we find. Goot! Mit throwings you are through!"

"You've got beyond the Dennis stage now, brother," said the Saint appreciatively, although he was now without a weapon of any kind. "I can only assume that you must have been reading the Katzenjammer Kids."

A rope was pulled tightly around his wrists, pinioning them together in front of him.

Again he was told to move, and he found himself ascending a spiral staircase of vertiginous steepness. Most of the treads were broken and rotting, and creaked alarmingly under his weight. The staircase wound itself like a corkscrew around the inner wall of a round tower, which rose straight up from what he had first taken for a sort of hall. At one time, no doubt, there had been a guarding balustrade on the offside, but this had long since ceased to exist, and there was nothing between the climber and a sheer drop to the flagstones below. At the top, he stepped off the last tread on to the floor of what might once have been a small turret room, but which was now hardly more than an unrailed ledge suspended over the black abyss. The only windows were two narrow embrasures, through which he could see nothing but darkness. He was placed against the wall away from the stairs and close to the edge of the floor, and the other end of the rope around his wrists was run through a heavy iron ring set in the masonry above his head and made fast.

"I can still kick," he observed solicitously. "Are you sure you're not taking a lot of chances?"

"That will not be for long," said the Z-Man.

A block of stone weighing about a hundredweight, with a rope round it, was dragged across the floor, and the rope was tied round the Saint's ankles.

"You vill kick now?" asked the Z-Man. "Yes?"

"I fancy—no," answered the Saint.

He moved his hands experimentally. His wrists were only held by a slip-knot. If he could drag a little slack out of the rope where it was tied to the ring he might be able to get them free. He wondered why he had been tied so carelessly, and the next moment he knew. As if in answer to a prearranged signal, Raddon stepped forward, and with an effort pushed the rock tied to the Saint's feet off the ledge. It dragged the Saint's legs after it, and the slip-knot came tight again instantly as the pull came on it. Simon hung there, excruciatingly stretched out, with only the cord on his wrists to save him from being dragged over the edge.

The Z-Man came closer.

"You know why you are here?" he asked. "You haff interfered with my affairs."

"Considerably," Simon agreed.

In that confined space, the light of the torches was reflected from the walls sufficiently to show the men behind them. Besides the Z-Man and Raddon, the third member of the party, as Simon had suspected, was Welmont, of taxi-cab fame. The two minor Z-Men stood a little behind and to either side of their leader.

The Z-Man put away his torch and took the Saint's own knife out of his pocket.

"You vill tell me how much you know," he said, "Tell me this, my Saint, und your fine looks vill still be yours."

He caressed the knife in his gloved hand, and brought it suggestively forward so that the light glinted on the polished blade.

"So we now attempt to make the victim's blood run cold, do we?" said the Saint amusedly, although his joints felt as if they were being torn apart on the rack. "I take it that you're in the mood for one of your celebrated beauty treatments. Why don't you operate on yourself first, laddie? You look as if it would improve you."

"Tell me vot you know!" shouted the Z-Man furiously. "I giff you just one minute."

"And after I've done the necessary spilling, I suppose you slit my gizzard with the grapefruit cutter and then bury my remains deeply under the fragrant sod," said the Saint sardonically. "Nothing doing, Slug. It's not good enough. I've made myself a hell of a nuisance to you, and you won't be satisfied until I'm as dead as—Mercia Landon."

"You fool," screamed the Z-Man. "I mean vot I say!"

"That makes us even," said the Saint. "But I'm not a film actress, remember. Carving your alphabetical ornamentations on my face won't decrease my earning capacity by a cent. I'm surprised at your moderation. Now that you've got me in your ker-lutches I wonder you don't flay the skin off my back."

His utter indifference to the peril he was in was breathtaking. The mockery of his blue eyes and the cool insolence of his voice had something epic about it, as if he had turned back the clock to days when men lived and died with that same ageless carelessness. And yet even while he spoke, his ears were listening. Events had moved faster than he had anticipated. The Z-Man's lofty eyrie, too, was a factor of the entertainment that Simon had not allowed for. Those crumbling stairs couldn't be climbed easily and quietly . . . Time was the essential factor now, and the Saint was beginning to realise that the support upon which he was relying was not at hand—while he was not so much at the mercy of a man as of a homicidal maniac.

The Z-Man was within arm's length of him now.

"No, I do not slit your gizzard," he said huskily. "I tell you vot I do. I only cut der rope vot hold you up. Und then der stone pulls you down, und we take off der ropes, und you haf had an accident und fallen down. Do you understand?"

The Saint understood very well. He could feel the dizzy emptiness under his dangling toes. But he still smiled.

"Well, why don't you get on with it?" he said tauntingly. "Or have you lost your nerve?"

"You crazy fool! You think you are funny! But if I take you at your word—"

"You're getting careless with that beautiful accent," mocked the Saint. "If you say 'vot,' you ought to say 'vord.' The trouble with you is that you're such a lousy actor. Now if you'd been any good—"

"You asked for it," said the other, in a horrible whisper, and slashed at the rope from which the Saint hung.

And at the same moment the Saint made his own gamble. The fingers of his right hand strained up, closed on the iron ring from which he was suspended, tightened their grip, and held it. The strain on his sinews shot red-hot needles through him, and yet he had a sense of serene confidence, a feeling of seraphic inevitability, that no pain could suppress. He had goaded the Z-Man as he had anticipated, and he had been waiting with every nerve and muscle for the one solitary chance that the fall of the cards offered—a game fighting chance to win through. And the chance had come off.

The rope no longer held him from plunging down to almost certain death, but the steel strength of his own fingers did. And as the rope parted, the slip-knot had loosened so that he could wrench his left hand free.

"Thanks a lot, sweetheart," said the Saint.

A hawk would have had difficulty in following the movements that came immediately afterwards. As the Z-Man gasped with sudden fear, a circle of wrought steel whipped across his shoulder, swung him completely round, and placed him so that his back was towards the Saint. Then the Saint's left hand snaked under his opponent's left arm, flashed up to his neck, and secured a half-nelson that was as solid as if it had been carved out of stone.

"We can now indulge in skylarking and song," said the Saint. "I'll do the skylarking, and you can provide the song."

To some extent he was right, but the Z-Man's song was not so much musical as reminiscent of the shriek of a lost locomotive. Some men might have got out of that half-nelson, particularly as the Saint was still crucified between his precarious grip on the ring and the weight that was trying to drag him down into the black void; but the Z-Man knew nothing about wrestling, and all the strength seemed to have gone out of him. Moreover the Saint's thumb on one side of his captive's neck, and his lean, brown fingers on the other, were crushing with deadly effect into his victim's carotid arteries. Scientifically applied, this treatment can produce unconsciousness in a few seconds, but Simon was at a disadvantage, for half his strength was devoted to fighting the relentless drag on his ankles.

Raddon and Welmont started forward too late. The Saint's wintry laugh met them at their first step.

"If anything happens," he said with pitiless clarity, "your pal goes over first."

They checked as if they had run into an invisible wall, and Raddon's gumpish face showed white as his torch jumped in his hand.

"For God's sake," he gasped hoarsely. "Wait—"

"Is dat you, boss?" bawled a foghorn voice far below, and the Saint's smile became a shade more blissful in spite of the wrenching agony in his right shoulder.

"This is me, Hoppy," he said. "You'd better come up quickly—and look out for someone coming down." He looked over the shuddering bundle of the Z-Man at Raddon and Welmont, still frozen in their tracks.

"There's no way out for you unless you can fly," he said. "How would you like to be a pair of angels?"

They made no attempt to graduate into a pair of angels. They stood very still as Hoppy Uniatz crashed off the stairs on to the ledge, followed by Patricia, and briskly removed their guns. A moment later an arm like a tree-trunk took the weight off the Saint's hand and hauled him back to the safety of the floor.

Patricia was touching the Saint as if to make sure that he was real.

"Are you all right, boy?" she was asking tremulously. "I was afraid we'd be too late. They'd locked the outside door, and Hoppy was afraid of making a noise—"

The Saint kissed her.

"You were in plenty of time," he said, and yanked the Z-Man clear of the edge of the floor. "Think you could hold him, Hoppy?"

"Wit' one finger," said Mr Uniatz scornfully.

With one swift hop that was in itself a complete justification of his nickname, he heaved the Z-Man to his feet from behind and held him in a gorilla grip. The Z-Man's struggles were as futile as the wrigglings of a fly between the fingers of a small boy. And the Saint retrieved his knife and tested the point on his thumb.

"Hold him just like that, Hoppy," he said grimly, "so that his tummy occupies the centre of the stage. I want to do some surgery of my own."

With a swift movement that made Patricia catch her breath and shut her eyes quickly, he thrust the knife deeply and forcefully into the Z-Man's protruding stomach. There was a loud, squealing hiss, and the patient deflated like a punctured tyre.

"I just wanted to see whether it would make a squashy noise or merely explode," said the Saint placidly. "You can open your eyes, darling. There's no mess on the floor. Mr Vell is mostly composed of air."

With a swift movement he yanked off his victim's hat, wig, glasses, and beard. "Miss Sheila Ireland, I believe," murmured the Saint courteously.

11

Patricia found her voice first.

"But I thought you told me Sentinel was the Z-Man," she said weakly. "We left Orace to tie him up—"

"I didn't say so," answered the Saint. "I told you that I'd met Comrade Sentinel, and I thought I knew who the Z-Man was. But I wanted you to tell the girls about Comrade Sentinel, because I knew she'd remember that he knew about her affair with Raddon, and I knew she'd be scared that he might say something that'd start me thinking, and I knew she'd get the wind up and feel that she had to do something about it—that is, if my suspicions were right. And I was damn right!"

"I wondered why she suddenly decided that she couldn't stay away from the studio a little while after I told her the news," Patricia said slowly. "But I never thought . . ."

"I did," said the Saint. "I did most of my thinking in Sentinel's office. He was twiddling a pencil—and all at once I remembered that when I was in Bryerby House the Z-Man had been twiddling a pencil too. Only the Z-Man had a different twiddle. Everybody has his own distinctive nervous habits. I started thinking about the Z-Man's twiddle, wondering where else I'd seen it, and all at once it dawned on me that it was exactly like the way Sheila Ireland had been twiddling her cigarette-holder last night when she was telling us her tale of woe. It nearly knocked me over backwards."

He looked across at the dishevelled girl who was still writhing hysterically in Hoppy's relentless grasp, with the smeared remains of her make-up disfiguring her face, and his eyes were hard and merciless.

"It wasn't a bad idea to make yourself up not only like a man, but a fat, repulsive Zeidelmann," he said. "You nearly fooled me, until I saw you running away from Bryerby House. There's something funny about the way a woman runs, and that started me thinking. Even then I didn't get the idea, but I was ready for it. You did the voice pretty well, too, but that was your business. You only fell down on the little details like pencil-twiddling. And of course nobody would expect you to be a woman. But you were woman enough to make Andy Gump go on putting his head in the noose to try and please you, even after he'd come out of stir for the cheques he forged to buy you jewellery. And you were woman enough to know what the threat of disfigurement would mean to a woman." The Saint's voice was like icy water flowing down a glacier. "You got it both ways. You put the boodle into your own bank account, and at the same time your rivals were having breakdowns and getting thrown out of the running and letting you climb higher . . . I wonder how you'd like it if we made the punishment fit the crime?"

The girl strained madly against Hoppy's iron hands. "Let me go!" she screamed. "You swine! You couldn't—"

"Let her go, Hoppy," said the Saint quietly.

Mr Uniatz unlocked his fingers, and the girl tore herself free and stood swaying on the edge of the floor.

"Would Andy still love you if you had a Z carved on your face?" asked the Saint speculatively.

He moved the knife in his hand in an unmistakable gesture.

He had no intention of using it, but he wanted her to feel some of the mental agony that she had given to others before he dealt with her in the only way he could. But all the things he would have liked to do were in his voice, and the girl was too demented with terror to distinguish between fine shades of meaning. She gaped at him in stupefied horror as he took a step towards her, and then, with an inarticulate, despairing shriek, she flung herself backwards into the black pit below . . .

Raddon started forward with a queer, animal moan, but Hoppy's gun whipped up and thrust him back. And the Saint looked at him.

"It's no use, Andy," he said, with his first twinge of pity. "You backed the wrong horse." He slid his knife back into its sheath and put an arm around Patricia.

"Where are we?" he asked, in a matter-of-fact voice.

"This is some sort of old ruin with a modern house built into one wing of it." She spoke mechanically, with her eyes still hypnotised by the dark silence into which Sheila Ireland had disappeared. "I suppose it belonged to her . . ."

The Saint buttoned his coat. Life went on, and business was still business.

"Then it probably contains a safe with some boodle in it," he said. "I know a few good causes that could use it. And then we'd better hustle back and untie Comrade Sentinel before he bursts a blood-vessel. We'll have to take him back to Weybridge and add him to Beatrice and Irene for the alibi we're going to need when Claud Eustace hears about this. Let's keep moving."

PUBLICATION HISTORY

Perhaps Hodders got their numbers wrong. Or maybe they simply underestimated the power of the Saint. Regardless, no sooner had they published the first edition of this book, in June 1937, than they had to rush back to the printers and order another batch, with a second edition appearing the following month. And just four years later, in October 1941, they were on their eleventh edition making this, initially at least, one of the Saint's best-selling adventures, particularly if you use the number of book reprints as a measure.

Yet curiously, since the 1940s reprints have been fairly thin on the ground; sure the coming of paperbacks in the post-war 1950s provided two or three editions, and of course there were a couple of reprints to tie in with the first TV series, but once you get passed the initial rush, this is one of the Saint and Leslie Charteris's less popular books.

This is echoed in the foreign sales as well, for translations were limited to a handful of reliable markets; the Dutch published *De Z-man* in 1939 but understandably renamed it *De Saint en de Z-man* when it came to reprinting it in the 1960s. The French opted for *Le Saint contre Mr Z . . .* in 1947, the Italians for *L'asso dei furfanti* (which translates as the rather excellent *The Ace of Villains*) in 1973, whilst the

Brazilians and Swedes published their respective translations in 1937 and 1945 respectively.

All three stories in this book were adapted for *The Saint* with Roger Moore: "The Beauty Specialist" was retitled "Marcia" and was first broadcast on 24 October 1963 as part of the second season. The following week saw the first broadcast of "The Work of Art," an episode based on "The Spanish War," whilst "The Unlicensed Victuallers" was renamed "The Hi-Jackers" and was first broadcast on 13 December as part of the third season.

ABOUT THE AUTHOR

> *I'm mad enough to believe in romance. And I'm sick and tired of this age—tired of the miserable little mildewed things that people racked their brains about, and wrote books about, and called life. I wanted something more elementary and honest—battle, murder, sudden death, with plenty of good beer and damsels in distress, and a complete callousness about blipping the ungodly over the beezer. It mayn't be life as we know it, but it ought to be.*
>
> *—Leslie Charteris in a 1935 BBC radio interview*

Leslie Charteris was born Leslie Charles Bowyer-Yin in Singapore on 12 May 1907.

He was the son of a Chinese doctor and his English wife, who'd met in London a few years earlier. Young Leslie found friends hard to come by in colonial Singapore. The English children had been told not to play with Eurasians, and the Chinese children had been told not to play with Europeans. Leslie was caught in between and took refuge in reading.

"I read a great many good books and enjoyed them because nobody had told me that they were classics. I also read a great many bad books which nobody told me not to read . . . I read a great many popular scientific articles and acquired from them an astonishing amount of general knowledge before I discovered that this acquisition was supposed to be a chore."[1]

One of his favourite things to read was a magazine called *Chums*. "The Best and Brightest Paper for Boys" (if you believe the adverts) was a monthly paper full of swashbuckling adventure stories aimed at boys, encouraging them to be honourable and moral and perhaps even "upright citizens with furled umbrellas."[2] Undoubtedly these types of stories would influence his later work.

When his parents split up shortly after the end of World War I, Charteris accompanied his mother and brother back to England, where he was sent to Rossall School in Fleetwood, Lancashire. Rossall was then a very stereotypical English public school, and it struggled to cope with this multilingual mixed-race boy just into his teens who'd already seen more of the world than many of his peers would see in their lifetimes. He was an outsider.

He left Rossall in 1924. Keen to pursue a creative career, he decided to study art in Paris—after all, that was where the great artists went—but soon found that the life of a literally starving artist didn't appeal. He continued writing, firing off speculative stories to magazines, and it was the sale of a short story to *Windsor Magazine* that saved him from penury.

He returned to London in 1925, as his parents—particularly his father—wanted him to become a lawyer, and he was sent to study law at Cambridge University. In the mid-1920s, Cambridge was full of Bright Young Things—aristocrats and bohemians somewhat typified in the Evelyn Waugh novel *Vile Bodies*—and again the mixed-race Bowyer-Yin found that he didn't fit in. He was an outsider who preferred to make his own way in the world and wasn't one of the privileged upper class. It didn't help that he found his studies boring and decided it was more fun contemplating ways to circumvent the law. This inspired him to write a novel, and when publishers Ward Lock & Co. offered him a three-book deal on the strength of it, he abandoned his studies to pursue a writing career.

When his father learnt of this, he was not impressed, as he considered writers to be "rogues and vagabonds." Charteris would later recall that "I wanted to be a writer, he wanted me to become a lawyer. I was stubborn, he said I would end up in the gutter. So I left home. Later on, when I had a little success, we were reconciled by letter, but I never saw him again."[3]

X Esquire, his first novel, appeared in April 1927. The lead character, X Esquire, is a mysterious hero, hunting down and killing the businessmen trying to wipe out Britain by distributing quantities of free poisoned cigarettes. His second novel, *The White Rider*, was published the following spring, and in one memorable scene shows the hero chasing after his damsel in distress, only for him to overtake the villains, leap into their car . . . and promptly faint.

These two plot highlights may go some way to explaining Charteris's comment on *Meet—the Tiger!*, published in September 1928, that "it was only the third book I'd written, and the best, I would say, for it was that the first two were even worse."[4]

Twenty-one-year-old authors are naturally self-critical. Despite reasonably good reviews, the Saint didn't set the world on fire, and Charteris moved on to a new hero for his next book. This was *The Bandit*, an adventure story featuring Ramon Francisco De Castilla y Espronceda Manrique, published in the summer of 1929 after its serialisation in the *Empire News*, a now long-forgotten Sunday newspaper. But sales of *The Bandit* were less than impressive, and Charteris began to question his choice of career. It was all very well writing—but if nobody wants to read what you write, what's the point?

"I had to succeed, because before me loomed the only alternative, the dreadful penalty of failure . . . the routine office hours, the five-day week . . . the lethal assimilation into the ranks of honest, hard-working, conformist, God-fearing pillars of the community."[5]

However his fortunes—and the Saint's—were about to change. In late 1928, Leslie had met Monty Haydon, a London-based editor who was looking for writers to pen stories for his new paper, *The Thriller*—"The Paper with a Thousand Thrills." Charteris later recalled that "he said he was starting a new magazine, had read one of my books and would like some stories from me. I couldn't have been more grateful, both from the point of view of vanity and finance!"[6]

The paper launched in early 1929, and Leslie's first work, "The Story of a Dead Man," featuring Jimmy Traill, appeared in issue 4 (published on 2 March 1929). That was followed just over a month later with "The Secret of Beacon Inn," starring Rameses "Pip" Smith. At the same time, Leslie finished writing another non-Saint novel, *Daredevil*, which would be published in late 1929. Storm Arden was the hero; more notably, the book saw the first introduction of a Scotland Yard inspector by the name of Claud Eustace Teal.

The Saint returned in the thirteenth issue of *The Thriller*. The byline proclaimed that the tale was "A Thrilling Complete Story of the Underworld"; the title was "The Five Kings," and it actually featured Four Kings and a Joker. Simon Templar, of course, was the Joker.

Charteris spent the rest of 1929 telling the adventures of the Five Kings in five subsequent *The Thriller* stories. "It was very hard work, for the pay was lousy, but Monty Haydon was a brilliant and stimulating editor, full of ideas. While he didn't actually help shape the Saint as a character, he did suggest story lines. He would take me out to lunch and say, 'What are you going to write about next?' I'd often say I was damned if I knew. And Monty would say, 'Well, I was reading something the other day . . .' He had a fund of ideas and we would talk them over, and then I would go away and write a story. He was a great creative editor."[7]

Charteris would have one more attempt at writing about a hero other than Simon Templar, in three novelettes published in *The Thriller* in early 1930, but he swiftly returned to the Saint. This was partly due to his self-confessed laziness—he wanted to write more stories for *The Thriller* and other magazines, and creating a new hero for every story was hard work—but mainly due to feedback from Monty Haydon. It seemed people wanted to read more adventures of the Saint . . .

Charteris would contribute over forty stories to *The Thriller* throughout the 1930s. Shortly after their debut, he persuaded publisher Hodder & Stoughton that if he collected some of these stories and rewrote them a little, they could publish them as a Saint book. *Enter the Saint* was first published in August 1930, and the reaction was good enough for the publishers to bring out another collection. And another . . .

Of the twenty Saint books published in the 1930s, almost all have their origins in those magazine stories.

Why was the Saint so popular throughout the decade? Aside from the charm and ability of Charteris's storytelling, the stories, particularly those published in the first half of the '30s, are full of energy and joie de vivre. With economic depression rampant throughout the period, the public at large seemed to want some escapism.

And Simon Templar's appeal was wide-ranging: he wasn't an upper-class hero like so many of the period. With no obvious background and no attachment to the Old School Tie, no friends in high places who could provide a get-out-of-jail-free card, the Saint was uniquely classless. Not unlike his creator.

Throughout Leslie's formative years, his heritage had been an issue. In his early days in Singapore, during his time at school, at Cambridge University or even just in everyday life, he couldn't avoid the fact that for many people his mixed parentage was a problem. He would later tell a story of how he was chased up the road by a stick-waving typical

English gent who took offence to his daughter being escorted around town by a foreigner.

Like the Saint, he was an outsider. And although he had spent a significant portion of his formative years in England, he couldn't settle.

As a young boy he had read of an America "peopled largely by Indians, and characters in fringed buckskin jackets who fought nobly against them. I spent a great deal of time day-dreaming about a visit to this prodigious and exciting country."[8]

It was time to realise this wish. Charteris and his first wife, Pauline, whom he'd met in London when they were both teenagers and married in 1931, set sail for the States in late 1932; the Saint had already made his debut in America courtesy of the publisher Doubleday. Charteris and his wife found a New York still experiencing the tail end of Prohibition, and times were tough at first. Despite sales to *The American Magazine* and others, it wasn't until a chance meeting with writer turned Hollywood executive Bartlett McCormack in their favourite speakeasy that Charteris's career stepped up a gear.

Soon Charteris was in Hollywood, working on what would become the 1933 movie *Midnight Club*. However, Hollywood's treatment of writers wasn't to Charteris's taste, and he began to yearn for home. Within a few months, he returned to the UK and began writing more Saint stories for Monty Haydon and Bill McElroy.

He also rewrote a story he'd sketched out whilst in the States, a version of which had been published in *The American Magazine* in September 1934. This new novel, *The Saint in New York*, published in 1935, was a significant advance for the Saint and Leslie Charteris. Gone were the high jinks and the badinage. The youthful exuberance evident in the Saint's early adventures had evolved into something a little darker, a little more hard-boiled. It was the next stage in development for the author and his creation, and readers loved it. It became a bestseller on both sides of the Atlantic.

Having spent his formative years in places as far apart as Singapore and England, with substantial travel in between, it should be no surprise that Leslie had a serious case of wanderlust. With a bestseller under his belt, he now had the means to see more of the world.

Nineteen thirty-six found him in Tenerife, researching another Saint adventure alongside translating the biography of Juan Belmonte, a well-known Spanish matador. Estranged for several months, Leslie and Pauline divorced in 1937. The following year, Leslie married an American, Barbara Meyer, who'd accompanied him to Tenerife. In early 1938, Charteris and his new bride set off in a trailer of his own design and spent eighteen months travelling round America and Canada.

The Saint in New York had reminded Hollywood of Charteris's talents, and film rights to the novel were sold prior to publication in 1935. Although the proposed 1935 film production was rejected by the Hays Office for its violent content, RKO's eventual 1938 production persuaded Charteris to try his luck once more in Hollywood.

New opportunities had opened up, and throughout the 1940s the Saint appeared not only in books and movies but in a newspaper strip, a comic-book series, and on radio.

Anyone wishing to adapt the character in any medium found a stern taskmaster in Charteris. He was never completely satisfied, nor was he shy of showing his displeasure. He did, however, ensure that copyright in any Saint adventure belonged to him, even if scripted by another writer—a contractual obligation that he was to insist on throughout his career.

Charteris was soon spread thin, overseeing movies, comics, newspapers, and radio versions of his creation, and this, along with his self-proclaimed laziness, meant that Saint books were becoming fewer and further between. However, he still enjoyed his creation: in 1941 he indulged himself in a spot of fun by playing the Saint—complete with monocle and moustache—in a photo story in *Life* magazine.

In July 1944, he started collaborating under a pseudonym on Sherlock Holmes radio scripts, subsequently writing more adventures for Holmes than Conan Doyle. Not all his ventures were successful—a screenplay he was hired to write for Deanna Durbin, "Lady on a Train," took him a year and ultimately bore little resemblance to the finished film. In the mid-1940s, Charteris successfully sued RKO Pictures for unfair competition after they launched a new series of films starring George Sanders as a debonair crime fighter known as the Falcon. But he kept faith with his original character, and the Saint novels continued to adapt to the times. The transatlantic Saint evolved into something of a private operator, working for the mysterious Hamilton and becoming, not unlike his creator, a world traveller, finding that adventure would seek him out.

"I have never been able to see why a fictional character should not grow up, mature, and develop, the same as anyone else. The same, if you like, as his biographer. The only adequate reason is that—so far as I know—no other fictional character in modern times has survived a sufficient number of years for these changes to be clearly observable. I must confess that a lot of my own selfish pleasure in the Saint has been in watching him grow up."[9]

Charteris maintained his love of travel and was soon to be found sailing round the West Indies with his good friend Gregory Peck. His forays abroad gave him even more material, and he began to write true-crime articles, as well as an occasional column in *Gourmet* magazine.

By the early '50s, Charteris himself was feeling strained. He'd divorced his second wife in 1943 and got together with a New York radio and nightclub singer called Betty Bryant Borst, whom he married in late 1943. That relationship had fallen apart acrimoniously towards the end of the decade, and he roamed the globe restlessly, rarely in one place for longer than a couple of months. He continued to maintain a firm grip on the exploitation of the Saint in various media but was writing little himself. The Saint had become an industry, and Charteris couldn't keep up. He began thinking seriously about an early retirement.

Then in 1951 he met a young actress called Audrey Long when they became next-door neighbours in Hollywood. Within a year they had married, a union that was to last the rest of Leslie's life.

He attacked life with a new vitality. They travelled—Nassau was a favoured escape spot—and he wrote. He struck an agreement with *The New York Herald Tribune* for a Saint comic strip, which would appear daily and be written by Charteris himself. The strip ran for thirteen years, with Charteris sending in his handwritten story lines from wherever he happened to be, relying on mail services around the world to continue the Saint's adventures. New Saint books began to appear, and Charteris reached a height of productivity not seen since his days as a struggling author trying to establish himself. As Leslie and Audrey travelled, so did the Saint, visiting locations just after his creator had been there.

By 1953 the Saint had already enjoyed twenty-five years of success, and *The Saint Detective Magazine* was launched. Charteris had become adept at exploiting his creation to the full, mixing new stories with repackaged older stories, sometimes rewritten, sometimes mixed up in "new" anthologies, sometimes adapted from radio scripts previously written by other writers.

Charteris had been approached several times over the years for television rights in the Saint and had expended much time and effort during the 1950s trying to get the Saint on TV, even going so far as to write sample scripts himself, but it wasn't to be. He finally agreed a deal in autumn 1961 with English film producers Robert S. Baker and Monty Berman. The first episode of *The Saint* television series, starring Roger Moore, went into production in June 1962. The series was an immediate success, though Charteris himself had his reservations. It reached second place in the ratings, but he commented that "in that distinction it was topped by wrestling, which only suggested to me that the competition may not have been so hot; but producers are generally cast in a less modest mould." He resented the implication that the TV series had finally made a success of the Saint after twenty-five years of literary obscurity.

As long as the series lasted, Charteris was not shy about voicing his criticisms both in public and in a constant stream of memos to the producers. "Regular followers of the Saint saga . . . must have noticed that I am almost incapable of simply writing a story and shutting up."[10] Nor was he shy about exploiting this new market by agreeing to a series of tie-in novelisations ghosted by other writers, which he would then rewrite before publication.

Charteris mellowed as the series developed and found elements to praise too. He developed a close friendship with producer Robert S. Baker, which would last until Charteris's death.

In the early '60s, on one of their frequent trips to England, Leslie and Audrey bought a house in Surrey, which became their permanent base. He explored the possibility of a Saint musical and began writing some of it himself.

Charteris no longer needed to work. Now in his sixties, he supervised the Saint from a distance whilst continuing to travel and indulge himself. He and Audrey made seasonal excursions to Ireland and the south of France, where they had residences. He began to write poetry and devised a new universal sign language, Paleneo, based on notes and symbols he used in his diaries. Once Paleneo was released, he decided enough was enough and announced, again, his retirement. This time he meant it.

The Saint continued regardless—there was a long-running Swedish comic strip, and new novels with other writers doing the bulk of the work were complemented in the 1970s with Bob Baker's revival of the TV series, *Return of the Saint.*

Ill-health began to take its toll. By the early 1980s, although he continued a healthy correspondence with the outside world, Charteris felt unable to keep up with the collaborative Saint books and pulled the plug on them.

To entertain himself, Leslie took to "trying to beat the bookies in predicting the relative speed of horses," a hobby which resulted in several of his local betting shops refusing to take "predictions" from him, as he was too successful for their liking.

He still received requests to publish his work abroad but had become completely cynical about further attempts to revive the Saint. A new Saint magazine only lasted three issues, and two TV productions—*The Saint in Manhattan*, with Tom Selleck look-alike Andrew Clarke, and *The Saint*, with Simon Dutton—left him bitterly disappointed. "I fully expect this series to lay eggs everywhere . . . the only satisfaction I have is in looking at my bank balance."[11]

In the early 1990s, Hollywood producers Robert Evans and William J. Macdonald approached him and made a deal for the Saint to return to cinema screens. Charteris still took great care of the Saint's reputation and wrote an outline entitled *The Return of the Saint* in which an older Saint would meet the son he didn't know he had.

Much of his time in his last few years was taken up with the movie. Several scripts were submitted to him—each moving further and further away from his original concept—but the screenwriter from 1940s Hollywood was thoroughly disheartened by the Hollywood of the '90s: "There is still no plot, no real story, no characterisations, no personal interaction, nothing but endless frantic violence . . ." Besides, with producer Bill Macdonald hitting the headlines for the most un-Saintly reasons, he was to add, "How can Bill Macdonald concentrate on my Saint movie when he has Sharon Stone in his bed?"

The Crime Writers' Association of Great Britain presented Leslie with a Lifetime Achievement award in 1992 in a special ceremony at the

House of Lords. Never one for associations and awards, and although visibly unwell, Leslie accepted the award with grace and humour ("I am now only waiting to be carbon-dated," he joked). He suffered a slight stroke in his final weeks, which did not prevent him from dining out locally with family and friends, before he finally passed away at the age of 85 on 15 April 1993.

His death severed one of the final links with the classic thriller genre of the 1930s and 1940s, but he left behind a legacy of nearly one hundred books, countless short stories, and TV, film, radio, and comic-strip adaptations of his work which will endure for generations to come.

> *I was always sure that there was a solid place in escape literature for a rambunctious adventurer such as I dreamed up in my youth, who really believed in the old-fashioned romantic ideals and was prepared to lay everything on the line to bring them to life. A joyous exuberance that could not find its fulfilment in pinball machines and pot. I had what may now seem a mad desire to spread the belief that there were worse, and wickeder, nut cases than Don Quixote.*
>
> *Even now, half a century later, when I should be old enough to know better, I still cling to that belief. That there will always be a public for the old-style hero, who had a clear idea of justice, and a more than technical approach to love, and the ability to have some fun with his crusades.*[12]

---

1 *A Letter from the Saint,* 30 August 1946

2 "The Last Word," *The First Saint Omnibus,* Doubleday Crime Club, 1939

3 *The Straits Times,* 29 June 1958, page 9

4 Introduction by Charteris to the September 1980 paperback reprint of *Meet—the Tiger!* (Charter), the last ever print edition.
5 *The Saint: A Complete History,* by Burl Barer (McFarland, 1993)
6 PR material from the 1970s series *Return of the Saint*
7 From "Return of the Saint: Comprehensive Information" issued to help publicise the 1970s TV show
8 *A Letter from the Saint,* 26 July 1946
9 Introduction to "The Million Pound Day," in *The First Saint Omnibus*
10 *A Letter from the Saint,* 12 April 1946
11 Letter from LC to sometime Saint collaborator Peter Bloxsom, 2 August 1989
12 Introduction by Charteris to the September 1980 paperback reprint of *Meet—the Tiger!* (Charter).

WATCH FOR THE

SIGN OF THE SAINT!

THE SAINT CLUB

And so, my friends, dear bookworms, most noble fellow drinkers, frustrated burglars, affronted policemen, upright citizens with furled umbrellas and secret buccaneering dreams that seems to be very nearly all for now. It has been nice having you with us, and we hope you will come again, not once, but many times.

Only because of our great love for you, we would like to take this parting opportunity of mentioning one small matter which we have very much at heart . . .

—Leslie Charteris, The First Saint Omnibus *(1939)*

Leslie Charteris founded The Saint Club in 1936 with the aim of providing a constructive fanbase for Saint devotees. Before the War, it donated profits to a London hospital where, for several years, a Saint ward was maintained. With the nationalisation of hospitals, profits were, for many years, donated to the Arbour Youth Centre in Stepney, London.

In the twenty-first century, we've carried on this tradition but have also donated to the Red Cross and a number of different children's charities.

The club acts as a focal point for anyone interested in the adventures of Leslie Charteris and the work of Simon Templar, and offers merchandise that includes DVDs of the old TV series and various Saint-related publications, through to its own exclusive range of notepaper, pin badges, and polo shirts. All profits are donated to charity. The club also maintains two popular websites and supports many more Saint-related sites.

After Leslie Charteris's death, the club recruited three new vice-presidents—Roger Moore, Ian Ogilvy, and Simon Dutton have all pledged their support, whilst Audrey and Patricia Charteris have been retained as Saints-in-Chief. But some things do not change, for the back of the membership card still mischievously proclaims that . . .

> *The bearer of this card is probably a person of hideous antecedents and low moral character, and upon apprehension for any cause should be immediately released in order to save other prisoners from contamination.*

To join . . .

Membership costs £3.50 (or US$7) per year, or £30 (US$60) for life. Find us online at www.lesliecharteris.com for full details.

Made in the USA
Monee, IL
01 September 2022